1638 EAST PALACE

1638 East Palace

A novel
by

Kathleen McElligott

Adelaide Books
New York / Lisbon
2019

1638 EAST PALACE
A novel
By Kathleen McElligott

Copyright © by Kathleen McElligott
Cover design © 2019 Adelaide Books

Published by Adelaide Books, New York / Lisbon
adelaidebooks.org

Editor-in-Chief
Stevan V. Nikolic

All rights reserved. No part of this book may be reproduced in any manner whatsoever without written permission from the author except in the case of brief quotations embodied in critical articles and reviews.

For any information, please address Adelaide Books
at info@adelaidebooks.org
or write to:
Adelaide Books
244 Fifth Ave. Suite D27
New York, NY, 10001

ISBN: 978-1-951896-02-7

Printed in the United States of America

Contents

Characters *7*

Starting Over… *9*

Part I *23*

Part II *115*

Part III *171*

About the Author *265*

Characters

Elaine	Santa Fe artist and former nurse
Colin	Elaine's grandson
Stephanie	Elaine's daughter, killed in a car crash in Ireland
Christa	Elaine's friend, a psychologist
Trish	Christa's partner, silversmith and at-home mom
Deshy	Trish and Christa's adopted son
Roxy	Elaine's daughter, a marine biologist in Chicago
Helen	Elaine's mother, also in Chicago
Maggie and John	Colin's Irish grandparents
Denise and Stuart	Elaine's sister and brother-in-law
Mercedes	Christa's former lover

Starting Over...

Elaine

Morning sunlight spills across the table as a grey vireo flits from branch to branch on the mesquite bush in the back courtyard. A horned toad races across the gravel, stops as if contemplating what he's forgotten, then promptly disappears under a rock. Today, Mother's Day, my world tilted on its axis. After today, nothing will ever be the same.

C'mon, Christa. Answer your phone, I pray, as if sheer will power can force her to pick up. I push my readers up my nose and rake my fingers through my uncombed hair. I lick salty tears from my lips, summoning the strength keep from shattering into pieces.

"Christa, thank God," I manage, my voice a quivering whisper.

"Elaine, honey, what's wrong?

For a moment I'm mute, unable to say the words that will change this nightmare into reality.

"Elaine? Are you alright? What's wrong?" Christa pleads.

"She was in an accident—my Stephanie. She's gone."

Christa gasps. "Oh my God!"

The words come spilling out "They were on their honeymoon in Dublin. Liam's in critical condition."

I collapse onto the chair. My cup crashes to the terra cotta tile, splattering coffee on the freshly painted walls of my casita. The acrid smell of burnt toast lingers in the tiny room.

"Colin wasn't with them, thank God." I manage, doubled over, eviscerated with grief. The physical pain is more real to me than Stephanie's death. It can't be true; they must have made a mistake, confused Stephanie and Liam with some other young couple motoring through the countryside on spring holiday. I just talked to her last week. She was pregnant, again. Imagining her in the front seat, her little baby bump the promise of a little sister or brother for Colin brings on a fresh wave of wailing.

"Anything you need, Elaine. You know I'm here for you."

I cling to her words like a drowning man clutching a lifeline.

"I want to bring her back to the States, have her buried here. There's so much to do—collect Stephanie's and Colin's birth certificates and overnight them to the embassy, and something called a Foreign Service Report of Death needs to be done."

"I'll go with you." Christa says without hesitation. "You can't do this alone."

Thank you is not enough for the relief and gratitude I feel.

"And poor Colin—he just turned three. He's coming home with me, too."

Maggie and John Casey will be keeping vigil beside Liam, their only child. But the cows have to be milked twice a day along with the endless chores of running a dairy farm. They can't possibly care for little Colin, too. My only grandchild needs to be here in Santa Fe with me. Bringing Stephanie and Colin home keeps me from splintering into a million raw shards.

I glance out the window as we prepare to land. The fields below are a patchwork of more shades of green than I knew existed. Christa and I collect our luggage, present our passports, and set off to find a driver who will take us to Listowel, a village near the Casey's farm and the mouth of the Shannon River. We decide to hire a driver. In my present state I couldn't possibly navigate in a tiny car with a stick shift on the wrong side of the road. Once word gets out, we have our choice of several drivers and accept the services of Kevin, a soft-spoken college student with a reddish brown beard. He loads our luggage into the boot and onto the roof of his incredibly small red Fiat. Christa's long legs are folded up to her chin in the passenger seat. A spring breeze whips her blond hair across her face until she captures it in a rubber band. My petite frame slides easily into back seat. I push my glasses up the bridge of my nose and brush the hair out of my eyes.

Away from the congestion of the city, sheep and cattle graze in pastures divided by stone fences; a jigsaw puzzle of greens, browns and golds. It's an idyllic scene, but my heart is like lead, heavy in my chest. I stare wordlessly out the window. Two hours later we turn onto a single-lane road, rutted, and barely wide enough for the Fiat. Kevin slows the car to a crawl. At the top of a hill the Casey's farm spreads out before us; an old clapboard house in need of fresh paint, and a shiny new barn. A calf trots alongside its mother. The choppy Atlantic menaces at the far edge of the rolling pastures. It's stark, yet sadly beautiful.

Kevin motors up to the door. A barking dog with huge paws bounds toward the car as a woman in a housedress steps out on the porch, wiping her hands on the apron around her ample waist. Her tight gray curls frame a grim, work-worn countenance with lips compressed into a thin line. "Shut up!" She yells at the beast.

This must be Maggie Casey. She regards us mutely; two American peas in a pod with our designer purses and matching luggage. I nervously adjust my glasses and tuck a wisp of hair in back of my ear. No one's talking, so I extend my hand. "Hello. I'm Elaine, Stephanie's mother, and this is my friend, Christa."

"You've had a long trip. Come in. I'll make the tea," she says without a hint of a smile, a civil greeting, or acknowledgment of my loss.

"This is for you," I say, extracting a two-pound box of hostess mints from my carry-on. "Thank you for having us."

"Humph." She says. "I'm diabetic, as is Johnny."

Christa glances toward me, eyebrows raised.

"But Father O'Malley at St. Brigid's got a birthday coming up. He'll be saying Mass for me poor Liam's departed wife later this month."

Yes, Liam's wife and *my* daughter. Is this woman's heart made of stone? The kitchen windows let in plenty of spring sunshine, but I'm chilled to the bone. Maggie puts the dented kettle on the stove, lights the ancient white contraption, and turns to Christa.

"What is it you do?" Her joyless eyes narrow, as interrogating us.

"I'm a therapist in private practice."

"We deal with our own problems here, or ask our priest." Maggie sniffs. "Are you married?"

"No, I don't have any children, so that's probably why I enjoy working with them so much."

"What about you, Elaine. You're a nurse?"

"Yes, I was a school nurse for many years. I recently moved to Santa Fe, New Mexico. That's in our Southwest." Christa and I are on our best behavior, Miss Manner's poster women from America.

"I know where it is." She scoffs. "What about Stephanie's father? Where is he?"

"We were divorced many years ago."

"Naturally."

God, I am so exhausted—and hungry, I realize. Forget this 'getting to know you' chit chat. Where is Colin? Doesn't Maggie know why we're here?

My stomach growls audibly and it finally dawns on Maggie that Christa and I are famished after our long flight and drive from the airport.

"Jaysus, I'm forgettin' me manners. I baked a nice soda bread over there in the breadbox."

"You sit, Mrs. Casey. I'll take care of it," Christa says, looking relieved at the mention of food. She places the round loaf on a platter in the center of the wobbly wooden table along with a knife, chipped teacups, plates, spoons and a saucer mounded with pale butter.

Christa and I devour thick slices of bread spread thickly with the butter produced here on the farm, as Maggie reminds us. Strong tea with plenty of cream and sugar washes it down. Slowly, I feel energy return to my limbs and some clarity to my brain.

"Where is Colin? Can I see him, now?" I ask meekly, like a kindergartener asking permission to use the bathroom. I shouldn't have to beg to see my own grandchild. He was born in the United States and lived under my roof for his first two years before Stephanie reunited her little family in Ireland. Still, we are guests here. But this is not a social visit. Far from it.

"He's havin' a wee nap. He was runnin' around so excited to be seein' yourselves that he wore himself out and could barely stay awake over biscuits and milk. You can go peek in on the lad. He's the image of his da, he is." She motions with her head to the closed door across the hall.

"Does he know?" My voice is a hint above a whisper.

"Ah," she says, "I told him his ma's gone visiting the angels and his da's away sick and will be home soon."

Not the truth by a longshot, but it's a start; Colin's mother is dead and his father is in a coma.

I slowly open the bedroom door. Colin's asleep in a tiny bed, clutching a well-loved stuffed bear, probably Liam's as a child. Faded curtains hang limply from the window. I long to gather him into my arms. Instead, I lean over and brush his forehead with my lips, light as a hummingbird. He slowly awakens and stares at me with green eyes, his mother's green eyes, and then blinks.

"Granma?" he cries, as he sits up and throws his arms around my neck.

I sit down on the bed and hug him tightly, my tears flowing freely. He's not a chubby toddler anymore; he's a sturdy three-year-old boy with unruly locks of reddish brown hair falling across his brow.

"Why are you crying, Granma?"

"I'm so happy to see you, sweetheart. I missed you so much." It's true. Since Stephanie and Colin moved here a year ago to be with Liam, I have missed him terribly.

"Granma, Granma," he bolts out of the bed, "C'mon, let's go to the barn. I want to show you Dora. She's mine. Grandpa gave her to me." He grabs my hand and I'm off to meet Dora, no doubt a four-legged creature of some kind.

At the dinner table that night, Colin pushes carrots around his plate and says without warning, "Where's Ma and Da?"

Maggie almost drops the platter of roast beef she's handing to John.

"Eat your carrots, Colin," he says, ignoring the question.

"And chew and swallow before talking," Maggie adds.

"Colin helps me feed Russell and the cats, doncha boy?" John says, pushing the limits of denial.

"He'll soon be big enough to be some real help around here, and God knows we need it," Maggie says.

Are the Caseys so grief stricken that they don't hear what Colin is asking, or is it a cultural thing? Are they planning to have Father O'Malley tell him that his mother isn't just 'visiting the angels?' If ever there was an opening to discuss Stephanie's death and Colin's future, this is it.

"Tomorrow we're going to Dublin, to the American Embassy." I tell the Caseys in a firm voice. "I'm having Stephanie's remains sent back to the States as quickly as possible."

"So soon? We were thinkin' of havin' the service for her in a week or so," Maggie says. "Surely, you're not taking her back before then?"

"Actually, we are. Her family's in Chicago; her father, her sister Roxy, and her Grandma Helen."

"We'll be taking Colin with us," I say with authority. "Kevin's driving. It's all arranged. You've been so kind giving us a place to stay, and we wouldn't want to put you out any more than we already have."

Maggie clamps her mouth and squints at me with raptor-like eyes.

"What do you mean, you're taking the boy?" Maggie says, her voice rising.

"Where, Granma? Where are we going?" Colin asks.

"Home to America, sweetheart. We'll need to get the papers in the city tomorrow. Then we're taking you on an airplane ride in a day or so."

"To see Ma and Da?" His eyes are as bright as search lights.

"That's enough, Colin." John interrupts.

"When are they coming back?" A panicked look erases Colin's hopeful anticipation.

"Eat your carrots, Colin." Maggie warns.

Enough. Have the Casey's lost their minds completely? Can't they see how Colin is struggling with the mixed messages he's receiving? 'Eat you carrots, your ma's with the angels, chew your food, your da's sick.'

"You come with me," I say, taking Colin by the hand and excusing us from the table.

Maggie sits in stunned silence. John rises from his seat to intervene.

"No," I tell him. "He has to know. She's his mother."

From Colin's room I hear the outraged cries of Maggie and John across the hall. Christa follows me into the bedroom and closes the door behind her. She's the expert, a certified counselor. I'll need all the help I can get telling Colin the truth.

The old rocker in the corner has plenty of room for Colin and me. I stroke his head and take a few moments to rock back and forth before saying the words that must be said.

"Your mother…" I begin.

"Is with the angels, Granma Maggie said," he interrupts.

"Yes, she's with the angels, Col. Up in heaven. She's not…" I struggle with the words, "she's not coming back." There, I've said it. His life is forever changed, the security of family and home stolen abruptly from him.

He looks up at me. "Me Da, too?"

I hug him closer. "No, your da's not in heaven. He's hurt. He was in a car accident. A crash."

"Where is he?" His voice rises to a frightened whine.

"He's in the hospital. Grandpa John visits him there."

"I want to go and see him!" He turns to look at me and my heart breaks at his clear, innocent eyes.

"Oh, sweetie, they don't let children go there."

Christa quickly adds, "But you could make a picture for him and Grandpa could take it to him. Your dad will know it's from you."

"He's coming back?" His eyes are wide with concern.

"I hope so, Colin. I hope he gets better soon and comes back." I tell him.

"Now! I want him now!" His face reddens as he wails and stiffens in my arms.

Oh, God. Did I say too much? Suggest too much uncertainty? But Christa says it's best to be honest.

"I know you do, but that can't happen now," Christa says. "He's hurt really bad."

"No he's not! I want him now!" I'm amazed at his strength as he struggles to free himself, butting his head against my chest.

"Listen to me, Col. Christa's right. Your daddy has to get better before you can see him. He was in a car accident with your mom."

He's made a connection. "My Hot Wheels get in crashes." He slams his fists together. "Bam!"

"I'll take care of you," I tell him, stroking his head as his mother did.

He associates my caress with his mother's and calls mournfully for her. "Ma, Mommy!"

"Oh, honey," I grasp him to me. "Your mommy's not coming back and I am so, so sorry."

"Mommy!" he wails, brokenhearted.

I hear chairs scraping the kitchen floor and brace myself. In an instant, Maggie and John are standing in the doorway. Maggie's face is contorted with rage. John's is lined with pain.

"For the love of God, leave the child alone." Maggie demands.

John stands silently as Colin continues calling for his parents.

"It's better for him to know it now, as fully as he can understand," Christa tells the Caseys in a calm, professional tone. "It's difficult and frightening at first, for all of us, but far more compassionate than giving him false hope."

Christa's assurance and conviction calm us all. Even Colin quiets. She pauses to let her words sink in, "We can help him together, or we can prolong his uncertainty and pain."

I have never been so proud of my friend. This is what she does—helps people, and she's good at it. We met back in Chicago when we worked at the same school, she as a psychologist and me as a nurse.

We return silently to the kitchen. The dinner is cold and untouched. It seems we've all lost our appetite. Christa and I help Maggie clear the table. Colin sits on John's lap, clutching a red crayon and dragging it across a sheet of paper, a picture for his father. Maggie produces a bottle of whiskey and glasses and pours drinks all around. John lifts his glass, "May God be merciful."

Amen.

Christa

I don't drink hard liquor, but Elaine and I are guests here, so I take a sip. It burns like acid then warms my gut like a hot ember.

Suddenly, Colin reaches for John's glass. "Me too, Grandpa," he says. When Elaine shakes her head he appeals to Maggie, "You know you let me." Does Maggie see this as nurturing him in some misguided way?

She must, because she urges, "Aye, Johnny, Give 'im a wee sip. It'll settle 'im and what can it hurt?"

John reaches for the glass, presumably to give the boy some whiskey. Elaine abruptly stands. "No, John, please. It's not good for him."

"And what makes you Miss Know-it-All?" Maggie challenges.

Colin chimes in, "Yes, Grandpa, yes!"

"No, John." Elaine removes her glasses and rubs her eyes. I'm shocked at the dark circles. Her hair, usually shiny, hangs dull and limp at her shoulders. She's exhausted and stressed to her limit. The sooner we take care of business and get the hell out of here, the better for everyone. Especially Colin.

"I will not allow you to give alcohol to my grandson." Elaine stands firm.

Maggie ignores this and defiantly empties her glass in one gulp, slamming it on the table.

All eyes turn to John. For a long moment he does not move. Finally, he says, "Colin, I've got a bit of a chocolate bar for you in me coat pocket. Let me get that for ye."

Elaine and I emit a collective sigh.

"As God is me witness, don't think you're taking the wee one to America." Maggie's cheeks are red and puffed with anger.

"Maggie, you don't understand." Elaine says. "Next to Stephanie, I'm the closest thing to a mother that Colin's had. I practically raised him, for God sake."

"Surely *you* don't understand." Maggie shoots back. "He is Liam's son and we intend to raise him until Liam comes around. Besides, Colin loves it here. What better place to raise a young boy than on a farm?"

She makes it sound like her son will soon be up and about. She's got a point, though; a farm is a good place to raise a boy, but not when whisky is the cure for all ills, including the loss of one's mother.

John winces and groans as he shifts his weight in the chair.

"It's me arthritis," he says. "Too many years of farmin.' With the stock needin' feedin' and milkin' twice a day and keepin' the stalls clean and the fences in good repair, it never ends. I can't do it alone—haven't for years. There's the hired help, but it's not the same."

John's paddle-like hands speak to his once substantial frame, but he's been whittled thin by years of endless work and worry.

"Aye, and they're all eejits, every one." Maggie says.

"Maggie, girl, we need 'em. It's harder than ever now with me visitin' Liam in the city. We need these fellas to keep everything goin.' With you seein' to things, having to run the farm on top of runnin' the house and doin' the laundry and cookin' and cleanin, it's too much.' He pauses for breath. "And now we've the boy."

We all turn our attention to Colin who's fallen asleep nestled on John's lap.

Maggie rises to close the window against an ocean chill. Slumping back in her chair she whispers, "Sure, I'm tired, Johnny, and not seein' Liam is breakin' me heart."

"With Colin in Elaine's safekeepin' you could come to the hospital with me, see Liam, and talk to 'im. Hearin' his ma's voice will do our boy a world of good. Colin won't be gone forever...he'll come back." John's voice softens and he stares out the window at the vast expanse of his property.

Elaine

The following Wednesday we're in the air, headed home to Santa Fe. I breathe a sigh of relief despite a lingering headache. It's no wonder. In a week I procured an expedited passport for Colin, filled out endless paperwork at the embassy, purchased airline tickets for the three of us and for Stephanie's casket in the cargo hold. Colin's seated between Christa and me, buckled into his seat. He arches his back and kicks the seat in front of him. "Out! Get me out!" he cries.

"Please! Control that child!" The elderly gentleman in the forward seat turns and gives me a nasty look.

"Here, Colin, let's put these on," Christa says, adjusting the headphones to cover his ears. "We'll watch a movie."

Colin clutches his stuffed bear and watches *A Bug's Life* for a while until he loses interest and begins kicking the seat again. The unlucky gentleman complains again and summons the flight attendant. The other passengers stare like they've never seen a fidgeting three-year-old.

Eight hours later, after one lunch, two snacks, another movie, three trips to the bathroom, pilot's wings from the flight attendant, and several Dr. Seuss books, we prepare to land.

Did I make the right decision? Should I have left Colin in Ireland with the Caseys? He loves his calf, Dora, and the other farm animals, too. Then I remember the Caseys' refusal to tell him the truth about his parents and Maggie's willingness to feed him whisky and I know I made the right choice, the only one I could make, in good conscience.

When the plane touches down, my tranquil life will be a memory. I'll be starting over, a single parent raising my grandson.

PART I

Elaine

Santa Fe, four years later…spring, 2003

Home is my casita, our "little house" on East Palace Avenue, vintage 1950s, and within walking distance of the Plaza, the heart of "Old" Santa Fe, my favorite part. Our five small rooms are big enough for the two of us and our cat, Callie. At three o'clock, Colin barrels through the door. He's breathless, as usual. I'm in our stand-up kitchen, preparing chicken strips for Colin's favorite meal, chicken tenders. I wave him toward me.

"Come here. I need a kiss. How was school?"

I bend over, bread crumbs stuck to my fingers. Colin pushes aside his coppery bangs and dispenses a duty kiss that barely brushes my cheek. An instant later his eyes cloud over. He holds out his hand and uncoils his fingers. There, smudged and crumpled, is a white ticket from his teacher. Some kids collect coins or Civil War memorabilia; Colin collects white tickets for disturbing the class, fighting on the playground, pushing in the cafeteria line, or any in a long list of infractions.

For kids with attention issues, acting out is part of everyday life. Mrs. Allen, his second grade teacher, and the administrators at his school are educators, so why don't they know that? And why don't they deal with Colin more effectively?

Today, Colin slugged a classmate. I cast him a quizzical look and wait for an explanation.

"Josh was bugging me."

"Didn't I tell you to ignore him?"

Josh is a little twit who knows exactly how to push my grandson's buttons. Each time he does, Colin lashes out. But it's Colin who pays the price. But he's safe at home with me now.

He drops his backpack onto the table. A couple of stubby pencils and three spitballs tumble out. "Granma, I have to make a family tree for school, and Mrs. Allen says no pro... procras..."

"No *procrastinating*. That means let's start on it right away." I've got a scant minute before his concentration skitters off and he realizes he's starving, or missing his favorite TV show, or needs to pee. The afternoon sun slants through the window illuminating golden particles suspended in the air.

"Tell me about it," I say as I dredge the chicken pieces in seasoned crumbs.

Colin flops onto the kitchen chair and immediately begins kicking the leg. I cock my head and give him my *we don't kick the furniture* look and he stops—for all of three seconds.

"I hafta make a family tree and write a really long paper," he says, his forehead creased with worry. "Everybody's gotta be there, too."

It should be a simple assignment; draw a family tree and write a few paragraphs about your family. But there are all kinds of trees and all kinds of families. Today, when my sweet, impulsive grandson carried home this assignment in his backpack, he launched both of us on a twisty journey, one that is sure to dredge up feelings of abandonment and loss.

Goodness, where to begin a family tree?

There's Roxy, my youngest, Colin's aunt. She visits us once or twice a year, when she can break away from her job at the Shedd Aquarium in Chicago.

Colin's mom, Stephanie, was an impulsive risk-taker with a glorious mane of red hair who decided to ride the wave of global prosperity in the mid-nineties and moved to Ireland. No dream job materialized, but she met Liam, her future husband.

Stephanie and Liam are a delicate subject; Colin knows his mom died in a car crash. He might remember standing at my side during Stephanie's funeral, but he was only three. Distant relatives fawned over him and clucked, "Poor motherless boy." But I doubt he remembers much beyond that. Liam, Colin's father, survived the crash, but lingered in a coma for more than a year and died without regaining consciousness, or seeing his son. Until Colin asks, I think it's best to say nothing about the details their deaths.

On the other hand, Colin should know how Stephanie didn't want to give birth in Ireland. Trying to make it back in time, she went into labor over the Atlantic. The plane's wheels were still hot on the Chicago tarmac as she was taken by ambulance to the nearest hospital. Stephanie lay panting and panicked on the gurney while little Colin made his grand entrance into the world a few short minutes after they arrived in the delivery room.

I took Stephanie and her infant son under my wing for two years until she brought her little family together in Ireland; Stephanie, Liam and Colin. That was the first time Liam had laid eyes on his son. They were married shortly after Stephanie found out she was pregnant again, but neither she nor her unborn child survived the crash. These are all things Colin should know—but doesn't.

Colin's Irish grandparents will be part of the family tree, too, Maggie and John Casey. Struggling with diabetes and arthritis, they still manage to run a dairy farm in County Kerry. Does Colin remember the bitterness between me and the Caseys after Stephanie's death? We were all devastated, emotionally raw and physically drained. But even as the Caseys were trying to cope with the tragedy of their son's coma, they assumed, wrongly, that they'd be the ones to raise Colin.

The family tree will include my mother, Helen, of course. She's in Chicago, wishing she could see Colin for more than just holidays.

Christa and her partner, Trish, my best friends, are here in Santa Fe. They're like family, along with their fifteen-month-old son, Deshy. They most assuredly belong on the tree.

"Granma, I'm talking to you!"

Colin's staring up at me, his eyes locked on mine; a trick I taught him. It gets his attention when nothing else works. At least he's learned something from me. I've read a dozen books about parenting a child with Attention Deficit Disorder, and yet every day is a struggle, but one I accepted when I agreed to raise him as my own. More than just raising him for Stephanie, I want Colin to have every opportunity despite his special needs.

"Sorry, sweetheart, Grandma's daydreaming."

Beyond writing a theme, collecting poster board, construction paper and glue, Colin's assignment means an emotional journey, one I'm not ready to begin, but one that can't be postponed. Who knows, this project may turn out to be a blessing, clearing the air and setting things straight.

Tonight after dinner we'll start drawing the tree from the roots up. Everybody who's family and everybody who's like family to us will be on that tree.

"I'll bet your tree is the best!" I say with as much enthusiasm as I can muster. Certainly the most unique.

"Mrs. Allen says we have to have pictures, too."

That's a problem. The only picture I have of Stephanie, Liam and Colin together is a copy of a photo taken at the dairy farm. When I brought Colin here to Santa Fe, I hung it in his room, thinking it would comfort him, but he cried so hard each time he saw it that I took it down and put it away. Maybe it's time to bring it out again.

Colin is scrounging in the cabinet for an after-school snack. If I don't cut him off, he'll eat until he spoils his dinner. When I moved here the cabinets were a wretched mustard color. In a burst of enthusiasm—and energy, I repainted them Indian red and all the walls Navaho white. From the kitchen I look out on the tiny courtyard and my cactus garden, all surrounded by a six foot adobe wall. Santa Fe was supposed to be my second act, and it was, but not as a watercolor artist painting desert scenes.

Raising a child at my age can be exhausting, but fifty-seven is hardly ancient, and raising him is my choice. I jumped through hoops to bring him here from Ireland and don't regret it for a minute. Sometimes I think about going back to work, but nursing is a demanding profession and my days are full; shopping for groceries and clothes, cleaning, cooking, helping Col with his homework and attending impromptu parent-teacher conferences. It seems like Mrs. Allen has my number on speed dial. My savings are dwindling, but we live simply and within our means. Thank goodness the Caseys have started sending checks that help make ends meet. And thank heaven they've stopped sending him picture books of tortured martyrs glancing toward heaven and oversized soccer jerseys from teams he's never heard of and doesn't wear.

"Here's a glass of milk to wash down that granola bar. Don't forget to feed Callie and give her fresh water."

It would be far easier for me to put out food and water for our little calico, but responsibility is good for Colin. I don't mind sweeping up a little cat chow or mopping up a few splashes of water.

Little boys need young, energetic parents; Colin's got me. Some mornings I can barely lift my head off the pillow, but on others the sun's rays energize me and I'm eager to face the challenge of another day. I can and will raise this boy. Handing Colin off to creaky old farmers in Ireland isn't an option.

The Caseys, though, they're stubborn. I know they're plotting to get Colin back somehow, and groom him to take over the dairy farm. Liam was their only child, so they ache to have Colin with them; I get that. I'm not sure how old the Caseys are, exactly, but Maggie and John, with their health issues and lifetimes of hard work, are too old to parent a boy, especially an active boy like Colin. So who else is there, but me?

Tom, my ex-husband, is divorced again and lives in a small apartment in Chicago. My sister, Denise, and her husband, Stuart, are childless, professional people accustomed to a sophisticated lifestyle. Denise is four years older than me, and talks about the exotic trips she'll take with Stuart when they retire. They'd lavish every material thing on Colin, hire a nanny and enroll him in countless activities. And they'd love their niece's little boy, but would that be what Stephanie would have wanted? More importantly, would that be what Colin needs? And his great grandmother Helen would love to cuddle and fuss over him, but believe me, Colin is not one to be cuddled and fussed over. He can't bear to be restrained, not for a moment. Even a perfunctory hug or kiss is a stretch. So it comes down to me.

Back in Chicago, when I was a school nurse, I worked with special needs kids and their parents all the time. One thing I learned is that sitting behind a desk and doling out bad news at a parent-teacher conference is worlds away from being on the receiving end. I used to think a firm hand and consistent discipline were the answer to keeping a difficult child in line. I assumed that the parents sitting across the desk from me were to blame because they couldn't control their bright but unruly child. Now I know better. Consistency is great, but not a cure-all. I've considered putting Colin on medication, but I haven't gone there…yet. Instead, I feed him unprocessed food, except for his favorite, boxed macaroni and cheese, monitor his schoolwork, and sign him up for soccer to burn off energy. Plus, I read everything about Attention Deficit Hyperactivity Disorder I can get my hands on.

"What's for dinner, Granma?" He's barely swallowed the last mouthful of granola.

To Colin I'm 'Granma' but I do all the things that a mother does for her child; cook for him, wash his clothes, help him with his homework, read to him, get him through the rough patches at school, and love him more than I ever thought possible.

After his bedtime ritual of teeth-brushing, face and hands washing, a story, prayers and a good-night kiss, Colin is tucked into bed and the house is quiet. I sink into the sofa and put my feet up on the coffee table. A feeling of foreboding washes over me. A family tree project—what was that teacher thinking? It's a big project, and we're so close to the end of school. And besides, doesn't she know about Colin's family situation? Hasn't he been through enough without dredging up the past? And what right does Mrs. Allen have to pry into our private life? I'm calling her tomorrow, after Colin leaves for school.

Get a grip Elaine! Things happen for a reason. This might be the least painful way for Colin to learn the details of his past. But, oh, the memory of my Stephanie giving birth in the Chicago hospital, barely an hour after she was wheeled off the plane from Ireland. I almost got in an accident speeding from the airport to the hospital after I found out what was happening. And the first time I held her little boy in my arms—I'll never forget the overwhelming love I felt for him. And the emptiness I felt when they returned to Ireland. And the complete devastation when Stephanie died, lost to me forever. I'm her mother, but I wasn't there to protect her, couldn't save her, and didn't even know she'd died until hours after she'd breathed her last. It nearly destroyed me.

I do my best to hide my raw emotions from Colin, and we work on the family tree for three nights. By the time it's finished, Colin is relieved and I am drained.

The following morning, I drive Colin to school. In the back seat the theme paper is clipped to the poster, the poster is rolled and nestled in a cardboard tube, and the tube is secured with a seat belt. This project represents our family, the living and the dead. It includes everyone we have ever loved and everyone we love to this day. It traces Colin's birthright, reveals his past, defines his present, and acts as a guidepost to his future. It represents a single family–ours–a family that has come to include those born to it, adopted into it, and embraced by it. It is a treasure, this unlikely family of ours.

Colin

Yesterday I handed in my tree project. Today, Mrs. Allen calls me up to her desk.

It's just before lunch and everyone is talking and I'm starving and...

"You did a great job on your family tree project, Colin." She's smiling, but then she gets a sad look on her face. "I didn't know..."

What didn't she know? She's sitting at her desk with her hands folded and she looks like she might start crying any second. I think she wants me to say something, but I don't know what, so she lets me go back to my seat. Phew! That was creepy, but it reminds me of my project and the picture that Granma hung in my room.

My ma had red hair and she used to sing to me at bedtime. I remember one song, "Hush little baby..." She had a pretty voice.

My da had black hair. It smelled good when he held me and tossed me in the air.

Now I live with Granma. Her hair smells like coconuts and her glasses are always falling down her nose. Once when she looked in the mirror and I heard her say, "I've got to do something about this gray!" She didn't see me standing in the hallway.

My friend, Rachel, lives with her Granma and sometimes her mom. Rachel says her mom is a crackhead. When I ask Grams what a 'crackhead' is, she says, "Where did you hear that?"

When I tell her it's about Rachel's mom, she says, "Oh, Sweetie, a crackhead is someone who uses drugs. I'm so sorry for Rachel."

Today Mrs. Allen gave me a sticker and I didn't even finish my worksheet. She never did that before.

Trish

My cell phone chirps, sounding loud in the park, which is hardly as packed as it soon will be when school's over for the year. "Hold on a sec, Elaine. Deshy's coming down the slide."

I scoop up my darling little boy before his feet touch the cedar chips at the bottom of the slide. I give him a twirl and he giggles, then quickly squirms free and toddles to the sandbox.

"Hi, Elaine. Are we still on tonight? Deshy's excited to see Colin—and play with his toys, of course."

It's Elaine's artist gathering and I'm happy to hold down the fort for a few hours while she visits with 'her people.'

I pluck a plastic bucket and shovel from my tote bag and hand them to Deshy. He plops down and wriggles his toes in the cool sand.

"Any chance you could come early?" Elaine says. "I could use some help with Colin while I get dressed. If you'd like, you and Deshy can eat here."

"Sure, but I'll need to stop at home first to get Deshy's dinner."

After we adopted Deshy, Christa and I agreed that nothing artificial would touch his lips. We're deeply committed to organic fruits and veggies, and free range chicken. Our little boy got a rocky start in life. The plane had barely touched ground in America when Christa began researching pediatric surgeons who specialize in cleft lip repair. We're determined to see that he has a happy, healthy childhood.

Elaine

"Colin, get the door. Aunt Trish and Deshy are here. Col... Colin?"

I step out of the shower, throw on my robe, and traipse to the front door, dripping water across the floor. Little Deshy toddles right in and heads straight for Colin's room where he's sprawled on the floor, staging a war between Spider Man and Bat Man, ably assisted by their minions.

I remember when Christa and Trish brought Deshy home and I got to hold him. He was sleeping peacefully, wrapped in a yellow blanket with blue moons and stars. Silken strands of black hair stuck out from under the matching cap. I ran my finger across his upper lip and he tried to suck. It broke my heart, how difficult that was for him, but by then I knew that Trish and Christa were women on a mission. As soon as he put on weight and was strong enough, his new moms scheduled his surgery with the best pediatric surgeon they could find.

Trish

Colin wraps his arms around Deshy and hoists him off his feet. The bear hug has both boys shrieking with laughter. But a few minutes later, Deshy trundles into the kitchen, wailing.

"Colin pushed me!" Deshy sticks out his chunky arms, mimicking the shove.

"Come on, let's go talk to him."

Deshy takes my hand and leads me to the bedroom. Colin's in full battle mode, staging hand-to-hand combat with his action figures, knocking out full regiments with the swish of an arm, bombing enemy headquarters with wooden blocks, and howling the agonizing screams of the injured.

"Colin?" I say.

He ignores me.

"You've got a good battle going, Col," I say, going for a low-key approach. "But Deshy says you pushed him. Did you?"

Colin lobs another block at enemy headquarters and, without glancing up, blurts: "He was knocking over my Army guys. I had to set them all up again."

"Colin, look at me. We don't push. Remember? No pushing."

"Oh-kay," he says, more annoyed than penitent.

Elaine

"How do I look? Not bad for a 57-year-old grandma, ya think?" I preen for Trish, showing off my denim skirt and red cowboy boots.

"Sweetie, you look great. I love the cowboy hat over the white kerchief. Very Georgia O'Keefe."

"I want to look good for my group." *Especially if Chuck is there.*

"Have a good time, and don't worry about us." Trish says.

I click my boot heels on the sidewalk as I walk a couple of blocks up East Palace to our meeting place, Sophia's shop, just off the historic Plaza. The night is mellow. The scent of mesquite drifts up from the Santa Fe River. Insects whir in celebration of spring. A night away from homework, grilled cheese, and TV reruns! This calls for a glass of wine…or two.

Heads turn when I enter Sophia's gift shop and gallery, an eclectic mix of visual art, hand-woven fabric, locally crafted jewelry, incense and CDs of local musicians. The regulars are all here. They know I'm raising my grandson; some have helped out by watching Colin when I needed a last minute sitter, or passing on gently worn boy's clothing. Sophia wraps her arms around me and I linger in her soft comfort. Before Colin, she sold some of my desert watercolors on consignment. The urge to paint is still there, but I haven't quite gotten back to it, yet.

Yvonne's shoulders are as broad as an Olympic swimmer's and her skin is as dry as an alligator's. Working on the road crew will do that, but the pay is good and she gets time off in the winter. She builds unique sculptures from the debris she finds on the road-side.

Ingrid's here, too. She's a potter with a Boston accent. Her hair is in an elegant French twist and she's wearing her signature flower print caftan.

Being surrounded by friends is a welcome break from my full-time role as a 'Granma-momma.' Best of all, *he's* here; Chuck, another sculptor. His creations are large scale metal designs. His silvery hair is pulled back in a slender pony tail. His jeans are soft and faded and spotlessly clean. The burnished leather of his boots suggests years of wear. You cannot purchase boots as well-worn and supple as these. He offers me a glass of wine.

"You can have this," he asks, sky-blue eyes registering concern, pinning me in place, "right?"

"Sure," I reply, "I'm raising my grandson, not joining a nunnery."

Be still, my heart! If Chuck only knew the erotic fantasies I have about him!

Trish

Elaine floats into the house, swishing her skirt and grinning like a schoolgirl. It's after eleven and she's jazzed.

"How did it go?" I sit up and toss a scratchy Indian blanket off my legs.

Elaine sinks into the nearest chair.

"It's always great to see my people. There's such a connection. Yvonne says 'hi,' by the way. How was Colin? No problem, I hope."

"Nothing major, but I had to put him in time-out for pushing Deshy. I gave him two warnings." *Am I making too much of this, being overprotective of Deshy?*

"You did the right thing." Elaine says. "Sometimes time-out is the only thing that works—that and taking his action figures away." Elaine sighs. She removes her boots and props her feet up on the coffee table. "You'll never guess who asked me to dinner."

"Hmmm…could it be the tall cowboy-artist who is also, oddly, a physics professor?"

"That's the one. I get tingly around him, so I guess there's still some life left in this old body. Is that crazy?"

"Tingly is good. Something I haven't felt in a while. Maybe it's being a new mom, but by the time Christa gets home I'm exhausted." I sigh, thinking about Christa and me and how distant we've become. "We haven't made love in a while."

Elaine pauses, choosing her words carefully, I imagine. "I remember when Stephanie and Roxy were little," she says. "I'd crash after I put them down in the evening. Even if Tom had been around, which he wasn't most of the time, I was exhausted and just wanted to sleep."

So this is normal? I should be relieved? "Before Deshy, Christa and I had such great times together. We were so in love, sometimes we never left the house. When we were trying to adopt a child we spent hours on the phone and internet, long into the night, until we found Deshy. Now Christa's back to focusing on her career, and I'm home all day with him. I can barely keep my eyes open past ten o'clock."

"Kids change everything." Elaine says with authority. "Stay the night, okay? No point waking Deshy."

"Thanks. He was so excited, sleeping in Colin's room, even if it's in his Porta Crib. I'll give Christa a call and let her know not to wait up."

Elaine

When Trish talks about Christa, her voice is as soft as a cooing dove, but that girl needs reassurance. And affection. And sex! Tomorrow morning I'm going to remind Trish that she's doing a great job with Deshy and offer to baby-sit so she and Christa can have some alone time.

It feels natural to give motherly advice to Trish. Her own mother and father weren't exactly supportive when she 'came out' in college. Trish told me her father threw her out of his house, while her mother stood silently by his side, unable or unwilling to stand up to him.

This maternal relationship with a young woman feels right. If Stephanie were alive, she'd probably still be in Ireland. No chance for long mother-daughter chats over coffee, only expensive long-distance calls. My friends tell me daughters become closer to their mothers after having kids of their own. But Stephanie and I were never close, not really. Unlike Roxy, Stephanie pushed every conceivable boundary…and my buttons. My biggest regret is that we didn't get a chance to become friends before she died.

In the morning, Colin's frantically searching for his backpack. When he finally finds it under his bed, he stomps on it so it will zip. It's overflowing with crumpled paper, candy wrappers and heaven knows what else.

"Your cereal has been on the table for twenty minutes," I remind him.

He sits down to a bowl of soggy flakes. "I'm not hungry," he says, pushing away from the table. He grabs his backpack, making to leave.

"Have you got your homework?"

"I guess," he shrugs.

I shake my head. "You guess wrong. I found it under the table." I unzip his backpack and slide the papers into a folder. He graces me with a quick kiss and slams out the door.

I pour fresh coffee for Trish and me, filling the kitchen with the aroma of hazelnuts. "I pray he gets promoted to third grade…then fourth… " I say. "A little divine intervention, please."

Trish finishes feeding Deshy and he squirms off her lap, heading straight for Colin's room.

"Let him go," I tell her. "I'll put everything back before Colin gets home. He won't even know Deshy was in there."

"It must be hard," Trish says, "raising him when you'd just started your new life here in Santa Fe. Last night I had to repeat myself three or four times before he listened. Is his hearing okay?"

"He's been tested at school and he's fine." Colin always was a handful. When he was just a toddler, Deshy's age, Christa had us over on Christmas Eve. She was serving hot cocoa and chocolate chip cookies when Colin grabbed a ceramic figure from her Christmas Village. She asked him for it and somehow it ended up sailing across the room and crashing into the fireplace. Cocoa spilled all over the carpet and her blouse. I had my suspicions before, but after that night I knew that Colin was, well, different. Not that I loved him any less because of it. When I think about how Stephanie and Roxy were at that age, there isn't any comparison. They're girls, sure, but Colin's brain is wired differently. They used to think these kids grew out of it, but the latest research says they don't. I've got a long road ahead of me, raising him.

"What about medication?" Trish says.

"Maybe, but there are so many side effects—loss of appetite, headaches, trouble sleeping. A good night's sleep is the one thing I can count on. I dread the thought of him wandering the house alone at night. His teacher is pressuring me to medicate him and I know she'll mention it again at the next parent-teacher conference. It would make her job easier, of course, but I know from experience she can't force it."

On to happier thoughts, like what to wear for my date with Chuck. I've never seen him in anything other than jeans and a Western shirt with the cuffs turned up, so I think a flowing skirt and peasant blouse is a safe bet. It's a treat to get dressed up for a night out. The last time I dated, before Colin, I wore a floral print dress. I wore it twice—once with a co-worker, a surgeon, and the other time with Tristan, my neighbor.

Turned out the good doctor had an ego the size of his bank account—enormous. He went on and on about his cruise up the Amazon, his country club and new Beemer. We had nothing in common except that we worked at the same hospital. After our date, whenever we ran into each other at work, we just said "Hi" or smiled. Eventually, we ignored each other when we passed in the hall. It was a relief, really, a relationship best forgotten.

But Tristan, well, he's my bona fide hero. While I was cooking dinner one night, Colin slipped out the door to ride his tricycle. Before I could catch him, he was careening down the street toward a busy intersection. Luckily, Tristan was jogging around the corner and intercepted him before he barreled into oncoming traffic. It wasn't pretty—Tristan went down

with a thud and Colin scraped his shin on the trike's fender. Tristan was scuffed up and momentarily dazed, but he carried the trike home while I carried Colin. That day, the groundwork was laid for a relationship between two unattached neighbors. Good old Tristan, who had me wondering if he was gay because he didn't kiss me good-night on our first date. Possibly it was because our date was dinner here, with Colin, who kept referring to the broccoli in Hollandaise sauce as 'trees.'
But nothing came of it, romantically. I guess Tristan and I are destined to be friends. Not a bad deal, when I think about it. But still, I'll always wonder why it didn't work out.

Maybe Chuck is the guy for me. When I'm with him my breath catches in my throat and my heart beats a little faster. Plus, the man could be a Ralph Lauren model gracing the pages of GQ, older, maybe, but more distinguished with his grey hair. And who'd believe that a physics professor creates massive metal sculptures? No doubt his science background helps him balance the heavy steel beams he uses for his art.

Colin is at Trish's while I primp for my date. The house is blissfully quiet. I take my time with my make-up; a dusting of blush, sable eyeliner, a hint of smoky perfume.

The doorbell rings. I check myself once more before I make my way to the front door, swaying my hips as I go. I want to purr in a faux Southern drawl, 'Hi, ya'll, come on in. Mint Julep?' Wisely, I resist.

Chuck's jeans outline his lanky frame; his boots are burnished brighter than a new penny and he smells like a Ponderosa pine. His hair is in its usual pony-tail held in place with a narrow strip of cowhide. In one hand is his Stetson, in the other a bouquet of flowers—black-eyed-susans, purple coneflowers, white daisies with yellow centers and violet prairie sage.

"How sweet!" I float to the kitchen for a vase.

"I thought we'd go to the Cowgirl Hall of Fame for dinner and dancing," he says, "How does that sound?"

"Fantastic. I can't remember the last time I went dancing. Do I look okay?"

"Perfect."

Bless this man!

Twenty minutes later, Chuck's pickup is crunching across the gravel parking lot. Country music is blaring right through the rough-cut wood walls. Inside, a wagon wheel chandelier hangs above the bar, casting a dim light on couples chatting over sweaty bottles of ice-cold of beer. Cattle horns are everywhere, as if a herd of inquisitive bulls had stampeded through the splintery walls, trying to join the party. The place is jammed—and LOUD. Conversations bounce to the beamed ceiling and down again. Tall amplifiers stand at attention like soldiers on the corner stage awaiting the band. No wonder the Cowgirl Hall of Fame has been on my list of places to go, and now I get to experience it on the arm of a handsome cowboy!

Chuck's mother raised a gentleman. He opens the door for me, pulls out my chair, and reassures me that I look fabulous and that everything here is delicious. The waitress is a perky cowgirl in jeans I swear she sprayed on and a blouse tied at the midriff revealing taut abs. Her nail polish is fire engine red and a Cupid's heart with 'Bobby' is tattooed above her right breast. She's here for our drink order. The choices are beer…or beer. I'm a Chardonnay gal, but how can you not order a cold beer at the Cowgirl Hall of Fame?

"So here we are," I say. My date-night conversation skills are a bit rusty.

"I noticed that your grandson wasn't home. I'd hoped to meet him."

This is promising. "He's with Christa and Trish, my two best friends. They have a little boy, too, Deshy." I may as well get all the details out in the open. But I stop right before *and my best friends are lesbians. You got a problem with that?*

He takes a long swallow of beer and leans over the table. Oh God, what if he's anti-gay and quotes a Bible verse about eternal damnation? I brace myself. He squints those piercing baby blues as if deciding how to phrase something critical. Finally, he says, "I think it's great that you've got such good friends."

I want to throw myself across the table and plant a wet kiss on his lips. So far he's passed with flying colors. If he didn't accept my friends this would be our first—and last—date.

"I couldn't have raised Colin without their help," I say, just to underscore my loyalty.

The evening's entertainment bounds onto the stage—a girl band wearing Daisy Dukes just this side of the law, shirts open to there, and cowboy hats accented with fans of bright orange feathers. They greet the audience with an energetic "Howdy!" The crowd erupts into whistles and applause as the lead singer charges into their first song, "All My Exes Live in Texas." I glance at Chuck. He's watching them, smiling appreciatively. This could be interesting.

The band quickens its tempo. It's the cue for line dancing. Chuck stands and extends his hand. I've never line danced before, but here I am, on a date with a gorgeous guy whose after-shave I want to lick off his neck, and he's asking me to join in the fun. So I try, I really do, to blend with the other dancers and imitate their moves. Chuck has obviously done this before, and I feel like a gawky fourteen-year-old at my first sock hop.

Hop to the left. Stomp. Hop to the right. Stomp, stomp. Keeping my balance without careening into the line of sure-footed dancers requires concentration. Chuck flashes a wide smile along with thumbs up. I try to relax, but I can't hide the fact that I'm a greenhorn in this bullring. Finally, the lights dim. The music shifts to a slow tune about whiskey, cheating hearts, and pick-up trucks. I melt into Chuck's arms and he holds me close as we dance to a ballad about good love gone bad. This is more like it.

Too soon, the evening is over. At the door Chuck gently raises my chin to meet his gaze. Nice move, straight out of an old movie, but he's a natural at it. His kiss is warm, lingering. "Thanks," he whispers, "I had a great time." He turns to leave.

"Would you like to come in for a glass of wine?" I open the door—wide.

We sit on the sofa and talk about painting, sculpting, how each of us ended up in Santa Fe. He was married briefly, no children, and relocated here from New Jersey to teach at St. John's College. Nobody's really from Santa Fe, I've come to realize in the six years I've been here. It seems like everyone is either reinventing themselves, running from their past—or both.

We finish the wine and sit quietly for a few moments. He leans over and kisses me, chastely at first, then deeply. I want this man. I think he wants me, too. Should I make the first move? Lead him by the hand into the bedroom? My mother's voice is in my head, spewing platitudes, like *why buy the cow when you can get the milk for free? Damn it, Mom, get out of my head!*

Before I can take this relationship to the next level, Chuck gets up and thanks me for a wonderful evening.

"Why don't you stay? I don't have to get Colin until morning."

"I can't. Sorry, but I'll call."

"You don't have to leave, you know." Do I have to spell it out?

He shifts his weight and looks at the floor. "I can't," he says, deflated. Then, slower: "I mean—I can't."

Oh my God. I am an idiot! He doesn't want to stay because he can't perform. It's not unusual for men around his age, mid-sixties I'm guessing, but they have those little blue pills now. The commercials make it seem like every guy over forty sucks them like candy. I'm at his side in an instant, looking up into his eyes. *Fix this, Elaine!*

"I'd like to see you again," I say, walking him to the door. How to salvage what has been, up until now, a perfect evening? "There's a way around this—modern medicine and all. Did I tell you I'm a former nurse?" This is way beyond awkward, but what more can I say? The next move is his. Either he'll call or he won't.

I watch him get into his truck and drive away. A cool breeze rustles the cottonwood leaves, insects drone an electric hum. I exhale deeply and gaze at the stars. I don't have to pick Colin up. One call to Trish and he could stay over, but Chuck's not spending the night so what's the point?

I want to cry. I want Chuck. I want to have hot, wet sex with a gorgeous sculptor who teaches physics. But tonight I'll go to bed alone, and lie there, aching with want.

Over at Trish and Christa's house, the door is unlocked. Trish is on the sofa, sound asleep. The television casts an electric glow over her slender frame. She hears me and bolts upright. "I had trouble falling asleep. Sometimes I watch TV until I doze off."

No need to explain, but doesn't she usually fall asleep in bed next to Christa?

"It's late. I'll collect Colin and we'll be on our way."

Trish disappears into Deshy's bedroom. After a few moments Colin appears, dragging his backpack behind him. I put my hand on his shoulder and usher him toward the door. Trish looks like she wants to say something. Worry lines crease her brow. There's something on her mind, that's for certain.

"Is everything all right?" I ask, but I'm tired and eager to get home. Trish surely understands that our conversation will have to wait.

"We'll talk tomorrow," she says, her tone dark.

The following morning, the breakfast dishes are drying by the sink and Colin's on his way to school. I'm finishing my second cup of coffee when I hear a knock at the door. It's Trish. Dark circles underscore her brown eyes. Her shoulders sag under the weight of Deshy and a huge diaper bag. She said we'd talk, but at nine in the morning?

"Let me get that." I slip the bag off her shoulder and start a second pot of coffee. Trish sits Deshy on the floor along with her car keys, and he's content. Colin was never that easy, I think. I ramble on about my date with Chuck, but Trish isn't listening. She's staring down at Deshy playing contentedly on the floor while the two steaming mugs of coffee cast dagger-like shadows across the table.

"What's wrong?" I ask, giving her my full attention.

Three little hiccups are followed by an onslaught of tears. Trish covers her face and sobs into her hands. I put my arm around her and wait for the deluge to subside. When it doesn't,

I rub her back and lightly massage her delicate shoulders. I've got all the time in the world. At least until three o'clock when Colin explodes through the door.

"It's alright," I say in a soft voice, "take as long as you need."

Another tidal wave. I drag my chair next to hers, swaying as I rock her, instinctively, as I did when my girls were babies.

Trish blows her nose into a crumpled tissue. "You must think I'm crazy." She straightens up and sips from the mug. "It's Christa. She's not happy. When I ask her what's wrong, she won't say. I can't pin her down. She's been working insane hours…seeing more and more clients. I ask her if it's something I'm doing, but she denies it. I can't reach her and it scares me."

"Has she given any clue about what's bothering her?" I'm on the edge of my chair, gulping coffee.

"That's just it, she won't talk about it. It's like she's forcing me out of her life. We're not close like we used to be. To tell the truth, we haven't been close, physically close, in months. Then last night there was a phone call…"

"While you were watching Colin?" My shoulders tighten.

"About seven o'clock a woman called, asking for Christa. When I asked who it was she hesitated then said—and I swear it's like she was taunting me—'Tell her it's Mercedes. She'll know.'"

"Mercedes. That bitch!" I gasp.

"You know her?" Trish's eyes are wide.

Suddenly, we hear Deshy's blood-curdling howl. We hadn't even noticed he'd left the kitchen. Trish and I jump up from the table and find him in Colin's bedroom, his sweet little face streaked with tears. He holds up his hand and we see an angry red crease across his palm. He must have pinched it in the closet door when he was searching for more of Colin's toys.

Trish nestles him in her arms. Looking at this Madonna and Child, I think that Trish is the best mother ever, and if Christa can't see that...

"Oh my God, what time is it?" Trish says. "I forgot that Deshy has a check-up across town."

"Can't you cancel it?" *We're in the middle of a crisis here!*

"If I do, they'll charge me. And for the next six months I'll only get crappy appointment times." She collects Deshy and the diaper bag and races out the front door.

I had no idea this was brewing. For the rest of the day I'm unsettled. There's an elephant in the room—named Mercedes!

Well, the day didn't start out great and it's taking a nosedive now. I'm late picking up Colin from soccer practice, and I feel terrible about it even though I'm sure Coach wouldn't leave him alone at the field. And I don't usually run late, but after a quick stop at the bank and post office I remembered that we needed coffee and milk. I ran into Sophia thumping cantaloupes in the produce aisle and we talked about her daughter, Chloe, who used to watch Colin. Then I got in the slow check-out line, dropped a bag of oranges in the parking lot, and had to rush like a mad-woman to the practice field.

So I'm speeding when I make a sharp left turn on a late yellow—or maybe it's an early red. A guy driving a black pick-up truck approaching from the opposite direction lays on his horn. Sorry—my bad. I shrug and wave, the Chicago version of an apology. Apparently he doesn't see it that way, because he keeps on honking and waving his fist out the window.

It's more than just a harmless mistake on my part; my driving record isn't good— it's terrible, in fact. One more moving violation and my insurance will drop me. My premium is already sky-high. Worse still, I could get my license taken away. I'm terrified this guy will call the police and have me charged with reckless driving. But there's no physical damage to him or his truck, so I guess I'm in the clear. Or not.

Another fifty feet, and he pulls alongside me and shouts out the window, "Stupid bitch!" Dark glasses and a Diamondbacks ball cap hide his eyes, but he's baring his teeth like an animal about to attack. I'll admit I cut in front of him, but there was no slamming on the brakes or near collision, not even close. This is not how a normal person reacts to typical Friday afternoon traffic; folks rushing home from work eager to start their week-end, mothers rushing to pick their kids up from sports practice. Everyone's rushing somewhere, so what's the fuss?

Road Rage Guy isn't letting up. I drive on a ways and he comes right alongside my car, nearly sideswiping it and cutting me off at every opportunity. What if he has a gun!? I manage to dial 911, keeping my cell phone low, out of sight.

"So, you cut him off?" the dispatcher jokes when I tell him what's happening, but I'm not laughing.

"I may have cut him off, but this guy's scary."

He asks if I want to press charges, but I tell him all I want is to be left alone to pick up my grandson at the soccer field without being forced off the road. He asks my location and I peer out the window for the nearest street sign.

Behind me, Road Rage Guy suddenly accelerates, as if he's going to rear-end me. My heart's pounding like a jack-hammer inside my chest. He swerves in front of me. I'm in a game of chicken with a psychopath bent on revenge. I pray he stays in his car; I have no intention of leaving mine. Hasn't he made his point and scared me enough? I swear I'll never turn in front of anyone on yellow again!

But now I do need to turn left at the intersection. Hopefully I'll lose him in traffic. But he brakes hard, tires squealing, and cuts a sharp left in front of me across oncoming traffic, barely missing an old man in a Buick. "Oh, no!" I suck a mouthful of air and hold it. The old guy shakes his fist, but the lunatic in the truck has already roared away. My lungs deflate with a sigh as I clutch the wheel for support.

The left turn arrow glows green. I'm on my way. Coach will be there with Colin and other kids waiting for their rides. The soccer field is right around this curve, beyond that clump of trees.

Oh no! There he is! His pick-up is parked across the access road to the park. There's not another car in sight. He's leaning up against it with his beefy arms across his chest, clutching a thick metal pipe in his fist. I scream, and I'm startled to realize I'm still on the line with the 911 dispatcher.

"Mrs. McElroy, are you alright?" he says, at last sounding concerned, "What's happening?"

I can't answer. I have to choose—stop and risk being dragged from the car and assaulted—or ram him. He's walking toward me, slow, steady, his shades pushed up over the bill of his cap. His eyes are slits of distilled hatred. This is beyond road rage. This is pure hate! I slow down and try to pass his truck on the gravel shoulder.

I try to tell the dispatcher what's happening, but the phone's gone dead. The stalker is three steps from my car. Sweat is pouring down his face. He's grinning like a maniac.

"I'll kill you, you stupid bitch!" he shouts and suddenly raises the arm with the pipe.

I jam my foot on the gas. The tires go into a terrifying skid, spitting loose gravel in a stream behind me. Road Rage Guy dives for the pavement. The tires grab the pavement and the car lurches around the curve toward the soccer field. I never thought I'd be so happy to see Coach's mini-van, parked in its usual spot. I screech to a stop and bolt out of the car.

Coach rolls down the window, but before he can speak I scream, "He's after me. Call the police!" I'm gulping air like a spent marathoner. Colin just stares, dumbfounded. "There's a crazy man in the road. My phone's dead. You have to call the police—now!"

"Stay in the car, Colin," Coach directs calmly. He gets out of the van and reaches into my Toyota, turning off the engine. Then puts his hand on my arm, walking me out of earshot..

"Calm down, Mrs. McElroy. Tell me what happened."

"He came at me in the road over there!" I point toward the bend in the road. "What are you waiting for?"

By the time the cops arrive the crazy guy is long gone, of course. Colin is beside himself with excitement when we get to sit in the back of the squad car. He sees the shotgun mounted on the dash and blurts, "Have you ever shot anyone?" The patrolman replies that his job is to keep people safe, not injure them. Thankfully, he doesn't go into a gory rendition of a cops and robbers shoot-out.

Suddenly, the dispatcher's voice breaks through the static on the radio. He's relieved to find out I'm alright, and I'm thankful because now Coach knows I'm not crazy; there really was a psycho stalking me.

It's long past dinner time when the patrolman finishes his report. On the drive home, my stomach is in knots. I'm lightheaded from hunger—and spent. Colin bounces non-stop, straining against the seatbelt. I put my hand on his leg, a reminder to bring it down a notch, but he's wired, asking question after question.

"Did he have a gun? What did he look like?"

I clutch the steering wheel. My hands are trembling, reliving the trauma.

Suddenly Colin falls silent. I look over. He's wrapped his arms around himself and he's rocking back and forth.

"Sweetie, I'm fine," I say, and I tousle his hair. "Everything turned out okay. The dispatcher on the phone helped me and so did the patrolman."

"Will they shoot that guy when they catch him?" He perks up at the thought of a gun battle, like on TV. "I could be a policeman when I grow up."

He's seen so many shows with the police portrayed as tough guys who get the job done. Sitting in the squad car and seeing a policeman on the job has sparked his interest.

"You never know." I say, although I envision Colin someday working in a skilled trade, perhaps an expert carpenter, maybe, or a master electrician, not a policeman strapping on a weapon before he goes to work every day. I don't want to discourage him, though. "They won't shoot him, Col. They'll give him a ticket and tell him not to do it again." An anger management course wouldn't hurt, either.

That night, a piercing scream startles me awake. It's mine. My nightshirt is stuck to my clammy skin. Colin runs into my room.

"Granma, Granma, what's wrong?" His voice is high and tight, his eyes scrunched beneath the worry lines on his brow. All the pain and loss he's experienced in his young life has returned, ready to overwhelm him.

"Just a bad dream, like you have sometimes."

A shadow darkens his face. "Was it a car crash?"

The memory is always there, lurking in a bruised corner of his heart. I wonder how his life would be if he had been raised by his parents, in Ireland—instead of here in Santa Fe, with me. The best I can offer him is my love and reassurance that I'll always be here for him. Sometimes I'm not certain it's enough.

"Not a crash, sweetie, just a silly bad dream. Don't worry, I'm fine." I stroke his head and he melts back to sleep alongside me. My breathing slows and I drift off.

Trish

The Ten Items or Less line at the check-out snakes halfway down the aisle. Its 5:15 and folks are rushing in after work, hurrying to grab something for dinner and settle in for the evening.

Christa's left work early. It's a treat for Deshy and me, since she usually gets home just as I'm putting dinner on the table. She's dressed in her 'professional attire'; black tailored suit and sling-back heels, a knock-out. No wonder people steal sidelong glances at our handsome family. In my cargo pants and Birkenstocks, they probably assume I'm the nanny. It's funny, I hate shopping for myself, but I get a kick out of picking out cute outfits for Deshy. I slip my hand around Christa's slim waist, draw her close, and give her a chaste peck on the cheek.

"I'm so glad you're home early," I say.

Christa

Trish has been "out" so much longer than me. She doesn't care that people are staring.

"Huh? Look a' that!" Says a paunchy, middle-aged guy in line behind us. He elbows his wife and nods in our direction. I glance in their shopping cart. It's filled with chips, jars of cheesy dip, and a gallon jug of wine.

Well, Mister, live and let live. Just leave us alone.

The wife glares at him. "Shut your pie hole, Lenny! Why do you give a shit?"

"I don't need to see a couple of dykes kissing." Everyone hears him and looks away.

Why do I need to be subjected to this jerk's homophobic rant? I glance at my watch, wishing the checker would hurry up. Trish clenches her jaw and busies herself brushing granola crumbs from Deshy's chin as he fusses. He grabs a candy bar within reach and bites into it, wrapper and all. Trish removes the wrapper and hands it to him; she must be rattled, allowing him junk food. I plant myself between the loud-mouthed jerk and my family. No need for an ugly scene. Let's just check-out and get the hell out of here.

Trish points to a display of disposable razors, just above loud-mouth guy's head. I freeze, careful not to make eye contact with this creep.

I reach for the razors and as I do he eyes me with a salacious grin and grabs his crotch. Disgusting! My stomach turns and bile rises in my throat. Apparently, this moron thinks that one go-round with him and my attraction to women will be forever quelled. Unbelievable!

It takes every bit of restraint I can summon not to punch him in the mouth. I could do it, too. I'm a head taller, years younger, and in way better shape. His wife shakes her head, mumbling. No doubt Lenny's unenlightened world view has reared its ugly head before.

"Let's go," Trish says.

I take a breath, throw my shoulders back, and glare into Lenny's little piggy eyes. "I don't know what your problem is, mister. Just leave us the hell alone."

"Yeah Lenny, just leave 'em alone," his wife chimes in, bolder now that I've confronted him. Apparently she thinks we share some sort of sisterhood because we're both revolted by her husband. *Sorry, Mrs. Lenny, you're on your own.*

"Whose side are you on?" he barks at his wife.

The people in line crane their necks to see what's going on, shifting their weight nervously. This confrontation is going to make their wait longer, but nobody has the guts to intervene. Trish unbuckles Deshy. "Enough. We're out of here," she says.

"Yeah, and take that kid with you," Lenny calls after us. I don't look back. "Won't have one of your own, but don't mind taking someone else's reject." That bastard means Deshy.

He starts to wail, as if he understands the ugly things being said about him. This guy Lenny is the lowest form of bigot. It's one thing to attack Trish and me, but Deshy? No wonder the world is so messed up—thanks to people like him.

We leave the groceries on the belt and storm past the checker. "What about your groceries?" she calls to us.

"Ask him!" I nod toward Lenny. He scowls and looks away.

"We're never shopping here again," I say, but I know it's not true. Why should we have to drive half-way across town because of people like that?

Trish

We drive home in silence. The ugliness at the store should bring Christa and me closer. It's a chance to share our mutual outrage over Lenny, and every bigot everywhere, whether it's about sexual preference, race, religion, nationality, or any other kind of discrimination. Instead we withdraw into our thoughts.

I guess because I've been 'out' longer and experienced homophobia many times it doesn't bother me as much. It still surprises me, though. I'm comfortable with who I am, and when I'm confronted by someone like Lenny, it reminds me that not everyone has evolved.

Christa's rattled. I can tell by the way she clutches the steering wheel and stares at the road. The muscles in her jaw clench and relax, then clench again. She'll be grinding her teeth tonight while I lay next to her wondering how to bridge the gap—chasm—that's developed between us, threatening to swallow us. I worry that we won't make it, but I try not to dwell on it.

Christa

One of the associates at the office is on maternity leave, and the rest of us have to pick up the slack. It's been a challenge, balancing the increased workload with the strain at home.

Tonight when I pull into the driveway I just about lose it.

I've asked Trish a million times to move Deshy's tricycle out of the way. It's not enough that I listen to clients' problems all day, now I've got to get out of the car, move the trike, and get back in before I can park in the garage.

"Hey guys, I'm home. Where is everyone?" I plop on the leather sofa and kick off my shoes. They hit the floor with a thunk. Deshy motors toward me, his round face beaming like sunshine. "Come here, you!" I hoist him onto my lap. He notices my dangly earrings and begins tugging at them.

"What a day I've had." I say loud enough so Trish can hear me in the kitchen. "Can you believe Lupe didn't show up for work, again? Not even the courtesy of a call. Now we've got to find another receptionist and we're already shorthanded. I can't believe how casual these people are about not coming to work, and if they do make it, nine times out of ten, they're late."

Trish

"These people?" Who is this woman I thought I knew?

"Trish, honey, I made a pitcher of lemonade last night. Could you get me some? With a splash of vodka?"

And when did I become her personal bartender?

"Please?"

Oh well, I suppose that makes all the difference. I'll get right on it.

Christa

Deshy threads his fingers through my hair, twisting and pulling. I release his grip and tickle his belly—round as a garden Buddha's—until he's breathless from laughter. All of a sudden, he stops laughing. After the briefest pause, he vomits purple ooze all over my new suit. A Donna Karan! Shit!

"Trish, come quick! And bring a damp towel! What are you feeding him? It's all over my new suit."

"It's grape juice, one hundred percent organic. Just like we agreed."

What's she so pissed about? I'm the one with grape puke in my lap.

"I've got to get this to a cleaner right now, before the stain sets. Is the one at the strip mall still open?"

"You keep forgetting, Christa. This is Santa Fe, not Chicago, where things stay open 24/7."

I get that, but by now it doesn't matter. This wardrobe investment's a total loss. I can't resist a final dig, though. "At least the people in Chicago have a strong work ethic. Dry cleaners there accommodate the schedules of customers with careers."

Trish

I resist the urge to fire back. We haven't eaten. And Deshy still needs to be bathed and put to bed.

"It must be frustrating for you," I say, a weak retort to Her Royal Highness.

Christa changes into a satin Vera Wang robe and Ralph Lauren skinny jeans, in sharp contrast to my sweats, blown out at the knees and splotched with stains after a day with an active toddler. Deshy shovels food in his mouth and spills it on the floor in equal quantities. All of a sudden, he swats his bowl into the air, and before it makes landfall it somersaults twice and spatters applesauce all over Christa, Vera, and Ralph.

"Oh well, that's how they learn, I guess," Christa says. "Deshy, sweetie, try to keep our applesauce on the tray, okay? Don't make more work for Mommy Trish."

Christa sounds like a condescending bitch. I never noticed it before. Funny, how a toddler's typical behavior brings out a person's true colors.

I mop the mess with a paper towel and settle back into my chair. It's time for grown-up talk with Christa.

"We were at the park today and there was this big, fat caterpillar—all fuzzy—right there on the ground. Deshy had to squat down for a better look and he wanted to touch it, so I held his hand and we did, together. I told him it was like his book, *The Very Hungry Caterpillar*. He tried to say it and it came out 'pilla pilla' instead of just 'pilla' like before. He's getting it more and more, even with big words." I'm bursting with pride at my—our—son.

Christa pats Deshy on the head. "That's my boy, right on schedule."

Instead of giving Deshy a thumbs up or saying "Good job", Christa tells him he's right on schedule. When did she become so clinical? Maybe she always was and it's one more thing I didn't notice. She's reduced our son to a developmental timetable. She'd enjoy him more if she'd lighten up and accept him as he is; an adorable, frustrating toddler.

Then she adds, "He's so developmentally on track." She looks to me for affirmation.

"Ah ha," is all I can manage.

Christa

Deshy's asleep and all I want to do is catch the news before going to bed. Trish drops a bombshell—Mercedes has been calling the house asking for me!

Damn, you Mercedes! Why couldn't you have stayed out of my life! All of a sudden, after years, you call me at home, and for what? I'm not even sure how you got my number. I certainly wouldn't have given it to you. I should have gotten an unlisted number, but who knew I'd ever need one? You dumped me—hard, so why would I take your calls?

Trish

I want to scream into the phone, "Stop calling here, bitch!" My God, months of this! But even though my hands are trembling, I'll be damned if I'll give her the satisfaction of hearing me rant. Who the hell does Mercedes think she is, calling here? Doesn't she know we have a child? Just because she's Christa's ex doesn't entitle her to anything. Either she wants Christa back or they're already hooked up. That must be why Christa doesn't touch me anymore. Well, if Mercedes thinks I'm going to quietly fade away, she's dead wrong!

Cheese bubbles over the side of the casserole I made for dinner—Christa's favorite—chicken enchiladas. The spicy scent of cilantro, cumin, and jalapeños fills the kitchen. I love cooking for her, but why even try? She has no clue what I do all day, and, worse, she doesn't care. I wonder what she'd say if I served frozen dinners from the microwave. She's so wrapped up in herself and her work, I doubt she'd notice.

I search the closet for the cashmere sweater Christa gave me last Christmas, the one I wanted to return because it was so expensive and impractical. I'll put on make-up, that'll get her attention. We haven't had sex since when I can't remember. Now I know what's stopping us—it's *got* to be Mercedes!

Deshy's napping. His silken hair is draped over his eyes; his chest rises and falls rhythmically with each breath. Baby Boy, if I let you sleep, you'll never go down tonight and I need Mommy Christa's undivided attention later. I brush his hair from his eyes and kiss his cheek. When he doesn't stir, I decide to take a quick bath then feed him an early dinner. The evening will be Christa's and mine.

I turn on the tap and sprinkle scented crystals into the tub. Before stepping into the water, I examine my forty-two-year-old body in the mirror; my belly is flat, my breasts are still perky, and my butt has managed to defy the forces of gravity. It's one of the perks of adopting—your body doesn't go to hell. But I'd loved to have nursed Deshy. I feel a tingling sensation in my nipples thinking about him suckling at my breast—the same sensation I used to feel when Christa did. I'm the older woman in this relationship by a couple of years and Christa loves to remind me. Even though she says she's joking, I can't afford to let myself go.

Suddenly, Christa's image appears in the mirror, startling me. I stand perfectly still, watching her gaze roam the length of me like she's appraising a lifeless statue in a museum. Then, without a word, she looks away.

Caught off guard, I try to sound calm: "You're early." I watch a flush rise to her cheeks because she hasn't seen me naked in weeks.

So many things have come between us. First, it was Deshy's surgery, and then it was the daily routine of a new mother; feeding him, walks in the park, endless loads of laundry, doctor's appointments, bathing him, bedtime stories. I've become my mother, something I swore I'd never be. I've neglected my relationship with Christa, wasn't available to her. I drifted from my silver craft and the friends I had before Christa, before I moved into her house, before Deshy. There was a time when we couldn't wait to be together at the end of the day. It hasn't been that way for a long while…but she's here now, we both are, in this moist, scented cavern.

"Want to join me?" I say. "Deshy's asleep." The mirror is clouded, the air heavy with jasmine.

She pauses. Even when she's home, she's not. My nakedness has no effect on her, and I have to have sex with her now, to prove we're still a couple.

"It's Thursday," she says, her voice flat but emphatic. "Everybody's trying for an extra session before the week-end. I have two more clients to see. I just stopped home for some files. What's for dinner? It smells delicious."

"What's wrong with you?" I scream, startled at the sound of my own voice. "Why won't you touch me? And why is a woman named Mercedes calling here?"

Christa looks up, the color drained from her face.

"Say something, dammit, Christa!"

In the scene playing in my head, Christa takes me in her arms and reassures me, and we tumble into bed, a jumble of intertwined arms and legs. Instead, I'm humiliated by her indifference. With tears scalding my cheeks, I rush to the bedroom and wrap myself in my robe.

"You are something else," I hiss. "You call yourself a therapist and you can't even keep your own family from falling apart."

"You're upset, Trish." It's her damn professional voice; I've heard it a thousand times when she's on the phone with distraught clients, the tone I've told her is irritating and condescending.

"Damn right. And don't give me that clinical crap. Have you taken a vow of chastity? Or are you screwing her?"

Having retrieved a thin stack of files from her desk, she turns to the door, and stops. "I can't talk to you when you're like this," she says.

"Like what? A woman who hasn't had sex in *forever*? And why is that, Christa? Is it because you have someone else? God dammit, say something!"

"It strikes me as odd that you want me to jump in the tub with you—out of the blue—today of all days. Especially since you're the one who hasn't shown the slightest interest in sex in years. How convenient for you, now, all of a sudden, just when it's impossible for me..."

I storm off to the kitchen and hurl the hot casserole in the sink. I made this for us—but now it seems there is no 'us.' Glass explodes everywhere. Red sauce, tortillas and chicken splatter the counter, stick to the wall, and stain my robe. Christa watches, horrified.

"Get out!" I scream. "You don't care about me...or Deshy! The only person you care about is yourself!"

She turns on her heel and escapes out the front door.

I pick up a crystal vase and cock my arm to throw it at the door, and then place it back on the table. Enough destruction for one day. Deshy's in his crib, wailing.

I wipe my tears on my sleeve and rake my fingers through my hair. Deshy needs me.

He's so forlorn, standing in his crib with his plump arms outstretched. I manage a weak smile, pluck him out, and hold him close.

"Down," he says. In a wink, he's at the doorway to the kitchen. I rush to scoop him up before he steps on shards of glass scattered across the tile floor, glinting in the afternoon sunlight.

Jesus, I did this, and it didn't accomplish anything. She doesn't want me and no amount of cooking, cleaning or mothering our son will change that. Did she ever really want me, except maybe in the beginning?

Later, I call the one person I know who will listen and understand, the friend who's been there for me, more than my own family.

"Elaine?" My voice is shaky. "Can we come over?"

"Trish, honey. You sound strange—is everything alright?"

"Yes. Well, no. I don't know." I choke back tears. Once they start, there'll be no stopping.

"Sure. Come on over."

Christa

"Mrs. Homolka, tell me more about the argument you had with your husband last night."

My client sits on the office sofa, prim as a Mother Superior, with hands folded in her lap and legs crossed at the ankles.

She's one of Santa Fe's premier matrons. Everything's perfect—hair, nails, outfit—everything except her life.

"I really wouldn't call it an argument. I was the one doing the talking—and screaming. He won't argue. It's like trying to talk to a brick wall."

"That must be very frustrating."

"It's infuriating. Whatever I was aggravated about in the first place is multiplied a hundred times. I want to throw something at him. If only he would say something—anything. He won't even acknowledge my frustration. Do you have any idea what that's like? I'm invisible to him."

"Would that make it better, if it was more two-sided?"

"When he doesn't respond I think he doesn't care. It takes two to have a decent fight. If he loved me, he'd argue."

"Hmmm."

Elaine

Trish has brought more stuff with her than usual; a Pack 'n Play, the diaper bag, a suitcase and a bag of groceries. She's moving in!

"I ruined dinner so I'll have to start over," she says, wheeling the oversized luggage into the house. Her face is drawn. She looks exhausted, as if talking is an effort. A cat yowls from the back seat of her car. She's brought Winston, too! She's brought the cat!

And his bed!

Minutes later, Trish is whirling around my kitchen, trying to remake the dinner she says she's thrown into the garbage at her house, but offering no explanation as to how or why that happened.

I station myself well out of her way. At some point I'll draw her out. Find out what's going on at home. "I know enchiladas are Christa's favorite. So what happened to the first batch—too much sour cream? I've done that."

Her chin quivers. "No, I wish." She assembles the enchiladas using pre-cooked chicken and a jar of Verde sauce.

"What then?"

"I trashed dinner—threw it in the sink." Trish won't look at me and won't stop fiddling with those damn enchiladas.

"Because…?" I'm wondering if I'll ever find out why Trish has moved into my house and taken over my kitchen.

She stops, wheels around to face me, her eyes blazing. "Because Christa is having an affair with that bitch Mercedes!"

Good God, no wonder Trish is a wreck. "You know this for a fact?"

"Christa came home early today. Dinner was in the oven. Deshy was napping. And I was stark naked, about to take a bath." She slides the casserole in the oven.

"I'm still not making the connection."

She plants her hands on the kitchen counter as if bracing herself. She slowly lifts her head. Her face is taut with anger. Her eyes are dark pools of pain.

"I threw dinner in the sink because Christa rejected me. She could have stayed and we could have made love. It's been so long. Instead she bolted back to work. She was disgusted by the sight of me naked."

Christa

It's been two days since our big blow-up, and Trish and I haven't spoken. I came home to an empty house with a trashed kitchen. Just a scribbled note about staying with Elaine, which might not be a bad idea since it will give her a change of scenery and maybe a different outlook.

Trish and I are on different planets. A big decision for her is what to make for dinner, or which laundry detergent to buy. I spend my days in the real world, wishing my life was that simple. But I signed on for this—me, Trish, and Deshy—our little family. I listen to people complain about their lives all day, every day; *"he's having an affair, she's let herself go, since the kids arrived there's no time left for us."* I assumed Trish and I weren't like that, but I was wrong. Just because we're two women raising our son doesn't mean we don't have the same problems as any other couple.

But the last thing I need is Mercedes back in my life. No doubt she wants to pick up where we left off. I hate that I'm still attracted to her, but if I let my guard down, I'll fall—hard—and then Mercedes will drop me, like before. I don't think I could survive that kind of hurt—again. I've told her to stop calling the house. I've got nothing to hide, but Trish has gone over the edge. I've never seen her so upset.

In graduate school, while I was writing my thesis, I hit a road block. The words just wouldn't come. I needed a break and some fresh perspective. Of course, nobody had money. I joined a group of students on a bicycle trip. We rode fifty or sixty miles a day and camped at night. I remember my bike; metallic brown and heavy. The experience was liberating, though, and one I've never forgotten. We rode past dairy farms and an occasional stream, talking and laughing as the miles flew by. I was able to clear my head and finish my paper. Back then we didn't wear helmets or bike shoes or have GPS. We just rode. I want that kind of freedom again. No work. No toddler. No pissed-off partner. And no ex-girlfriend on the phone.

Know what? I needed that break then and I need it now. I'll call Trish as soon as I get home tonight and...

"Trish, I know it sounds crazy—a bicycle trip, especially now, But I've got to do this, got to have some time and space to sort things out, and need to do it before the summer heat gets fierce. I'll be back in a week, and you can reach me on my cell anytime."

What I don't say, but what hangs heavy in the air, is that this separation might be our last chance to stay together. Or it might be our breaking point.

I rummage around the garage and finally locate my bicycle behind Deshy's infant seat and a deflated wading pool. I dust off the cob webs, pump air in the tires and lube the chain. Then, I take it for a long ride up Aspen Vista Trail until my legs give out and I realize how out of shape I am. But, the feeling of freedom, the wind in my hair and the sun on my face, slowly returns. It's like flying without wings.

Elaine

Trish is sniffling. She and Deshy—and Winston—have been here for two days. Since they've arrived, Callie only creeps out of her hiding place at night.

Christa left this morning on some sort of bike trip, and Trish is devastated.

"I can't believe it." she moans, watching listlessly as Deshy wheels toy trucks around my sun-drenched courtyard. This small, private space is one of the main reasons I bought this place. It's so authentic Santa Fe. The casitas on East Palace Avenue aren't extravagant. They were built back in the 1950s, long before upscale developments here pushed the housing prices sky high. Two bedrooms, a cozy kitchen, stucco walls, a beehive fireplace, and my courtyard. I fell in love with it immediately.

"More coffee, Trish? It'll only take a minute to make another pot." I start to get up, but I'm not sure she's even heard me.

"My 'estranged partner' (she does air quotes) has gone off on a biking-camping tour, reliving a trip she took back in grad school—when she was single. She won't be back for over a week." Trish raises her coffee to her lips before she realizes, with a start, that it's empty.

Who knows what's going on in Christa's head? I don't want to pry, but I encourage Trish to explain. Gingerly, I ask, "Is Mercedes involved in this?"

"Deshy's 'other mommy' (more air quotes) informs me that she is *not* with Mercedes."

That's a relief. "And the phone calls?"

Trish shrugs. "All I know is that Christa says she hasn't done anything to encourage her, and I guess I have to believe her."

I remember Mercedes. She's the kind of woman who's not easily put off. She takes what she wants and won't take "No" for an answer. Trish has no clue what she's up against.

Oblivious to the escalating crisis, Deshy loads his plastic truck with pebbles from the walk-way, dumps the stones in a pile, and levels them with a stick. Watching him, it occurs to me that building a road is far easier than repairing a relationship.

Christa

The equipment I've collected for my trip is spread out on the garage floor—panniers, a rain jacket, helmet, bike shorts, gloves, jerseys, tent, sleeping bag, spare tubes, water bottles, energy bars. Santa Fe to Boulder in seven days will be a challenge—and a welcome break from my stifling routine. I wonder how I'll measure up to the other riders, fourteen of them and two guides. Will I be the oldest rider, the youngest, perhaps the most out of shape? No matter, I'm ready to jump right in.

Trish

I haven't been back at the house since I trashed the kitchen. I can't revisit that ugly scene just yet. Let Christa fix her own dinner, pick up the cleaning, do the laundry and scrub the bathroom. Maybe then she'll appreciate everything I do. Deshy and I are staying here with Elaine, at least for the time being. I do the laundry, help Colin with his homework, cook and clean the kitchen after meals. It keeps me busy, enough so that I'm not yearning for Christa every minute of every day.

Elaine's neighbor, Tristan, has been out of town on business. Elaine asks me if I wouldn't mind going next door to feed his parrot. She hands me the key and I head over. Tris and I are friends; I used to live on this same block before Christa and I set up housekeeping in a more upscale neighborhood across town. He must have remodeled since I was last here. He's installed track lighting, slate floors, and stainless appliances. No surprise, he's a successful architect.

Christa

Every muscle in my body is screaming. I'm exhausted, too, but after fifty scorching miles hauling thirty pounds of gear, I can't fall asleep. Go figure. It's so close in my tiny, one-person tent that I can't even turn around. And I have to pee, again. The guides told us to drink plenty of water during the day, so I did. Now my kidneys are working overtime.

I unzip the sleeping bag and the tent flap, grab my flashlight, find my flip-flops, shimmy out feet-first, and plod into the dark to the campground bathroom, a cinder block cube. Milky light from the bug-encrusted bulb above the door is my beacon to relief.

Trish

Stanley, Tristan's parrot, gives me a sidelong glance from his perch and backs two quick steps away. He cocks his head, staring at me with bright, beady eyes, deciding whether I'm friend or foe. Birdseed crunches underfoot as I slowly approach his cage.

"Hi, Stanley, pretty bird. How's the pretty bird?" I coo, all sing-songy. I slowly open the door to his cage a crack. The bird's fierce, button eyes track every move.

Christa

I keep my head down and follow my flashlight beam to the bathroom where I nearly collide with Dave. He's the super-ripped dude who pedaled today's brutal miles effortlessly. We talked at the lunch stop and again at dinner. He told me he's got a vacation condo on Maui. Seems like money's not a concern. He's shirtless. I'm bra-less beneath my T-shirt.

"Everything OK?" he asks.

"Fine. Just gotta pee." I hop from foot to foot, crossing my arms self-consciously over my chest. The stars are luminous gems scattered across a velvet cape of sky. An animal howls mournfully in the distance.

"Amazing, huh?" I say, staring at the heavens.

"Yeah," he says.

I move past him and he flashes a toothy grin.

"This is the men's side,' he says.

Mortified, I trudge to the other side. He calls after me, "Your tent is really small. If you want company, mine's right next to yours."

"Oh, I know." I call back.

Trish

Without warning, the bird shoots out of the cage and pecks my hand with his sharp beak.

"Damn!" He's drawn blood. What is it with him? Does he somehow smell my cat on me?

Stanley flaps around the ceiling, squawking. He lights on a high teak cabinet, and when I stand below, calling to him, he bombs me with a milky splat.

"Shit!"

Christa

Clearly, Dave's attracted to me. I'm turned on by him, too. The spark, the energy, it's how I felt when I first met Mercedes. Time hasn't dimmed the memory of her touch. I was my best—at work and with my friends— when I was with Mercedes. Now it's the daily grind of limited career prospects, and family obligations. I'm just so drained and worn down— as much from Trish's rejections as from the day-to-day routine.

With Mercedes sparks flew. With Trish, well…she's great with Deshy.

Trish

"Whoa, what's going on?"

It's a man's voice, and he's right behind me. It's Tristan. He's home early.

"I didn't expect you for hours. I thought I'd have time to clean up this mess. Sorry. I have no idea how to get him back in his cage."

Tristan is drop dead gorgeous and as stylish as his home. His hair's a little grayer than I remember, but he wears it well; tortoise shell frames highlight his kind grey eyes. He's not tall, but he's Richard Gere sexy.

"It's good to see you, Trish. I haven't seen you since you moved. Don't worry, I'll take it from here."

He admonishes the bird in a low monotone, moving slowly toward it, but stops abruptly when he sees my injured hand.

"You're bleeding." He reaches for my arm. "Let me get a clean towel." By the time Tristan returns, Stanley's in flight again. Downy feathers drift to the floor.

"Has he done this sort of thing before?" I ask.

"I don't think so. Elaine never mentioned a problem when she helped me out. I can't tell you how sorry I am, Trish."

Instead of moving slowly, this time Tristan simply extends his arm as a perch and Stanley flies down to him.

"Sorry, old man." Tristan says as he walks Stanley to his cage. The bird glares at me and pecks hard on Tristan's arm. Tristan deposits Stanley summarily in the cage. "Looks like he got both of us," he says.

Blood seeps through his ripped sleeve, but he seems more amused than concerned.

Christa

I feel like Alice down the rabbit hole. This tent's closing in on me. It's late—or early—and I can't sleep. I thought that after riding hard all day I'd collapse into oblivion. But no.

The air is chilly and dry as a cracker. Are those coyotes howling? Wolves? I know for sure snakes are out there. What if one slithers into my sleeping bag! No wonder I can't sleep! I hear a tent flap unzip, see a moving beam of light. Somebody's headed to the bathroom. And, *I need to pee again.* Surrendering to the urge, I unzip the sleeping bag, grab flip-flops, throw a hoodie over my T-shirt and open the flap. All is quiet, but I notice an inviting glow inside Dave's tent.

Trish

"Come on," Tristan says, leading me to the bathroom. I hesitate, gazing at the earth-tone marble floor and walls, the cavernous walk-in shower and elegant waterfall fixture. A cleverly placed sky light gives the illusion of showering outdoors. It's magnificent, out of the pages of Architectural Digest.

"I designed it myself," he says proudly.

At a marble basin, he runs warm water over my injuries—a couple of small puncture wounds between my thumb and index finger and an angry red scratch along my forearm. He cleans and dries them with a fluffy white towel. I relax and I lean into him, feeling suddenly woozy.

"Have you eaten anything?" He eases me onto a wooden bench.

This is where Scarlett O'Hara would flutter her lashes and purr, "Why no, Cap'n Butler, I don't believe I've taken any nourishment today. Please, sir, some smelling salts and a fainting couch." I reply, "I don't remember."

"I'll take care of that." He says, softly rubbing antibiotic ointment onto my hand and arm. Tristan is as gentle and caring as his bird is feisty and peckish.

He takes off his shirt and inspects the torn sleeve. "This is ruined."

He's naked from the waist up and I'll admit it's not an unpleasant sight. With no brothers and a father who never walked around shirtless, it's unexpected. I glance at his muscled pecs and quickly look away.

He pulls on a polo shirt and glances at the top of my head, frowning.

"My bird got you—there." He points and apologizes. "Sorry. You're going to need a shower." He turns on the spigot and hands me a plush, terry robe. "Towels," he says, and points to a glass shelf with snow white linens. "I'll start an omelet."

Cascades of soothing water caress me. I'm in heaven.

Christa

"Dave? Are you awake?" I whisper. "It's me, Christa." He unzips the flap and peers out into the darkness.

"Come on in," he says like he's been expecting me. The lantern hanging from a tent pole casts the inviting glow. His tent is palatial compared to mine. He's got a clothes line strung along the back with socks and bike shorts, and there's even a little mesh pouch for his cell phone within arm's reach. The effect is positively cozy, confirming my need for an upgrade in the tent department. Dave is a welcoming host, clearing a spot on the floor for me to sit, plus I can stretch out my arms and legs without touching nylon.

We talk about how we ended up on this tour—he does two long rides a year to stay in shape, for what he doesn't say, and he's certainly succeeding. I tell him that I'm taking a break from seeing clients and that I'm working through some personal issues. I tell him about my grad school biking experience. Neither of us asks if the other has a partner. He's not wearing a ring and neither am I. It's like we're united in a common cause—tackling daily miles through desert flats and mountain foothills. The people we left behind are temporarily forgotten. Being in the elements forces us to live in the moment, confronting each obstacle as it comes.

Dave encircles me in his muscled arms and draws me close. When I don't resist, he kisses me, tentatively at first. My entire body relaxes into his welcoming warmth. I close my eyes and the memory of lost passion returns, so powerful I feel tears welling. I wrap my arms around his neck and eagerly return his kiss.

Trish

What an unexpected pleasure, being pampered and fussed over by a classy, handsome man. I linger in the shower, sampling Tristan's high end body wash, shampoo, and conditioner—impressive for a single guy. How extravagant—and sexy—my every need is anticipated.

My clothes are in a pile, stained with blood and bird poop. I pull Tristan's plush terry robe around me, inhale its citrusy scent, and pad into the kitchen. He's busy at the butcher block chopping red peppers and green onions. A pan sizzles on the stove. It smells like breakfast at a diner—a very upscale diner. He stops to take a sip of white wine from a sweating crystal flute.

"I should call Elaine and tell her what happened," I say.

"Not to worry; she called while you were in the shower. I told her I was making dinner for us. It's the least I can do. Oh, and I fed and watered the beast, too."

Is this a dream? If it is, I don't want to wake up—ever.

"How was your shower—find everything?" He hands me a glass of chilled pinot grigio.

"Fabulous. Your house is so modern and cozy at the same time—an oasis, really."

"Here's to an interesting afternoon." He raises his glass to me as if saluting some heroic deed I've performed.

"Yes, interesting." A flush warms my cheeks and I'm not sure why I'm feeling shy. I quickly take a generous sip of wine.

Christa

I wake up refreshed—and sated—in Dave's tent. The sky is turning pearly grey.

"Up to you, want to stay?" he says, propped up on his elbow, grinning broadly, as if triumphant.

Oh sure, I'm a feather in his cap. Everyone will know we spent the night together. We'll be labeled a couple—Christa and Dave. Sex with Dave was a powerful reminder of what I've been missing—explosive orgasms that melt away months of pent-up frustration—but I'm not ready to be paired with him for the rest of the trip.

"Nah, think I'll head back to my tent."

One day melds into another; eat, sleep, ride. Each day is a little easier. My legs are getting stronger and I'm charging up the challenging hills without gasping for breath. Nothing beats riding hard all day, a warm shower, and a huge bowl of pasta drowned in red sauce and Parmesan cheese, plus garlic bread slathered in butter. I've burned so many calories that I can eat a spaghetti dinner without guilt, knowing that it won't go straight to my hips.

Despite the exercise, fresh air and full belly, I can't help lying awake at night wondering what will happen when I return to Santa Fe. Will Trish and I salvage our relationship? Do I even want to? And every night, I end up in Dave's tent. At first I fought the urge; now I don't even try. He's always got a condom handy if I'm ready—and I'm always ready. It seems too good to be true—mind-numbing sex with no strings attached.

Trish

Before we sit down to dinner, Tristan tells me that he has a daughter who's about my size. "Her jeans look like they'll fit you, and here's a clean shirt." The shirt is crisply laundered, and on a hanger.

"Tristan, I couldn't. Not one of your monogramed shirts."

"Why not? It'll look great on you." He grins and offers me the shirt. "Don't take too long, dinner's almost ready."

I shimmy into the jeans, roll up the shirt sleeves, and rejoin my host. Wearing his shirt makes me feel sexy and desirable. A way I haven't felt in a long time.

We linger over dinner, talking and laughing easily. His life is clearly more interesting than mine. He tell me about design work he did for a wealthy matron who had no qualms about inviting him to bed for an afternoon tryst while her husband was away on business.

"To her, I was just a fringe benefit of the job." He shakes his head and throws up his hands in mock resignation.

"Did you take her up on her offer?" My eyes are wide. Why am I shocked? This sort of thing probably happens all the time to men like Tristan—and to women like Christa.

Face it Trish, your life sucks.

"Nope." He shoots me a mischievous grin, his gray eyes sparkling. "But now I know how it feels to be a sex object."

After he loads the dishwasher and neatly folds the dish towel, we go to the living room. Stanley is blessedly sleeping. From the teak cabinet, Tristan selects a bottle of tequila and carries it to the kitchen. Ice cubes clink. A blender whirrs. He returns with a pitcher and two margarita glasses. Coarse salt clings to the rims, just as it should.

"To Trish," he says, "who got more than she bargained for today."

I take a generous sip. "Mmm, I could get used to this." I say, licking my salty lips.

We settle into the leather sofa and talk and drink and laugh and drink some more until the pitcher is empty.

Christa

This affair, arrangement, or whatever it is with Dave, is just a moment in time. His body is gorgeous and the sex is an explosion of built-up tension, but when the ride is over I'll go back to Santa Fe and he'll go back to Maui, or to climb his next mountain. I'm okay with that. Neither of us has a claim on the other, but after everyone is zipped in for the night and the camp is quiet, I'm drawn to him, to his stories of exotic adventures, to the hot, eager sex, and to the rapturous sleep that follows.

Trish

"I can't remember when I've had so much fun," I giggle.

I stand to leave, wobble, and plop back onto the sofa, laughing like it's the funniest thing in a long time, and it is. Tristan and I say nothing for a few seconds and then burst out laughing. He slides closer and kisses me. I kiss him back, surprised at my willingness, allowing his tongue to search and probe. It feels good—so very good. He lifts me effortlessly onto his lap. I wrap my arms around his neck. His hands slip under my shirt—his shirt—and over my breasts. Shock waves travel like electricity from my nipples down to my sex.

Do I want this? If I don't, I need to say something right now.

He lifts me effortlessly, nuzzling my ear, and carries me to the master suite. I giggle like a ticklish child. He sets me down on his huge bed and grabs a foil packet from the bedside table. I've never actually *seen* a guy put on a condom. I watch wide-eyed as he rolls it over his erection. Am I ready for this? Do I even know what to do? At my all-girls Catholic high school sex education consisted of ladies from the parish telling us that sex was wonderful—when you're married. So basically, don't give in to temptation—and don't *even think* about it until your wedding night. I'm unbuttoning his shirt and then he's on top of me, kissing me fiercely. I feel him, hard and ready.

I push him off.

"Wait." I say breathlessly. "I have to tell you something."

He rolls to his side, sighing, as if the wind's been knocked out of him.

"It's okay, Trish," he mumbles and turns to get up.

I pull him back to me. "I want to, but there's something you need to know." I hesitate, then struggle to find the words, "I'm…you're…"

This is way beyond awkward. My heart is thumping wildly in my chest, as much from excitement as from fear that he'll laugh at me, at my inexperience. "I've never been with a man," I whisper, searching his eyes. *Now what?*

He grins like a kid on Christmas morning. "That is so unbelievably hot!" And with that, he finishes unbuttoning the shirt and happily continues kissing me, moving from my lips, to my nipples, to my inner thighs. There's no turning back now.

I hold him, sliding my fingers over his muscled back while I struggle to catch my breath beneath his weight. Finally, I let go and relax into his rhythm. A tantalizing glow like molten silver radiates from my belly to my breasts—filling me up.

Tristan's arm is draped across my shoulder as I nod off and when I awake, fuzzy-mouthed and headachy from the margaritas, he's already in the shower. I long to snuggle under his light-as-air comforter, but I can't. I'm long overdue at Elaine's. She's had to feed and bathe Deshy and read him a bedtime story, something I normally do. He must be wondering what's up. Not to mention Elaine. I was supposed to feed and water Stanley as a favor to Elaine. I failed in that mission, but somehow I succeeded in getting drunk and sleeping with the devil bird's owner. Would I have slept with him if I weren't drunk? No matter, it's a done deal.

I scoop Tristan's crumpled shirt off the floor and shimmy into the jeans. I shout a quick "Good night, thanks for dinner," through the bathroom door. It's as graceful an exit as I can manage under the circumstances. My soiled clothes lay in a clump on the bathroom floor.

Oh my God! Tristan and I slept together—had sex—did the 'nasty'. Now what? I don't want to lose his friendship because we tumbled into bed after having too much to drink; white wine before dinner then a pitcher, a large pitcher, of margaritas afterward. But I told him, in my booze-y haze, that I'd never slept with a man before, and he loved it!

Elaine's asleep in an armchair and the house is quiet as I stealthily make my way toward the bathroom and unceremoniously smash my toe on a metal truck left on the floor. "Dammit!"

Elaine is up in a flash. I'm standing before her, disheveled, reeking of alcohol, and wearing Tristan's shirt and his daughter's jeans as Elaine looks me up and down, shoots me a look that knocks the breath from me, and heads to her room.

BUSTED!

Christa

After a quick dinner of sandwiches and chips, everyone retreats to their tents and hunkers down for a stormy evening. A howling wind pummels my tent, threatening to rip it from the ground, stakes and all, and send it swirling into the mountains. Desert storms can be deadly. I've read about sleeping campers who were swept away in a sudden deluge. I hope I pitched my tent on high enough ground.

Tumbleweeds somersault across camp, grazing my legs as I sprint, head down to Dave's tent. Dirt and grit scour my flesh like sandpaper. My shins are crisscrossed with angry, red scratches.

"Looks like you got tangled up in a mess of barbed wire." Dave says and shepherds me inside. He takes charge, cleaning my wounds, rubbing antibiotic ointment on them, and covering the worst ones with extra-large Band Aids. He's even got a snake bite kit, reminding me that Nature—and snakes—are not my friends. Outside a full-blown storm is brewing. The tent poles rattle and the fabric flaps non-stop. Sleep is out of the question, so I cuddle in Dave's arms. For once I don't have to be the strong one, the head of the household, the breadwinner, the one who pays the bills on time and keeps it all together. For once, I'm the one who's sheltered and protected. Eventually, we fall asleep in each other's arms.

Later that night a shaft of light spears into the tent. It's one of the guides warning everybody to head for higher ground. Now. Flash floods are predicted in the area.

"Time to go, Christa," Dave says.

"But my stuff, my tent..." I stammer.

"Leave it!" They command.

Dave and I join the others, heads bent into the wind, protecting our eyes as best we can from the gritty mixture of sand

and debris. The trail upward is narrow and spiked with rocks that I feel through the flimsy soles of my flip-flops. I stumble and grab Dave's hand. We hike about an hour until we come to a shelter at the top of a ridge. It's nothing but a pitched roof and three walls on a concrete slab. We arrive just before the rain hits; marble-sized drops that splat against the hard-packed earth. We squat, knees to chest—and wait.

"Relax. It'll blow over sooner or later," Joe says. Ten minutes pass. Twenty. I see him watching the steep rise we climbed, an expanse of rocky soil that, even now, is sliding off in thick, wet clods. We talk in hushed tones, listening to the wind and rain tear at the roof over our heads; weathered boards held in place by rusty nails. I lean into Dave and nestle into the crook of his arm. By now I don't care who knows that we're together. We could all die here, sucked under a massive mud slide, clinging to each other as we suffocate. *Stop it, Christa!* I close my eyes, but the image keeps reappearing.

By first light the storm has blown itself out. We slog through reddish muck down to the campsite, checking the damage. Some of the tents have collapsed, tangled clumps of sodden fabric. Others are nowhere to be found. Bikes lay in the mud. My tent is still staked into the ground, but is sadly deflated like a spent birthday balloon. And wouldn't you know it—Dave's tent is upright and splattered with mud but otherwise as good as new!

Trish

I was in high school when I realized, with certainty, that I was attracted to girls, not boys. I tried to blend in by styling myself with long, straight hair, lip gloss and eyeliner. Maybe the cover-up was for my parents, who refused to see what was right in front of them. I didn't date and my only real friend was Buddy. My older sister was a hippie—complete with bell-bottoms, granny glasses, and the drugs that were readily available. Most of the time we didn't know where she was or with whom. On one of her rare appearances at home, she challenged me, in front of the family, "You're not fooling me one bit, little sister. You're gay!" My mother was shocked; my dad, repulsed.

It's easier to hide being gay if you're a girl. Buddy was gangly and effeminate; an easy target for the bullies. This was Kalamazoo, Michigan, the center of America's conservative heartland. Once a group of thugs stuffed Buddy in his locker and slammed the door. Buddy screamed and banged until a teacher freed him, but did nothing to stem the onslaught of bullying. Every time he walked down the hall he risked being slammed against the wall or called a fag. Before prom, in a frenzy of male testosterone, the guys on the football team beat him up in the school parking lot. His parents were clueless, or in denial. He told them he fell down the stairs, and they mocked him for being clumsy. I lent him make-up to cover the bruises, but word traveled fast.

Buddy asked me to his senior prom. Who else would have us? My parents were over the moon. "Our Trish is finally dating someone, and such a nice boy! So handsome, too."

That charade would be our revenge against the all kids who had been mean to us. We would have a great time impersonating a straight couple; I'd be in a gown and heels, Buddy in a rented tux and cummerbund with matching boutonniere. We'd take our performance over the top. The dress I bought was lilac with a fitted bodice and full sweep skirt. My shoes and purse were dyed to match. Mom was so happy she made an appointment for me at her salon; an elaborate upsweep with a ton of bobby pins and hairspray. Dad kept bitching about the expense, but beamed from ear to ear when I made my grand entrance down the stairs. His little girl really was 'normal.' His pride at my supposed normalcy broke my heart.

In the gym that night, we mingled with others like us, artsy kids on the fringes. Buddy and I slow-danced to Fleetwood Mac's "Dreams." I flung my arms over his shoulders and our feet barely moved. After the dance we parked in Buddy's old Chevy. He had hidden a flask of whiskey in the glove compartment. It burned my throat going down. We coughed and laughed with every sip, and made a pact that this would be our last night as virgins.

We passed the flask between us, joking and mocking the prom king and queen. It seemed like our promise wasn't going to happen until Buddy abruptly planted his hand over my breast. I guided his hand under layers of chiffon and a fortress-like brassiere, and I was surprised at how good the touch of his hand felt. He needed help in the kissing department, though. His kisses were hard and slobbery, and when I pulled back, he looked so hurt and scared that I leaned over and said, "Like this," kissing him softly.

Soon, Buddy was breathing harder, his kisses more urgent. He placed my hand on his bulging crotch and it shocked me. I pulled my panty hose down to my knees. All systems were 'go' until he unzipped his fly. My first thought was, how will *that* ever fit in me? My second thought was, *no way.*

We finished the whiskey. Buddy drove me home. He was disappointed. I was relieved that I didn't have to go through with it. He was my best friend.

That was a lifetime ago, and the closest I came to having sex with a man—until tonight.

Christa

Three more challenging days and we're done. Our guide pours champagne into red plastic cups, "No injuries and everyone finished," he says. Dave and I toast each other. I'm stronger, tanner, and in need of a manicure, pedicure, and a deep conditioning treatment.

On our final night together, Dave and I lay curled up next to each other, lost in our thoughts. Sure, we made love with abandon, and I forgot, for a little while, the problems awaiting me back home, but now I feel empty inside. I know so little about him. What's his favorite movie, his Sunday morning ritual, does he prefer e-books or paper? It's a hollow feeling, but we agreed; no promises, no strings, and no regrets. Nothing's resolved with Trish and now I've got this week hanging over my head. Do I tell Trish? Can I live with myself if don't? It's time for me to get back to the real world.

I want and need someone in my life, and resolve to give it one last try with Trish. We have history and a child together. Who knows me better than Trish? Nobody, except Elaine. She's seen me at my lowest.

Little did I know that my first relationship with a woman would be like plunging off a cliff and bobbing to the surface, gasping for breath. I was deliriously happy with Mercedes until the inevitable; I was unceremoniously slammed to the curb for a younger, hipper woman, a photographer, whose career was headed for the stratosphere. At thirty-eight I'd felt ancient and nearly gaunt, getting thinner by the second. Elaine had noticed my weight loss and depression, enough so that she'd commented on it—caring enough to ask. It was Elaine who suggested I move to Santa Fe. At the time it was one of the few places openly welcoming of gays and lesbians. If not for her encouragement and support, I'd still be back in Chicago, depressed and alone.

Elaine

The next morning Trish and I sit at the kitchen table sipping coffee. Sunlight streams in the window and warms away the night's chill but not the frosty silence between us.

"I can explain!" Trish blurts. She thrusts her bandaged arm at me. "That bird of his is possessed! Look, he attacked me!"

I'm not making the connection. Bird. Bandage. Booze. She went over there around two in the afternoon. It was after ten when I fell asleep in the chair and she still wasn't back. Then she came stumbling in well after midnight reeking of tequila and wearing Tristan's clothes! Obviously they weren't talking about the weather all that time. A jagged shard of hurt festers where I've been carrying a torch for Tristan all these years. Colin was just a little boy when Tristan saved him from certain death, grabbing his tricycle before he careened into oncoming traffic.

But that was ages ago. *Time to let it go, Elaine. But can I?—I never thought it would hurt so much.*

Trish stares at her coffee cup, avoiding eye contact with me. "Stanley attacked me when I reached into his cage to feed him." she says. "He flew around the room squawking and crapping all over the place. Not only did he draw blood, he shit on my head!"

Huh? All those times I looked after Stanley, he was never a problem. We got along great, especially when I gave him peanuts in the shell. *What did you do Trish? Yeah, really—just exactly what did you do to that poor bird?*

"Tris came home at the height of the chaos. He took care of everything."

I'll just bet he did.

"I showered in his fabulous bathroom; he gave me his shirt and his daughter's jeans to wear. He made dinner for us, and a big pitcher of margaritas, too." She has a faraway look in her eyes when she says softly, "It was the wine—and the margaritas, definitely the margaritas."

You ungrateful slut! You slept with Tristan, and he was supposed to be mine!

Trish and Deshy have been staying at my house for a week. If she and Christa don't patch things up soon, I'll have to start charging Trish rent! Raising one little boy is hard enough, but I'm about to lose my mind with the constant bickering between Deshy and Colin over action figures and Legos. And the cats! Callie's come out of hiding, but all day long, they're slinking around and hissing at one another. And keeping Trish's pricey organic fruits and vegetables separate from my generic produce is more than I bargained for. Even Winston gets organic! Once I accidently gave Callie a can of his preservative and gluten-free, all-natural and organic brand by mistake, and Trish shot me a dirty look. It costs twice what I pay for Callie's food—but that's a small price for free lodging!

Trish gets up from the table and steps out into the courtyard to take a call. She's out there for a while and while I can't hear what she's saying, she gestures and nods enthusiastically, returning to the kitchen with a smile brighter than I've seen in weeks.

"That was Christa. She's on her way home from Boulder. She wants us to start over, try and make it work." I watch as the tension and uncertainty of the week (has it been just a week—it feels more like a month!) drain away in moments; her shoulders relax and the crease on her brow disappears. I'm just as relieved as Trish, but if this reunion is going to work, Trish could use a new look to go along with the fresh start of their relationship. She needs to lose the worn T-shirts, baggy cargo pants and strands of gray in her hair. I'll mention it gently— and out of her throwing range.

"I'm so happy for both of you, Trish." And I truly mean it. Colin and I will be getting our lives back. I'll keep quiet about her and Tristan; I wouldn't dare tell Christa and jeopardize their reunion.

At dinner Trish tells me that she and Deshy will return home tomorrow and get everything ready for Christa's homecoming. It's the best news I've heard in a while. I'll miss her, though; lingering over coffee in the morning and chatting after the boys are asleep in the evening. It's silly, but even though I have no claim on Tristan, and Trish knew that I was attracted to him, I'm hurt that she slept with him and tried to hide it from me.

Christa

I'm home. No trike in the driveway is a good sign. I'm ready to launch myself into domestic life, the closest to marriage vows for two committed women raising a child. I make a point to come dutifully home after my last appointment of the day, part of our agreed-upon reconciliation. It means a lot to Trish that we have an unhurried dinner together as a family. She doesn't realize, though, that for me it's a missed opportunity to socialize with the other therapists. The lack of strong connections with my colleagues means that I might not be chosen to attend a conference or lecture. Being new to a practice is more than just establishing a client base. It's all about fitting in, networking, representing the group at community meetings, paying my dues.

Even though I'm an experienced psychologist, New Mexico law requires indefinite supervision because my training and degree are from Illinois. My boss, Dr. Bernard Goldfarb, doesn't constantly look over my shoulder like the supervisor I had for my pediatric rotation back in Chicago. And he doesn't treat me like a second class citizen because I didn't earn my degree in New Mexico. Sometimes I feel that way, though. I could practice here for thirty years and still not achieve the same status as a psychologist educated here. That lower rung on the ladder is frustrating, but unless I enroll at a New Mexico university and earn a doctorate, I'm stuck. I knew that when I moved here, of course, but I didn't realize the resentment would build up, would affect my feelings toward my work, and Trish, too.

There's nothing I would rather do after listening to clients all day than relax. Listen to music. Have a drink. But Trish is primed for animated conversation. I make the effort—asking about her day, listening. Deshy loves it when I get down on the floor and horse around with him. I'm trying, but I never thought it would be this exhausting.

Trish spends more time on her appearance since I returned, even wearing some makeup and nail polish, a first for her. Her clothes are nicer, too. We're both trying hard, but it shouldn't require this much energy and effort to keep our relationship going. Or maybe that's *exactly* what it requires—hard work and energy. Does it ever get *any* easier, though?

And then there's what's *not* happening. We've made love a couple of times, but it's forced and predictable. With Dave, out on the trail, sex was spontaneous and uninhibited. I've suggested counseling, but Trish is skeptical. She says I have an advantage there, given my profession. So we have late night conversations about our relationship, fueled by a martini for me, a glass of wine for Trish, and the talk goes in circles, accomplishing nothing.

In the beginning, before I moved from Chicago to Santa Fe, our separation and my visits every few months fueled pent-up desire. But we were different, even back then. I thought it would be fun to try phone sex, but Trish just couldn't bring herself to talk dirty on the phone. She would switch the subject to her latest jewelry creation or a new recipe she would fix the next time I visited. I didn't hear any yearning on her part. When we were together, she seemed eager enough, but I shouldn't have ignored my nagging doubts about our relationship. I was just so relieved and happy to be part of a couple again that I swept everything, including our mismatched sexual needs, under the rug.

It's ten o'clock. Trish turns off the TV and I close the journal I've been reading. Just when I'm ready to pull the covers up and settle in for the night, Trish says, "You've been so edgy the last few weeks, Christa. What's wrong? What aren't you telling me?" She pouts for a moment then blurts, "Was Mercedes with you on the bike trip? Were you and that woman together?" Her eyes glisten with unshed tears.

"Of course not!" I reply, unable to hide the indignation in my voice.

What I can't share with her, yet, is that my period is late… since Dave, but it's never been regular, especially when I'm stressed out. I had to run to the drug store at lunch today and check the aisles for anyone I knew before buying a pregnancy test. I left it locked in my desk at the office. Dave used protection every time, but everyone knows a condom isn't fail safe.

Something inside me might well be growing just as my feelings for Trish are fading. Trish's touch is soothing, a mother's touch. With Dave, I was flooded with a sense of urgency. With Mercedes, every touch was electric. Nothing else mattered.

I was at a low point when Trish and I got together. After Mercedes, my heart felt like a bloody gash for everyone to see. Add to that a terrifying encounter with a rattlesnake in Elaine's courtyard. No wonder I fell for Trish, the proverbial nice girl next door. She ministered to my wounds on the outside, and inside my broken heart began to mend. But is kindness and gratitude enough to sustain a relationship? Should I have sent flowers and a thank-you note instead of falling into bed? Trish was Mother Theresa, but I need more than a saint.

Elaine

Trish calls to tell me about a new gallery opening in town. It's at the space where I exhibited my water color paintings a few years back, although it seems like another lifetime. The gallery has been vacant for a while and finally has a new owner. The grand opening of El Diablo will be the first show of the Santa Fe season. The buzz extends all the way to Taos and Albuquerque, thanks, in part, to the name: El Diablo, *The Devil*. Trish insists that I come to the opening party with her and Christa—a girls' night out with dinner afterward. It sounds like fun and a break from my boring routine since I'm usually in bed by ten.

In contrast to my show, when my watercolors were presented to Santa Fe art patrons along with a few bowls of mixed nuts, at tonight opening there's lots of lavish catered food. The new owner is sparing no expense; a showy bird-of-paradise centerpiece, bowls of salsa, baskets of blue corn chips, jumbo shrimp and cocktail sauce. Plus, there's Sangria with orange and lemon slices, white and red wine, and bottles of pricey sparkling water. Waiters in crisp uniforms roam the room, holding trays aloft and bending gratuitously as they offer flutes of champagne to the guests. We sip our wine and stroll through the exhibit; raw textile art that begs to be touched and paintings of rocky vistas thick with layers of pigment.

Michael the mountain man is in his glory. He's a local character, a poet/mathematician, who lives in a shack in the foothills. He attends all the openings (for the free food, no doubt) and looks more weathered every time I run into him. I'd like to give him some skin care tips like using facial moisturizer with sunscreen. Michael's showing a lot of skin tonight. He's scantily clad in a pair of Spandex biker shorts, a clingy jersey, and a feather boa. His arms and legs look like hairy bean poles. Depending on your point of view, Michael is a vision…or a nightmare.

He balances a plate with broccoli and cauliflower florets in one hand and stuffs a mini-sandwich in his mouth with the other. Trish and Christa grin in tandem.

Christa's wearing a black pencil skirt, purple silk blouse and a turquoise necklace. Trish is in black from her turtleneck to her jeans, bangle earrings, and both wear the matching bands she designed for them. They are an attractive couple, complementing each other's style. This is the first time I've seen them together—and happy—in a while.

Two women from my artist group wave me over. They're all smiles seeing Christa again and I introduce Trish as "Christa's partner, an artist in her own right." Christa proudly displays the necklace Trish made for her. Both women admire the fine craftsmanship.

We're all talking about the spectacular opening, when a young man in a tuxedo announces, "Welcome to El Diablo and our first exhibit of the season. We're delighted this evening to exhibit some of the most exciting new visual art of the region." People pause briefly then continue their conversations. He finishes with "…the new owner—La Diva Martinez." The crowd quiets. A striking Latina woman in a form-fitting scarlet dress that's slit to mid-thigh strides through the opening they have cleared for her, her stilettos clacketing like lightening with every step. She is breathtaking.

I glance at Christa. Her face is white as a Geisha's. Then it hits me.

The gallery's spectacular new owner is Mercedes, Mercedes Martinez, the woman who captured Christa's heart back in Chicago, and then tossed it to the curb when a younger, hipper woman caught her eye.

Mercedes scans the crowd. Her dark hair hangs loosely past her shoulders. She moves seductively in a haze of smoky perfume. The woman radiates heat like a blow torch. She pauses occasionally, recognizing a lucky few who glow in return.

Christa is stunned. Trish looks confused. Then she turns to me. This is *so* not good.

Mercedes spots Christa among the guests and makes her way toward our little group, smiling and greeting other guests along the way, air-kissing men and women alike. It's difficult to gauge who is more enthralled by her—the men whose gazes inevitably drop to her décolletage, or the women who are dumbstruck with jealousy.

Christa

She's headed right toward me! I can't move. My feet are anchored to the floor. Suddenly she's here, in front of me, air-kissing one cheek then the other. She takes half a step back, assessing me. I feel naked and vulnerable in her gaze. Without warning she locks her lips on mine. Her scent and the insistent pressure of her kiss send fiery impulses to places that were asleep and are suddenly awakened by currents of sexual energy. I pull away from her lip-lock to catch my breath. *Damn you, Mercedes! Only you have this effect on me.*

Trish

What the hell is going on? How dare they put on a display for everyone to see! Is this the promised 'show' at El Diablo? Did Christa and Elaine know about this? Apparently not. Elaine looks stunned. Christa takes a half step back. Her cheeks are flushed.

"Mercedes," Christa struggles to collect herself, "this is my partner, Trish. She's a silver artist." Christa fingers the silver necklace I made for her. "She designed this piece for our anniversary." Mercedes puts her hand over Christa's, an intimate gesture meant to mark her territory? What nerve!

Without thinking, I raise my glass toward Mercedes—and fling the contents at her. She lurches back, but the damage is done. Red wine dribbles down her face, her chest, her dress, all the way down to her killer shoes.

A collective gasp emanates from the onlookers. Elaine's mouth is a perfect 'O,' but no sound escapes. Christa appears to be frozen in place, a look of shock on her face.

"Come on," I say, grabbing Elaine by the arm. "We are out of here."

Christa

The crowd draws closer, aiming their cell phones at us. The guy in the tux reappears, as if on cue, with paper towels and seltzer water.

"I've got to blot this stain before the dress is ruined," Mercedes says. She's oddly calm, but my nerves are jangling like keys in a toddler's fist. I scan the crowd for Trish, but she and Elaine are nowhere in sight, vanished before I can explain that I had no idea...

"There's a bathroom in my office. We can blot the dress there," Mercedes directs. "Coming?"

The crowd closes in, jostling us and firing questions. I have no choice but to escape with Mercedes.

"Ms. Martinez!" It's a reporter wearing a press pass. "Who assaulted you...and who is this with you now?"

He's from *The Spotlight*, an online newspaper. He steps in front of us and snaps several pictures. Just what I don't need—photos of Mercedes and me splashed across the Internet. Santa Fe is a big small town. If this goes viral, and it will, it will seriously affect my practice, not to mention my already shaky relationship with Trish.

"Ms. Martinez, will you press charges?" The guy is gleeful, and why not? In the news business, a chick-fight tops a gallery opening any day of the week.

"No comment," Mercedes says, with a Mona Lisa smile. Taking my arm, she guides me to a back room, her office, and locks the door.

Everything inside is modern and sleek; a thick glass-top desk with chrome legs, oyster-colored carpet and a black leather sofa. "Help me with this zipper," Mercedes says. Before I know it she's pulling the damp dress off, pushing me onto the sofa, and laughing like it's all a delicious game.

Mercedes' bra and panties are snippets of filmy red lace, quickly tossed to the floor. Her kisses quickly turn red-hot, probing and demanding. Without a moment's hesitation, I hike up my skirt while Mercedes unbuttons my blouse, reaches around and undoes my bra. I surrender, without an ounce of resistance, hating myself for losing control, yet flooded with absolute joy. We must be hard-wired to be together; two bodies entwined like ravenous vines. Our sex is urgent—primal. There's no Trish, Deshy, no spilled wine or reporter, no crowd just beyond the door.

Afterward we lay motionless on the sofa for a while and Mercedes holds me, stroking my hair and shoulder, murmuring to me in Spanish, and all of it washing over me, over us, coming back together after missing and loving each other. I catch my breath and rest my head in the crook of her neck.

Just as I'm about to nod off I roll to my side, away from her, and rummage in my purse for my cell phone.

"Who are you calling?" Her voice is wounded, verging on accusatory. I don't want to hurt her, I really don't. She continues, "Your girlfriend, who doused me with *my* wine in *my* gallery? One elegant eyebrow arches as she glances at the ring I'm wearing.. "Needless to say, she's permanently off my guest list." She scoops her bra and panties off the floor.

"Stop it, Mercedes. She's my partner. We have a child together."

"Oh please. Tell me you were worried about that five minutes ago. No? No, indeed. You didn't put up a fight, did you?"

I put my phone back in my purse, hook my bra and button my blouse, which is a wrinkled mess and try to smooth my creased skirt. From a closet filled with gorgeous clothes, Mercedes plucks a short black dress. "Actually, your mousey friend did me a huge favor. I couldn't have asked for better PR, dumped, literally, in my lap for free."

"I need to go," I say combing through my tangled hair with trembling fingers. My mind is racing.

"Do that. I've got a gallery show to host." In an instant Mercedes has switched from wounded lover to curt businesswoman.

She throws her luxurious mane forward then back, assesses herself in the floor length mirror, and applies her signature red lipstick. "You'll come back for more, mi amor. And tell…Trina is it? Tell her thanks. She's the mousiest looking woman I've seen in ages. Is she that mousey in bed, too?"

With that, Mercedes waltzes out the door and closes it behind her. I stay back, trying to figure out how the hell this happened. It would be easy to argue that she took advantage of me, but she didn't. Our hands and mouths were all over each other, equally so. What I felt was the passion I've been longing for.

My chest is tight, my breathing fast and shallow. I think I'm having a heart attack! Okay, maybe not a heart attack, more like an attack of heart. No, more like an old-fashioned attack of guilt.

Trish bolted without waiting for an explanation. If she'd stayed, I'd have assured her that I had no idea it was Mercedes' gallery, and reminded her that it was Mercedes who kissed me first. And I'd have impressed on Trish that had she refrained from flinging wine at our hostess, I wouldn't have ended up on a back-room sofa. Trish doesn't realize that throwing that wine and walking out of the gallery was the worst thing she could have done. She played right into Mercedes' hands. She is a calculating woman who can turn a fiasco into an advantage. She's a woman who gets what she wants, but it's thrilling to realize that what she wants—is me.

Michael the Mountain Man

Everyone's texting, looking up from their tiny screens now and then to catch a glimpse of Mercedes wearing something new and stunning as she emerges from her office—alone. The reporter is doing interviews and taking crowd shots, killing time. Fortunately, there's still food and wine being served.

It's a classic lovers' triangle. When it's my turn I'll say, "I remember a couple of years ago, when Elaine, the blonde's friend, had a show of her own here, desert scenes mostly and one gorgeous nude of a young man I still dream about. I'm guessing Mercedes has history with the attractive blonde."

I fling my feather boa over my shoulder, hoping the reporter will take my picture and headline it "Fashionista Speaks on Lovers' Spat at Gallery Opening." A little publicity can't hurt—I'll be on the "A" list for all the openings.

Christa

There's got to be a back door to this gallery. No way am I walking through that crowd. My make-up is smudged, my hair is tangled, and my skin is damp. I look like I just had sex and I smell like it, too. But I'd do it again in a heartbeat. Still, I've got to make Trish understand that it wasn't entirely my fault. As soon as Mercedes spotted me in the crowd, I was a goner. She locked onto me like a laser on a target. What a God-awful mess! She knew I was living with someone, so what was she doing? Proving she could get me back any time, just because she could? Of course.

Since Trish morphed into an Earth Mother, all militant recycling, damning high fructose corn syrup, and wearing only natural fibers, I can count on one hand the number of times we've made love. And the few times we did, she kept sneaking glances at Deshy's baby monitor on the dresser. Did she think I wouldn't notice she was *so* not into me, into us? That it had gotten so bad?

When did it all start to go downhill? There's no date on a calendar that I can point to and say, "There! That's when Trish became obsessed with motherhood and began neglecting us."

Sometimes we'd sit at the kitchen table after Deshy was asleep and at Trish's insistence we'd play Scrabble, of all things. It had special meaning for her because her family used to have tournaments. Trish and her father were the ones to beat. I guess that it felt like family for her, but since I'm an only child, it didn't stir up homey memories for me.

I would much rather have gone out for dinner and drinks with Trish, or movies and plays, but she wouldn't hear of it. She wouldn't let anyone else watch Deshy besides Elaine. We seldom took advantage of her offers to babysit, maybe because Trish was happy to have me sit home with her. She didn't want to spend meaningful time alone with me, though, especially in bed.

Maybe all Trish had ever wanted was a child to replace the family she'd lost and she saw the perfect opportunity with me—still heart-broken over Mercedes, my feet bandaged after that terrible hike on the Aspen Vista Trail, and scared to tears by that rattler in Elaine's courtyard. I was a wreck, and Trish came to the rescue. After all, what did she have going for her—no girlfriend at the time, a minimum wage job, and just a sporadic trickle of money from her jewelry sales? She had no real hope of ever getting a place of her own, let alone a three-bedroom house half again as large as her casita with a small grove of piñon trees in the back yard. Our house—mine, really— has a second kiva in the master bedroom. We've only made a fire in it a couple of times in our five years here, back when I still hoped to have anything remotely like the passion I had with Mercedes. I should have known better. If that burning connection isn't there in the beginning, you can't make it happen. Once the newness with Trish and the pent-up need of a long distance relationship was past, I had to ask myself, 'what happened?' Maybe we were never so terrific together, but hadn't there been at least something to build on?

Was Trish more of a comforting presence—a convenient relationship to fall into?

Oh, God, I sound like some uppity snob who 'married down,' taken advantage of by a scheming opportunist. Trish is no opportunist, and she has a big heart. She'd honestly give some poor soul the shirt off her back—but she'd cover up fast if she thought *I* was within sight, dammit. So make that a *horny*, uppity snob.

Would I have moved to Santa Fe if Trish hadn't been waiting for me, welcoming me? Maybe, but it galls me when I think that my many career opportunities in Chicago vanished when I relocated. It's been a big step down, professionally. For Trish it's been a big step up. She's gotten a nice house to live in, no worries about money, and even the child she's wanted. It could have been different, but Trish can't let go and love me the way I need to be loved.

The sad thing is that I see this all the time in my practice but I never thought it would happen to me—to us. I once almost laughed out loud when a client told me he'd asked his wife, "What do I have to do to get laid around here?" I'm not laughing now. There's been a brick wall standing between us. I can't change that, and she won't even try.

If Trish had stayed after flinging that drink, if she'd fought for me... Instead she abandoned me, leaving me totally humiliated—and vulnerable—so of course I wanted the woman who clearly wanted me—Mercedes.

I open the office door a crack. The gallery's back door is nearby. A few steps and I'm out of here. Hopefully, Dr. Barry and my Mosaic Mental Health colleagues won't hear about this. I can just imagine the raised eyebrows, the snickers and sideways glances on Monday morning. What happens if my clients read *The Spotlight*?

I step out the door. Bursts of light bombard me as I stumble into the gallery's back lot.

"Ms. Thompson, I'm from *The Spotlight*," shouts the pudgy, balding reporter.

"How do you know my name?" I fire back.

"By now everyone knows your name. Get used to it."

He aims his camera and takes another series of shots. I shield my eyes against the blinding flash of the strobe.

"What's your relationship to Ms. Martinez?" He demands.

"No comment." I turn heel and run. He follows me briefly, but quickly falls back, gasping for breath.

My thoughts are swirling as I wander down the side streets I'd normally avoid in the car. This is one hell of a scandal. I might not have a job on Monday. I'm grateful for one thing, though, that my father isn't alive for this. He'd be mortified—and furious. He'd stare at me a long while then turn away, disgusted. I crossed a line tonight; broke every rule, violated every boundary. I hope it's not too late to talk to Trish, *if* she'll even listen.

I pass an outdoor café festooned with faded paper flowers. Mariachi music blares from a tinny speaker. The acrid odor of stale beer and urine waft up from the crumbling sidewalk. From the bar I hear whistles and cat-calls. As if I'm not humiliated enough, I feel like a used tissue, crumpled up and tossed into the trash. There's no one in the world to protect me. I walk faster though my feet are aching from these heels. Damnit—even my feet have turned against me!

After a few blocks, my stomach cramps and I feel moisture oozing between my legs. My period. My chin quivers and I double over, clutching my knees, completely undone. "Why?" I cry out to the deserted street. Tears dot the pavement. The one thing that's kept me going—the hope of new life—is gone. I never told anyone that I suspected I was pregnant, not Trish or Elaine or Dave. This grief is mine alone.

Closer to home now, the houses are less cookie-cutter tract homes and more upscale adobe with red-tiled roofs. I think about my parents. Neither of them could have imagined their daughter being attracted to women. I was long out of their house before I was certain myself. Maybe my failed relationships with men were red flags I chose to ignore.

My folks would have been shocked at Mercedes and me, together as a couple. They raised me to be a "good girl, go to church, and avoid temptation," let alone give in to it. Maybe that's why sex with Mercedes is so fantastic; there's no thought, no judgment, no guilt—until later when my mother's voice reverberates in my head. How to explain all this to Trish? The scary part is that I can't swear I won't do it again. Everyone should experience sex like that at least once in their lifetime. Once you've had it, though, you want it…need it…again and again.

Am I willing to risk everything for Mercedes? Trish is all about home and family, being a fabulous mother to Deshy and an exceptional silversmith, too.

Then there's Mercedes, all glitz and glam and unlike anyone I've known before or since. She's exciting, worldly, and fun. I remember a romantic weekend we spent at Chicago's

Four Seasons. We went to the symphony, then to an elegant French restaurant for dinner, and window shopped along the Magnificent Mile. I'll never forget the horse-drawn carriage ride to end the evening. We held each other close against the chilly night air. Another time Mercedes took me to a charming used book store where we uncovered a volume of Spanish love poems that she read aloud to me with emotion she'd never expressed in English. The other patrons stopped their conversations, drawn to her beautiful voice and the way we gazed lovingly at each other. We ended the day at a café down the street where we lingered over cinnamon lattes.

I have tender memories of our time together, but Mercedes can slip through my fingers like water. She did once before and I barely survived it.

There's Elaine, who might well turn her back on me if I leave Trish for Mercedes. Elaine saw me sink to my absolute lowest after being dumped. If I risk it again, I could be on my own. I must be insane to even consider choosing Mercedes over Trish.

But this decision needs to be made with my heart—not my head.

Elaine

Trish is trembling with righteous anger. We shot like bullets out of the gallery with all eyes on Mercedes and Christa. Was it spontaneous drama or a scripted stunt? Cell-phone cameras by the dozens caught Trish looking explosive, Mercedes looking splattered, and Christa looking stunned.

What on earth was Trish thinking? Aggression is so out of character for her. Well, she does have a penchant for throwing things, though, like that casserole dish filled with scalding-hot enchiladas in her kitchen.

We arrive at a dimly lit restaurant where Trish and I can have a quiet conversation in peace. She's like a deer in the headlights; I practically have to guide her to the door. Hopefully, she won't clam up—or throw something!

We slide into a booth. I'm not sure what to expect, so I brace myself for tears, jealousy and anger. Trish stares at the menu without seeing it. Let her be the first to speak.

Christa should be here, sitting across from Trish, not me. They're supposed to be a couple. What am I doing here?

A waitress approaches. Trish suddenly looks up. "Pinot grigio for my friend," she says. "Vodka, straight up for me. Grey Goose, and make it a double."

"Better order some food," I tell her.

"Of course," she says, sounding sardonic. "I've got to keep my strength up so I can be a mother to Deshy and a freakin' maid and housekeeper for that selfish bitch, Christa."

I don't dare say what I'm thinking, that Christa didn't plan this. She didn't throw her arms around Mercedes. Trish shouldn't have thrown that glass of wine, but if she'd slapped Mercedes, it would have been a down and dirty, hair-pulling, nail scratching cat-fight. Thank god we got out of there when we did!

The waitress brings our drinks and takes our order.

"Chicken soup and a toasted cheese sandwich," I tell her. It's all my stomach can manage. I'm relieved when Trish orders a salad. I hope it comes with plenty of croutons to soak up some of the alcohol.

"Damn her," she says with conviction. "Damn them both to hell!" She takes a gulp of vodka, narrows her eyes to slits, and scans my face for tell-tale signs of complicity. "Did you know about this?"

"God, no." I throw up my hands, deflecting any hint of involvement.

"But you know her. *You know Mercedes.*" She slugs down more vodka. If looks could kill I'd be dead. But knowing Mercedes—knowing of her through Christa, really— doesn't make me an accomplice.

"Yes, I told you once before that she and Christa were in a relationship. It ended badly. That's no secret. But did I know about tonight? No way, Trish. I had no idea that Mercedes is the new owner of El Diablo." My voice sounds strident, defensive.

"At first I thought it was staged," she says, "I thought you and Christa were in on it and I was the only one who didn't know." She takes another gulp of vodka.

"I'm as shocked as you are, Trish, honestly. Besides, I would never throw you under the bus like that." *The video in my head of The Kiss and The Great Wine Fling keeps playing over and over.* "I'm exhausted."

"Well, I'm ready for another." She indicates her empty glass.

Thank God I drove!

And now she catches the eye of our server. "Another of the same."

Oh, my God! Trish is full of surprises tonight. But how do I open the door a crack so she'll hear Christa's side of the story? Trish is in no mood for anyone's hurt but her own.

We eat in silence, Trish alternating bites of salad with gulps of vodka . This drama hasn't played out yet, and it won't be until Christa and Trish confront each other. With any luck I'll be asleep with the phone turned off when they have at it.

Finally we're done eating. Trish sobs and mumbles about betrayal on the way home. "Will you be alright?" I ask her at the curb.

"Fine!" she snaps. *Ungrateful bitch! Now you know how I felt when you stumbled in from Tristan's. Besides, I saved you further humiliation tonight—and cab fare!*

I pay the sitter, a neighborhood girl, and watch her walk home. I check my phone messages. The first is from Yvonne. "Get on your computer, Elaine. Go to www.thespotlight.com. Right now!"

This is awful—video of The Kiss and The Wine Fling and of Mercedes and Christa disappearing into the back office. It's the lead story with sidebar interviews of Yvonne, Ingrid, and Michael. Michael is practically leering into the camera. I can't help but notice that everybody at the gallery opening looks great for their fifteen minutes of fame on the web site video. Except me—I look like a dish rag; limp and used up from tending to everyone's needs but my own.

Worse still, I'm getting a migraine. I can feel the pressure lurking behind my eye sockets and over the bridge of my nose. If I don't take something now, I'll be out of commission for days, lying in my darkened bedroom with a cold cloth over my forehead. But I've got to break the news about the video to Trish, do it now, and do it as gently as possible.

Trish

I pay the sitter, and close my eyes for a moment when Elaine's call slaps me awake. I can't believe what I'm hearing! I bolt up from the sofa to watch the train wreck online; first the lip-locking kiss, then *my* wine in Mercedes' face, and a chorus of gasps. Mercedes whisks Christa to a back room, the video goes to the announcer, pans the gallery, the reporter interviews a few people, including Michael, who goes on and on, and then Mercedes reappears in a different dress, a little black number. There's a glimpse of Christa, that tousled slut, sneaking down the back hallway! Well, I've got news. I won't make it easy for them and simply disappear. I'm digging in for a fight.

When I check on my boy he's asleep, clutching the moon and stars blanket I swaddled him in as an infant. The front door creaks open and I catch a glimpse of Christa before she disappears into the bedroom. I remain in Deshy's room, dimly lit by a nightlight. A few minutes later, Christa's standing in the doorway, wearing a robe and slippers.

"I hope I didn't startle you." she says. "How long has he been asleep?"

"You're asking how long he's been asleep, but what you really want to know is how long I've been home and how much do I know? The answer is—I know plenty." I steady myself against the door way as I walk to the kitchen. My heart pounds hard and fast. The floor feels unsteady beneath my bare feet.

"What do you mean?" Christa lowers herself onto a chair. Surely, she knows that the photos are out there and someone has tipped me off. "I can explain," she says, searching my face for what? Forgiveness? This is a far cry from the woman who's usually so confident. Arrogant, even.

I've got the upper hand, but how to play it? "Explain what? That you've waltzed into our house stinking of sex with your "former" girlfriend? Stop playing me for a fool. I know you're unhappy. I know things haven't been the same between us since we brought Deshy home. But I'm through turning myself inside out for you—trying to be someone I'm not." My voice is getting shrill. I fight back tears. That will come later. Right now, the last thing I want to do is break down in front of her. I fold my arms across my chest, closing myself off from her.

"Lots of couples with kids have problems, even Elaine said so, you told me yourself." Christa says. "And with Deshy's medical issues early on…"

Christa runs her fingers through her disheveled hair, only making it worse. She'd never allow herself to be seen in public with a hair out of place—except for now. For some reason this hurts almost as much as her infidelity, the fact that she can change, but never would for me. The image of Christa and Mercedes together is like a hot poker branding my heart. Yet, it's also cold and empty, twisting inside, and not letting go. I draw in a long, deep breath and let it out.

"I know you love her. I know you don't love me anymore and it's tearing me apart. Love shouldn't hurt so much. I can't do this anymore. I'm done." I unclench my hands and twist the silver band off my right ring finger, setting it on the table between us. "There's one thing I need to know. Since we've been together, is Mercedes the only one you've been with?" Christa takes a small, sharp breath, but says nothing. "What about the bike trip?"

Christa's blue eyes darken. So, there it is.

"Why won't you answer? You were with someone while you were gone, weren't you? Well, that goes both ways," I say, hating the smug sound of my own confession.

Christa's head snaps up. "What? Are you saying that you slept with someone while I was on the bike trip?"

I've got her undivided attention. I guess it takes mutual infidelity to even the playing field.

"Who was it, let me guess. Mary Ellen from the library or Rachel the barrista?" Christa's eyes narrow. Her jaw clenches. "It's not like you haven't had relationships in the past. Every time I go to the library, there's Mary Ellen, big as life behind the reference desk, staring at me."

"Mary Ellen may be my ex, but..."

"*One* of your exes." She pauses. "Like I don't see Rachel every morning at the drive-up window on my way to work?"

"That may be true, but when I run into her she doesn't lock her lips on mine like she's giving me mouth-to-mouth resuscitation. We smile, we nod, and talk about the weather. Who the hell does Mercedes think she is?"

"So, who was it?" Christa demands.

"You're the one on trial here, not me! Stop trying to turn the tables. I don't need your guilt trip." Christa sighs and looks away, momentarily defeated. Before she starts in again I say, "Besides, that little guy sleeping in the next room means more to me than you'll ever know, so much more than any former lover. As far as I'm concerned he's the most perfect and beautiful creature that God put on this earth. We'll be fine without you."

We fall silent. After a long while, Christa looks up and says, "Where will you go? To Elaine's?"

"I'm not leaving without an order of eviction!" She just stares at me. "That's where you come in, Christa." I steel my gaze and set my shoulders. "You've heard of palimony?"

"You're suing me for support?" she says, incredulous. "You're joking, right? It's *my* house!"

"It's no joke. Deshy and I are not leaving. You want to stay—stay." My shoulders sag and I feel the toll this night has taken. "I'm exhausted and Deshy will be up early for his breakfast. We can talk tomorrow, but I won't change my mind. You've forced me out of your life, and it's too late to go back. I'm going to bed."

In the bedroom, our bedroom, I close the door, sprawl across the mattress, and cry myself to sleep.

I wake to the familiar sounds of Deshy stirring, talking to his stuffed animals. There's no sign of Christa. Or a good part of her clothes and shoes.

Christa

I need time and distance to sort through everything that's happened, so I rent one of those so-called executive suites on a weekly basis. Only it's just a glorified motel room with a kitchenette and a tiny dining area, a flat screen TV and a queen size bed. Ha! A lot of good that will do me. And if I don't have enough on my plate already, the thought of facing everyone at work on Monday looms like a dark cloud.

At the grocery store on Saturday I realize that I don't know where anything is because Trish always does the shopping. Coffee, fruit, milk, cereal and a pre-made veggie wrap are the only items in my cart, standard fare for the newly single. From now on I'll make coffee at home, I decide. I'm definitely not up to facing Rachel. By Sunday morning the walls are closing in so I lace up my shoes and go for a run, something I haven't done in ages. Seeing couples out walking and families with small children playing in the park is a bummer, but I continue running until I'm beat, then head back to my new "home." It's an ongoing struggle not to call Mercedes. Instead I concentrate on what I'll wear to work. Outfits are strewn across the bed; the navy blue suit is too severe, my purple silk blouse too sensual, and a long skirt and top too casual. I settle on black slacks, a white blouse and a camel blazer.

I check my make-up in the car visor, and head into the office. It dawns on me that I look like a real estate agent in this outfit, but it's too late to change. When I open the door, the young receptionist, a notorious gossip who's constantly checking social media, flashes a canny smile and purrs, "How was your weekend, Ms. Thompson?"

I nod and retreat to my office, closing the door behind me. If Miss Brittany Busybody knows, *everybody* knows! The phone rings. It's Dr. Barry. He wants to see me in his office at the end of the day.

Oh, my God! End of the day! This is so not good. Will this be the last time I'll be seeing some of my clients? How upsetting for them—and me—but I really can't say anything until I know for sure. So if I'm thrown out on my ass, who will contact them? Someone they don't even know? Ours is a relationship based on trust. To have that broken, snapped in two without warning would be terrible for my already fragile clients. Closure's essential, for both the client and the therapist.

Would Barry really fire me after five years of loyal service to Mosaic? But who knows what he's thinking? What could she have told him? It was that little receptionist—had to be. No doubt it'll be the top story here for at least a week—until something juicier comes along.

And how would I get a new job? I'm the head of the household. Oh, this is bad. I have to go check that contract I signed. How will I defend myself if it comes down to that?

For all I know, they'll search me before I'm escorted to my car by a building security guard—confidential medical records must be guarded at all costs.

Brittany buzzes me. "Ms. Thompson, your first client is here." Oh, great. Time to put on my professional face.

Even though I can't eat a thing for lunch, getting out of there gives me time to read my contract. A park bench under a tree serves as my office, but I can't decipher this legalese for the life of me. If I'm fired, I'll get a lawyer and go from there.

I've got to have a job and a steady source of income. And maybe, so does Trish. She's perfectly capable of finding day care now that Deshy's four, which would free her up to find work and help out. Dammit, why have I let this all fall on my shoulders?

When will this day end? It would have gone faster with back-to-back clients, but it's Monday, and the wait between the two of them has been torture. And when is he going to call me in and end this misery? Just shoot me and get it over with!

Finally, a call.

"Have the seat, Christa." He walks around to the front of his desk and sits on the edge, his arms folded across his chest.

Oh, shit.

"I'll get right to it. We've valued your contributions to Mosaic Mental Health these five years, and you're well liked…"

Oh, no. Here it comes.

"Of course, anything that jeopardizes the reputation of Mosaic is a serious issue."

Just get it over with. I can't take the suspense any longer.

He clears his throat and meets my gaze. "You've been in the, uh, news, lately—a lot in the news, and what you do in your personal life is none of my business," he says, not unkindly, "but when there's the chance it could negatively affect your therapeutic relationships with your clients, I need to step in. You know we don't discriminate, so it's not about your orientation per se…"

Uh, oh. He's started gazing at the potted plant in the corner.

"…But just the hint of scandal, however unfounded…" he continues.

I cut him off mid-sentence, completely undone.

"I'm so sorry, Barry. I can explain." *But can I, really? How to explain The Kiss and the Wine Fling? And our disappearance into Mercedes' office?*

"You don't have to explain, just try to keep it out of *The Spotlight* next time." He grins and walks back to his chair, a sign that we're done with this conversation.

"It won't happen again." *Damn straight it won't! I want to hug him, but that would be wildly inappropriate. Do I dare ask who clued him in? Better leave it alone.*

PART II

Trish

Christa drops in and out of our lives, picking up clothes and files as needed, dispensing hugs and kisses to Deshy before she goes back to her office—and to her lover, Mercedes. It's liberating, in a way. No more dinner on the table by six and Deshy to bed by eight. He and I have our own rhythm now, and it doesn't include worrying about Christa's client schedule or whether Deshy's sticky fingers will soil her designer suit. That's not my problem anymore. I wonder if Mercedes listens to Christa complain about the low caliber of help in Santa Fe. I was so willing to give up my freedom and creativity for a comfortable existence with Christa, but it never materialized. Part of the attraction, I admit, was living in a nice house in an upscale neighborhood with lots of space, and an open kitchen to die for. I cooked more often then, and with just the two of us, I would experiment with different cuisines—Thai, Indian, even French. Christa used to say I'd wear out Julia Child's *Art of French Cooking*. It was a welcome change for Christa, who'd been living on Lean Cuisine frozen dinners and deli take-out in Chicago. She loved that I'd come home from work in the boutique, roast something that I'd been marinating, and prepare a lovely dinner for the two of us complete with an organic salad and veggie. I'd even started dabbling with desserts, and we discovered the joy of freshly-made mango sorbet with a sprig of mint. The unhurried dinners and talk, especially in the cool weather when we lit the fireplace and the flames cast such lovely shadows on the wall and gave the terra cotta floors a rosy glow.

We were still getting to know each other, even though we'd hit it off when we'd first met at Elaine's. Those long weekends when Christa would fly in and stay with me; how long ago that seems–eight years. Where did all that go? Where did 'we' go?

Well, that's just a memory now. My old house, the little casita next door to Elaine's was for rent and I signed a one-year lease. I'm right back where I started, but a lot wiser. I learned a hard lesson: never again will I fall for someone who's just come out and never been in a long-term relationship—on the rebound, too. Forget about the palimony thing. I haven't got money for a lawyer, but Christa faithfully sends generous support checks. A little guilt goes a long way; a lot goes further.

I miss her, though—a lot. After she moved here from Chicago we'd try a new restaurant or café for dinner every week. We'd savor out time together, enjoying our meal and a bottle of wine until just before closing. All that changed after we brought Deshy home. I don't know if it was my trying to keep him to a schedule, or Christa who hoped we'd have some quiet time together after I put him down. It was dinner on the table by six and Christa was clearly irritated when it wasn't.

When I'd first brought up the subject of adopting a baby, I could tell she wasn't as into it as I was, but she never discouraged me. In fact, she seemed caught up in the whole challenging process, maybe because her job here offered her less stimulation and opportunities than her position in Chicago. But I wanted a family—no, I was *ready* for a family again. Christa's an only child, but I had four older sisters, though it wasn't perfect, God knows. I'll never forget the night I came out to them. Mom sobbed uncontrollably. Everyone else stood there in shocked silence and deferred to Dad, that self-righteous bastard, who kicked me the Hell out of *his* house. At least it wasn't in a storm or a blizzard, so I had *that* to be grateful for at least.

There wasn't a single friend left in Kalamazoo I could turn to, so I set out on that drive all the way back to Boston. It was tough going since I'd only slept for a couple of hours at a rest stop. I was exhausted by the time I got back so I just crashed, too drained to feel much of anything. The next day it hit me—I had no family, no home, and no real job; just a grant and a part-time teaching assistantship in the Fine Arts Department. Devastated and disowned, I was totally alone, and facing a tough future in the arts. I hoped the whole rotten lot of them felt guilty as Hell—and still do.

Life without Christa is less stressful, though I miss her almost every day, and think about her when I'm chopping cilantro for her favorite dish. She'd never tasted it before coming to the Southwest. Still, I realize I'd been walking on eggshells trying to please her, and along the way I'd become needy, the kind of woman I promised myself I would never be. Christa became the center of my social life, my lifeline to adult conversation. But the joy that Deshy brings into my life keeps me going. Healing takes time. I don't plan to rush into a new relationship anytime soon.

The sheets are changed and the laundry is washed and folded. The sun is shining. It's a perfect afternoon to take Deshy to the park.

A young Latina woman shares one of the park benches with two others, nannies, likely. She leans to show them her silver necklace. Springtime sunlight glints off the delicate chain. I step forward for a closer look. Her smile is as warm as the Santa Fe sun. The craftsmanship of the piece is impressive. It looks beautiful against her dark skin.

"It's lovely. I should know—I used to make jewelry." In saying so, I realize that all my tools and stones are packed away in the garage. I'd put my craft on hold, just like everything else. My grandmother's oak dining table is the only thing in the house I can say is truly mine. I vow to begin making jewelry again.

"It was a gift," the young woman says softly, fingering the necklace, "from my boss. He says I should call him Adam, not 'Mister.'" The woman next to her looks away. She and I know, it's a story as old as time.

Deshy's sudden yowl sends me to the sandbox. He's crying and rubbing his eyes. "He threw sand at me," he points to a younger boy.

"Stop rubbing, you'll only make it worse. Let's go wash it out at the drinking fountain."

After the sand is washed away, I push Deshy on the swings, standing alongside two women pushing their charges. I can't help but overhear their conversation.

"The missus, she treats me like I am, I don't know how to say, like I had no schooling."

The other nanny nods, "Dumb. Like you're stupid."

"Yes, like I know nothing. I learn English. I graduate. But the missus treats me like a dog. 'Do this way, not like that. Hurry up,' she says. No respect." Her eyes darken, likely from anger long repressed.

"No respect." The other woman echoes.

"Only the mister, he treats me nice, but not in front of her."

I have to wonder if I'm the only mother in Santa Fe available on a weekday to take her child to a park. So many kids are handed off to nannies while the parents work. Deshy is my life, not just a job. It's a life I wouldn't trade. It's as important as Christa's, but without the salary or status.

Christa

With Mercedes, I'm like a kid in a candy store; more free to explore new things than I was as a child. I never experienced true joy and the freedom to be myself until I was with Mercedes. But sometimes that fear returns that it won't last. Mercedes has told me that my relationship with Trish was a leap of faith. Loving Mercedes is an even bigger leap. I was hurt, badly, and risking that again is a huge.

Merc and I are rebuilding trust, one baby step at a time, opening up to each other, sharing our past. We've signed up for a basket weaving class taught by a Native grandmother whose journey is etched in the lines on her face. She gently guides our hands with her gnarled fingers. Mercedes says she'll incorporate some of these Natives motifs into her paintings. For me, time stands still and my worries about Deshy's future and child support to Trish are temporarily forgotten.

I've come to accept that Deshy's better off with Trish. After all, she was the one who wanted a child. I love Deshy with all my heart, but Trish is a better mother. I could take him from her at any time; his adoption papers are in my name, but I would never do that. She would be devastated. What would be the point? I only want what's best for him.

I still wonder who Trish was with during my bike trip. It could have been Rachel or Mary Ellen, or someone I don't know. Could it have been somebody's mom she met thru Deshy's school? I feel a stab of jealousy sometimes, but how can I even let myself feel this way? I'm just as guilty.

Mercedes

I never stopped loving Christa after our year together in Chicago. It was a blur of quiet dinners, exploring antique bookstores, the theater, a romantic carriage ride along Michigan Avenue, and more. So lovely, but I was her first woman, and clearly, neither of us was ready for a serious relationship. She may have thought she was at the time, but it wouldn't have worked, she was too new to the lifestyle. When I l suddenly broke it off for a young photographer Christa was devastated, but I always knew that someday we would be together. It just wasn't the right time for us. She came to mean more to me than I'd realized and even though I tried to put her out of my mind, I missed her for a long time.

After eight years of moving from city to city, trying different jobs in galleries and an auction house, I was ready to open my own gallery. Before I committed to Santa Fe, I asked around and learned that Christa had relocated here. She wasn't hard to find; I checked the listings for therapists, and—voila! She was listed under Mosaic Mental Health.

Local realtors were eager to talk to me, especially since there were a couple of prime gallery spaces available. Not only did I want to return to my own painting in a serious way, but also it made sense to have my own place, especially in a climate where I could work outdoors all year. It also meant providing opportunities for up and coming artists. It was a risk, but it paid off; Christa's back in my life, my gallery is thriving, and I've returned to my art.

Trish

At the local farmers market on Saturday I run into Tristan while I'm searching for red leaf lettuce and Deshy's sampling organic granola from a local vendor. Even though I haven't seen Tristan since 'our night' weeks ago, my heart spikes a blip on my imaginary EKG. He looks amazing; tan, sunglasses, and a baseball cap. He strides toward us.

"Trish. You look well—no bird crap or bandages, anyway." He smiles at Deshy. "This must be your son."

"This is Deshy. He loves tasting the samples on Saturdays. Everyone here knows us. Say 'hi,' Deshy."

He does, mumbling the word, so Tristan crouches, level with him. "That granola looks mighty good, buddy. I'm a big fan, too." He stands back up and smiles his killer smile at me. *He seems really happy to see me.* "I was called in on a major project in New York, and it was one crisis after another. Since I came back, I wasn't sure where you were living, but things seem to have quieted down at Elaine's place." *So—he's been looking for me?*

"I've still got your clothes at my house," he says, "freshly laundered, of course.

"Actually, we're practically next door neighbors again. We're back at my old place, next to Elaine's." It's hard to meet his gaze. "Christa and I...well, we're separated." I look down at the pale strip on my bare ring finger.

"I'm sorry. I hope it wasn't because of…well, you know." He glances toward Deshy who's now happily munching a gluten-free cookie.

"No, not at all. Our break-up was a long time coming, and now that we're apart it's a relief, really. No more uncertainty. She's with someone new, or not new, really—an old girlfriend. And I'm with…" I hesitate and look toward my son. "I'm with Deshy, the love of my life."

Tristan nods. "I remember when my wife and I divorced—so much pain. The women I've dated over the years, mostly professionals, were more interested in their careers than starting a family. I always wanted more children, though. My daughter, Susan, is happily married, but it looks like grandchildren are not in my future."

"That's too bad. I couldn't imagine my life without Deshy."

Tristan hesitates. A look of uncertainty crosses his brow. "I hope you weren't upset, I mean, at how we wound up…that night." He glances toward Deshy. "I had a really good time talking, getting to know you better, and learning about designing jewelry. I had no idea what goes into it." He takes off his sun glasses and holds them, squinting into the sun's glare. "Let's go to dinner…at a restaurant with waiters and candle light and no crazed parrot attacking you."

Tristan's asking me on a date. I've never been on an authentic, honest-to-goodness date outside of Prom with Buddy. The women I've been with—we grabbed a bite at a local eatery, maybe caught a movie and then went to one of our apartments. Deshy is grabbing my hand, wanting to move on to the next booth, so I've got to make a decision, now. "I'd love to hear about your job in New York." I'm smiling and looking back at Tristan as Deshy pulls me toward the homemade fudge booth.

Tristan and I go on a couple of dinner dates; very chaste with good night kisses shared at the front door. It's clear we enjoy each other's company so what's wrong with an expensive dinner with a handsome man who's great at conversation? Absolutely nothing.

Elaine's been chilly toward me since she caught me coming back that night in Tristan's clothes, so I've found another sitter, a part-time college student who needs the extra cash. I'm dipping into my meager savings, and now that Deshy's started kindergarten, I'll find a part-time job that syncs with his school schedule. In the meantime, I volunteer as a room mother to help plan his class parties, chaperone on field trips, and to get out of the house and meet other moms.

I'm teamed up with Victoria. Her twins are Drew and Cameron. Dieter is their father, a globe-trotting corporate attorney. Right off the bat, Victoria asks me if she can drop off the twins at my house "for a play date" while she's in Taos for the day. It's all good; Deshy's played at their house so it's our turn. Oddly, Deshy isn't thrilled when I tell him the twins will be spending next Saturday with us. It's good for him, though, being an only child with no hope of a sibling for companionship. I worry that he's too shy.

The boys arrive at eight—unfed. Victoria apologizes before zooming off in her light blue BMW convertible. It turns out that plain Cheerios, even with sugar sprinkled on top, are not sweet enough. And no, Cameron, we don't have frosted shredded wheat or colored marshmallow cereal, or cow's milk. He wrinkles his nose at soy milk. They like the apple juice and I don't dare tell them it's organic. I dole out toast with butter, cinnamon and sugar (white, which I keep on hand for guests).

The twins tell me their mom trims the crusts, so I do, too. Deshy watches in amazement.

After playing in Deshy's room for a while, they're all back in the kitchen. "We're hungry," Drew whines. Deshy nods in agreement.

"Do you have bacon, Miss Trish?" Cameron asks.

Nice, he's being polite. There's a pound of uncured bacon in the fridge, so I smile and ask how crispy they like it. "A lot crispy," Drew says. A half-pound of bacon sizzles in the frying pan. For good measure, I make more toast. Deshy clearly enjoys the bacon, a special treat, but Drew complains, "It's too crispy." And with that, both twins push away their plates. Coming from a big family, I have no frame of reference for kids who refuse perfectly good food.

"All right, how about peanut butter and jelly, guys?" I'd never let Deshy get away with this kind of behavior, but they're our guests, after all.

"Do you have pepperoni pizza?" Cameron wants to know.

"No, but I have peanut butter and jelly." Surely Victoria would have told me if they're allergic to peanuts.

"Crunchy?" He asks.

"Both crunchy and creamy!" It's my moment of triumph, at last.

After scarfing down peanut butter and jelly sandwiches washed down with more apple juice, they head back to Deshy's room. I peek in every few minutes. All his toys are strewn across the floor—Transformers, action figures, Legos, even Lincoln Logs passed down from Colin. House rules are to play with one toy at a time and put it away before taking another, but I let it slide. They play quietly for a while I work on my grocery list in the kitchen. Suddenly, a high-pitched scream sends me rushing to see who's injured and how badly. Drew is pummeling Cameron, clawing at him, trying to dislodge the Transformer he's clutching to his chest. Cameron's holding fast, gritting his teeth against his brother's assault.

"It's mine. I called dibs," he yells.

"What's the problem, guys?" I'm calm. I guess this is typical boy behavior.

They ignore me. Deshy watches wide-eyed.

"Stop it!" I scream, which gets their attention. I pry the toy from Cameron's sweaty fingers and hold it above my head. Drew jumps up for it, the little stinker; he could have any one of the dozen or so Transformers on the floor. Defeated, he folds his arms across his chest and lets out a "Humph."

I'm getting guff from a five-year-old *and* I've got four more hours with these spoiled brats.

"Let's go outside and play." I say. "I don't want you guys bleeding on the carpet." It's a phrase my Dad used when us kids got too rowdy, but, of course, it's lost on them.

We're off to the back yard, where Deshy keeps his dump truck and plastic shovel for building roads. Before I slip into the house for a much needed bathroom break, I remind the boys to play nice and make for the bathroom. I'm almost finished when I hear Deshy's terrified howl, "Mommmeee!"

I'm out the door in a flash, zipping my jeans as I go.

It's not a snake. Thank God. No, it's a fight to the death! Drew is jabbing the pointy end of a Tiki torch at Deshy's belly. Deshy is whimpering, trying to grab the business end of the torch. I yank the bamboo pole from Drew and demand, "What do you think you're doing? Who said you could pull this out of the ground?" And who knew a tiki torch is a lethal weapon?

Deshy clings to me, rubbing his belly and sobbing. From the corner of my eye I see Cameron smirk with pleasure at his brother being caught red-handed.

Drew is unrepentant. "It's a bayonet," he says matter-of-factly. Then, pointing a finger at Deshy, he adds: "And he's a dirty Jap."

I'm stunned. This one, Drew, will make headlines years from now, and it won't be for winning a Nobel Peace Prize. Wait 'til I tell Victoria about her little darlings.

"Drew," I get down, in his face. I want to throttle him. "Deshy is not Japanese, he's Chinese. But that's not the point. It's wrong to call people bad names. Your father is from Germany, but you wouldn't like it if I called him a name because of where he was born. What you said to Deshy was very mean. Do you understand?"

Drew glares at me through narrow slits, sending a chill through my body.

It's obvious that these three can't be out of my sight for a moment. Ugh, and I've got all afternoon with them. "Okay, boys, we're playing inside, now. I'll put in a movie and make you guys a snack."

"Do you have any war movies, Miss Trish?" Drew asks sweetly. Either he really doesn't have a clue or he's deliberately pushing my buttons. I'm beginning to wonder if I have a budding sociopath on my hands.

"No war movies, but I'm sure we have something you'll like."

When the boys are ensconced the sofa, each with a bowl of popcorn on his lap, I pop *Kung Fu Panda* into the DVR. It's just the thing I swore I'd never do; plop Deshy in front of the TV with food, but this day calls for extraordinary measures.

I'm in the kitchen, loading the dishwasher, when I hear footsteps behind me.

"Mom...Mommy...I've got a tummy ache."

Of course you do, sweetheart. Today's been hard for you. Try going to the bathroom, Okay?" I shepherd him inside and close the door.

Maybe *Kung Fu Panda* wasn't the best movie choice. The twins, I gather, take martial arts class and they're putting on a demonstration in the family room, complete with jumps and kicks. Cameron completes his move and comes down hard. He lands on the edge of a blanket they draped over a table to make a tent. A lamp crashes to the floor. Shards of glass scatter like confetti.

"Nobody move." I shout, running for the broom and dustpan. My cell phone rings. It's Victoria.

"Trish, is everything okay? You're out of breath."

"Fine, fine," I lie. "You're on your way, right?"

"Trish, honey, I've been in an accident."

"What!?"

After a long pause she says, "I'm all right, but I can't say the same for my car. I was barely out of Taos when one of those huge construction trucks wandered into my lane and clipped me. I'm going to have some nasty bruises, but thank God for seatbelts and airbags. An ambulance is on the way, just a precaution. Anyway, I'm not going to make it back to Santa Fe tonight."

Feeling lightheaded, I slump into a chair. She's *not* coming for the twins!

"What about Dieter? Can't he pick them up?"

"Trish, sweetie, Dieter's in Bonn on business. Believe me, if there was anyone else, but neither of us has family here."

"Oh." I whisper.

"Drew wears Pull-Ups to bed but he's terribly self-conscious. Could you pick up a package but not make it a big deal? Of course, I'll reimburse you."

Spending the night. Good God. My head is spinning. "What do I feed them for dinner?"

"Trish, I've got to go. The officer wants my statement."

No way can I manage the twins alone. Damn, I wish I could call Christa, but she's off on another long weekend with Mercedes. Elaine is my only hope. I know she's pissed that I'm seeing Tristan, so I appeal to the 'I can fix this!' side of her personality, and explain that Deshy and I are in imminent danger from the twins—especially Drew—and it works.

But it's two hours later before Elaine's at the door with frozen pepperoni pizza, a gallon of milk, Lucky Charms, Pull-Ups—and Colin in tow. Still, she's here, and I'm grateful.

"We have to stick together," I warn her, "or we won't survive the night."

"Oh, come on," she snaps, "you're from a big family and I've worked with kids for years. We'll be all right."

Colin's settled on the sofa watching TV. Now it's bedtime for the three younger boys. Baths would be an exercise in mayhem; water all over the floor, fighting in the tub, not to mention possible drowning. I try to keep it as low key as possible. At bedtime each twin gets one of Deshy's T-shirts. I hand Drew a Pull-Up discreetly tucked into a pair of Deshy's Transformer underpants. Cameron gets a pair of Batman briefs. Cameron snatches the Transformer briefs, lets loose with a triumphant war whoop, "I got the Transformers!" He shakes the underpants in the air and the Pull-Up falls to the floor.

"Drew's a baby. Drew's a little baby," Cameron chants.

Drew shoves his brother into the sharp corner of the vanity. It happens in an instant; there's nothing I could do to stop it. Cameron's on the floor bawling, clutching his arm. Drew runs out of the room with the Pull-Up and underwear clutched in his mean little fist. How does Victoria put up with this day after day? No wonder she was so hot for a day in Taos *without* the twins.

Once a nurse, always a nurse, apparently. Elaine persuades Cameron to let go of his arm so she can inspect the damage. It's only a scratch. Elaine takes over, washing and bandaging Cameron's injury and getting the boys ready for bed. Finally, after three bedtime stories, Elaine dims the light and closes the bedroom door.

I've already opened a bottle of Merlot and poured two glasses. Minutes later, Cameron's complaining, "I can't sleep. I miss my mom."

"Mommy's coming in the morning," I reassure him. "The sooner you close your eyes and go to sleep, the sooner she'll be here."

All is quiet for a few minutes, and then Drew appears in the kitchen. "Cameron's farting."

"Drew, it's time for bed," Elaine says, taking him by the hand.

"You're a mean old lady and I hate you," he says. "I want Trish to tuck me in."

This kid is a master manipulator. If I were Victoria, I'd be luxuriating in a bubble bath in a four-star hotel right now, savoring a respite from my two rotten kids. It's the parents' doing; clearly the twins get no direction or discipline. I almost feel sorry for them, the key word being 'almost.' I don't let Drew off the hook for his latest outburst. "You hurt my friend's feelings." I tell him. "You hurt your brother, too."

Drew considers this, and blurts, "I'm sorry."

"That's not good enough, Drew. You're going to have to apologize to them both in the morning—and mean it." He climbs into bed, pulls the covers up to his chin, and scowls at me.

In the morning, Victoria returns with beaded Indian headbands for the boys.

"Are you okay?" I ask her, trying to remember if she's wearing the same clothes as yesterday. I look closely for bruises without appearing too obvious, but see none. *Was there really an accident or a clandestine rendezvous?*

That instinctive parental question, "How were they?" never crosses Victoria's lips. Probably because she damn well knows the answer. It's just as well. I was prepared to tell her the truth. I know one thing for sure: I don't want Deshy with the twins outside of school.

Deshy and I return to our routine once he's done testing me—talking back and refusing to eat sandwiches with crusts, like Drew and Cameron. He quickly settles down and our lives flow along smoothly, like a stream over pebbles, until one October day when nothing seems right. Deshy whines and has no appetite. Winston the cat paces at the patio door. It could be a snake, but I don't see anything in the backyard.

By eight o'clock I'm restless, too. The Weather Channel says a massive storm front is sweeping across the desert toward Santa Fe.

The windows rattle as I tuck Deshy into bed.

"What's that?" he asks with wide, fearful eyes. Outside the wind howls and sand scrapes the house like dry rain.

"It's OK, sweetie, it's just the wind. Go to sleep." I rub his back and he dozes off.

The wind blusters, then retreats. Between cycles I nod off, too, until Deshy's shriek jolts me awake. A mother knows her child's cry, but I've never heard this sound from him before; it's like a wild animal with its paw caught in a steel trap.

Deshy thrashes about, red with fever and moaning. Sheets and stuffed animals tumble onto the floor. His cheeks are glowing like hot pokers. I have to cool him down—fast—or he'll start convulsing. I scoop him into my arms and rush to the bathroom.

His little fists clench his pajama top. When I try to loosen his grip, he howls, "No!" I feel his heat through the fabric. Fevered and frantic, he kicks wildly. The only way to get him into the bathtub is to press him to my chest and climb in with him.

And still he screams—jagged, terrifying sounds. My little boy is like a frightened animal, all teeth and nails, biting and clawing at me.

"Let me go! Put me down!" he shouts, but I can't. I've got to get his temperature down. I reach for the shower handle, pull it toward me. Cold water blasts down like a barrage of stinging, icy arrows.

I feel Deshy shiver in my arms. I hold him tighter and rock back and forth. After a moment, I realize—he's not breathing!

"Deshy!" I cry and shake him, hard. Nothing. I slap his cheek. His head lolls, his limbs flop like noodles. "NO! Wake up! Breathe!" Suddenly, his chest inflates and he gasps for air.

"Mommy! Mommy!" he shouts.

"I'm here, honey. I've got you." I stroke his head.

"Let me go. I want my mommy. I want Christa."

It's a punch to the gut, but I know I've got to cool him down. He thinks I'm being cruel, so of course he wants his other mommy, the one who brings him presents, but doesn't have to correct him. Finally, he calms. I stroke his arms and legs with cool water and he curls up against me. But when my hand brushes his ankle he lets out a sharp cry. Above his right ankle is an angry welt. It looks like a spider bite, the nastiest I've ever seen. No wonder he was hysterical. I've read that brown recluse spiders live in Santa Fe, and their bite can be deadly. We're at least twenty minutes from St. Vincent's Hospital—and that's on a good day without a sirocco raging outside.

By the time I get both of us into dry clothes, Deshy feels a bit cooler. The poor little guy is wrung out, resting his head on my shoulder.

I buckle him and his Bear into his car seat, and notice that the angry welt around the bite is getting bigger. There's no time to lose. Out on the road, dust blows across the landscape in towering waves, and the car's headlights are useless. Visibility is practically zero. I fix my eyes on the yellow median and inch forward, staying well to the right. Soon, a fuzzy halo of lights appears up ahead. An oncoming car. I whisper a prayer, and clutch the steering wheel.

What was *that?* There's a thud as the car's wheels go over something soft—a bump in the road. Oh my God, what did I run over?! Deshy wakes up and starts to whimper. I can't stop, can't even open the car door a crack to see what it was. Dust and grit would whoosh inside. It's not worth the risk. What if I hit someone's dog? I'm so sorry—there's nothing I can do.

Deshy wails louder, the shrill, piercing sound of a child crazy with pain.

Finally, the glowing Emergency Department sign is visible ahead. I pull up under the entrance canopy. A guard approaches with a flashlight. The wind is fierce.

"Ma'am," he chokes, holding a bandanna over his mouth, "you can't leave your car here."

I ignore him and lift Deshy from the car seat, pressing his face to my chest, and sprint through the sliding glass doors. "I'll move it later," I shout back.

The triage nurse doesn't seem too concerned about his fever and poor appetite, but when I show her his ankle, she's all business. Walking briskly, she leads us to a curtained cubicle. I hold him while a nurse takes his blood pressure and temperature, and when she tells me it's 104, I steel myself for what's coming—an IV and a blood draw.

A clerk from billing appears, inquiring about insurance. I hand her Christa's card. It lists Deshy as her dependent. My name, of course, is nowhere on it. At this point, according to the law and the hospital, I have no connection to Deshy.

"You're Christa Thompson?" the clerk asks, her tone perfunctory.

"No, but…"

Her head snaps up, eyeing me intensely. "What is your name and your relationship to the patient?"

She takes in Deshy's almond-shaped eyes and straight black hair, and my round eyes and brown hair. All she sees are the differences, not the bond we share.

"The patient's *name* is Deshy," I say through gritted teeth.

"…and your name and relationship?" She appraises me suspiciously.

"I'm Trish Hoffman, his mother." I say in a clipped tone, every muscle tense.

"Then who is Christa Thompson, and what is her relationship?"

"She's his mother, too…the one with the insurance."

"I see." She stares at me over her readers. "I'll need to inform my supervisor."

As if I care! She doesn't see and she doesn't understand how powerless I feel.

At the curtain, she turns and fires one last question, "And where *is* Christa Thompson?"

"She's on her way." Not exactly true, but she will be as soon as I call her.

Who does this insurance clerk think she is? This is a hospital, for God sake. My son is sick. We drove here through a dust storm, and she's interrogating me like I'm a criminal!

Enough of my righteous indignation. I call Christa as soon as the clerk's out of earshot.

I'm the 'other' mother—the one with no insurance, no money, and no legal connection whatsoever to my son, so Christa better get here fast. If ever I needed her, it's now!

But I'm Deshy's mother just the same, and have to hold him down as he screams and struggles as the nurse sticks him for the third time. Slowly his blood fills four vials while he sputters and grits his teeth. It's a nightmare. When she's done we transfer him to a cooling mattress. He's sobbing when the nurse gives him something for pain. I want to cry, too, but I have to stay strong, at least until Christa gets here. He drifts into a fitful sleep, clutching the stuffed bear he brought from home. The one that Christa gave him.

It's after midnight. I need to move my car. The security guard gives me a nasty look and I shoot one right back at him. The keys are in it. He could have moved it himself.

Back in the cubicle, I nod off in a straight-backed chair. Every so often, my head drops to my chest and snaps back up. Finally, a young doctor appears, swatting aside the curtains. A protective mask dangles from his neck. His badge says he's an Infectious Disease specialist. He asks about Deshy's wound, his fever, and appetite. He wants to know if he's been around anyone who's been hospitalized recently.

"But it's a spider bite, right?" I say, confused and half asleep.

"Not necessarily. The blood cultures will tell the story, but there's a strong possibility that it's MRSA— Methicillin-Resistant-Staph Aureus. It's an infection that's on the rise, one that's resistant to standard antibiotic treatment."

"But he hasn't been around anyone who's been sick or in the hospital."

"There are two types of MRSA," he tells me, "hospital-acquired and community-acquired. The second type usually occurs among kids who play sports like soccer or football."

I'm trying to take this all in. If only Christa or Elaine were here. Where the hell *is* Christa?

"The infection gets passed around by shared equipment like knee pads, shin guards, shoulder pads, that sort of thing."

"He doesn't play organized sports, but he's with other kids at school and some of them have older brothers and sisters. I noticed a small scrape on his ankle a couple of days ago, but I didn't think anything of it. Is there something I should have done?"

"No," he reassures me, "you did the right thing bringing him here tonight. We'll know for sure when the blood cultures come back. In the meantime I'll have to incise and drain the wound."

"Tonight? He's been through so much already."

"It's important to clean the area and get a culture of the infectious material." He pauses. "Do you have any questions?"

I have a million questions, but he's already halfway down the hall, taking his self-assurance and youthful good looks along with him.

In sleep, Deshy's chest rises and falls rhythmically. He's still clutching Bear. If only I could protect him from what's coming.

Christa

I hold my breath and run from my car to the hospital's glass doors.

"My son is here, Deshy Thompson," I tell the desk clerk while I exhale.

The young woman at the reception desk scans her computer screen without looking up.

"It says here his mother's with him." She looks up, quizzical.

"That's his other mother. I'm the one with the insurance," I hand her the card and my drivers' license.

"You're Christa Thompson?"

Duh, yes. It's not rocket science. "Can I see him now?"

"You'll need to sign here, here, and here."

"What's this for?"

"That you're the one responsible for his hospital bills."

I scribble my name in the appropriate places and toss the clipboard on the counter.

"Where is he?" I'm frantic to see my son.

The clerk is impassive. She takes her sweet time, peering at the photo and then me. Then she disappears to a back room, to make a copy, I suppose. It's her job, but really—is it because we're two women together?

Trish

I feel a whoosh of air as the curtain flaps open. My head snaps up. It's Christa! Finally, I'm not alone. Took her long enough! Her hair's a giant tangle. She looks like she came here without a thought to her appearance; pink flip-flops, a sleep shirt and no bra. She must have wrenched herself away from Mercedes, crawled out of bed, and jumped into the car. Oh, Jesus—she's not even wearing panties!

Christa

"Is he okay? I came the minute you called, but the storm…I've never seen anything like it. What does the doctor say?"

I'm hyped up on adrenaline, awakened from a sound sleep snuggled next to Mercedes.

Trish looks like hell. "He has an infection. On his ankle." she says with a dry cough. "It isn't good."

"How...?"

Trish waves away my question before I can finish.

Trish

"I don't know. He had a scrape there a couple of days ago and I didn't think anything of it, but the doctor thinks it might be MRSA."

"Oh, no." Christa says. Her worried look is not reassuring. "I've read about MRSA in the journals. It's serious..."

"We won't know until the tests come back. The doctor's going to cut it open and...dammit, dammit, God dammit!" I screech. "I—we—needed you—*here!*"

"I had to do everything myself. I held him in the shower to get his fever down. I drove him to the hospital, in the storm, and I couldn't see a thing. When I ran over something on the road I didn't even stop, for Christ's sake! When they started the IV, he fought so hard. I had to hold him down. And after that, they took blood, so much of it..." I rock back and forth in the chair, clutching my arms. "It was horrible, Christa." My cheeks feel hot, like Deshy's fever. "You wouldn't believe the crap they gave me—what relation am I to Deshy? How could I be his mother when everything's in your name? Dammit, Christa, you should have been here!" I'm yelling like a crazy woman. Suddenly I'm spent. I cover my face and sob.

We're separated from the other cubicles by a thin curtain that could be swept aside at any moment and just because we're no longer against the law doesn't mean we're safe to be who we are—a lesbian couple with a child. This is a Catholic hospital.

They could throw one of us out the door, probably me. My name's not on anything having to do with Deshy and there's not a thing I can do about it. At the end of the day, in the eyes of society, we're outlaws—me especially. I'm nobody where this family is concerned, except there wouldn't be a family if it weren't for me. I'm the first face Deshy sees in the morning and the last face he sees at night. That's what's important, and it has never, ever been true for Christa.

I wish that she would put her arms around me and reassure me. Instead she gives me her canned response. "I'm sorry you had to do this alone," she says, an oasis of serenity, "but I'm here now. I'll stay with him."

"The hell you will!" I scream.

She nods toward the bed. "Deshy's asleep. We're going to wake him if you don't quiet down. He needs his rest before…"

"I'm his mother," I shout.

"So am I!"

"Ladies!" A short, stout woman parts the curtain and glances from Deshy to Christa and then to me. A cap of short, gray curls rings her head like a halo. The wood crucifix around her neck is a give-away. Her fake smile's like the Cheshire Cat's.

"I'm Sister Mary Margaret from social services. How are we doing?"

"Fine!" Christa and I retort in unison.

"Well, let's keep it down, shall we?" She stands at my boy's side, makes the Sign of the Cross, folds her hand and prays—silently, but I can see her lips forming, "Hail Mary, full of grace," like the nuns in school who insisted on calling me Pa-TRISH-a HOFF-man whenever they suspected wrong doing on my part.

My favorite teacher from high school left the order to marry an ex-priest. Lots of them left in the sixties. It wasn't unusual to hear that our Math or English teacher would not be returning, code for she left the convent to get married or went to live in a commune in California.

I can't help it. I'm up and pacing. Finally, the good sister leaves, and I collapse back in the chair.

"You and I need to calm down," Christa says authoritatively, like a mother chastising her child. "We're both upset."

I've got a come-back, but it'll have to wait. The Doogie Howser clone is here again along with a nurse. She's holding a white tray, sealed in plastic and marked, "Sterile." My mouth goes dry.

"I've got this," Christa says with a tight smile. "Why don't you take a break, go get something to eat?"

In the lobby, I stare out the window past the parking lot to a convenience store across the street. The storm's blown itself out. The eastern horizon brightens to a sherbet orange glow. I'm beyond exhausted. I phone Elaine and she assures me that I did the right thing. Deshy will be in the hospital for a couple of days, she says, and on antibiotics for weeks. After we hang up, I lean against the window, drained. How I wish I could l find an empty bed, pull the covers over my head, and sleep for a week.

Three days later Deshy is released from the hospital, Christa actually takes a half day off work. We both stand in the kitchen smiling with relief as he devours a grilled cheese sandwich washed down with a glass of milk. He's lost weight. I'll make all his favorite foods: spaghetti and tofu meatballs, veggie pizza, chili, and homemade oatmeal cookies with raisins and walnuts. He'll be back to his sweet self in no time.

The responsibility for changing his dressing and giving him his medication falls on my shoulders, unlike the aftermath of his cleft-lip surgery when Christa and I were a team. She's got her own life with Mercedes now, and I've got mine, and somewhere in the middle is Deshy. Christa visits, and takes him on some weekends, but Deshy doesn't ask about her as much as he used to.

Weeks later, I'm thrilled to sell a turquoise bracelet at Sophia's shop. It will pay for our Thanksgiving dinner, my first contribution to our household expenses in a long time. It's amazing how easily I slipped into being financially dependent on Christa. At first I'd enjoyed the increased income and social status, but it robbed me of my identity. How long will Christa keep paying the bills, though? Baby steps, I tell myself. I'm not ready to work outside the home yet. For now, selling this one bracelet is a start.

Christa and I agree that holiday traditions are important for Deshy's sake, so we'll have Thanksgiving dinner here along with Elaine and Colin; our little group, our extended family. Just like before, only not.

By noon on Thanksgiving Day, the savory aroma of roasting turkey and sage stuffing fills the house. A pot with giblets and onion for gravy simmers on the stove. Elaine and Colin are at the door. He's carrying the slow cooker wrapped in dish towels. It holds Elaine's yummy sweet potato casserole.

She's hefting a shopping bag with a pumpkin pie balancing precariously at the top.

"Trish, the house looks beautiful," she says. "I love the centerpiece."

"Deshy made it at school," I say proudly. It's only dried flowers and leaves, but to me it's a masterpiece.

Elaine plugs in the cooker and deposits the pie and a jug of cider in the refrigerator. "Christa's coming?" she asks. I nod.

Deshy appears, cute as kittens, in his holiday outfit; gray corduroys and a rust-colored sweater with a yellow leaf stitched across the front.

"Look at you," Elaine says, bending to give him a hug. "You get more handsome every time I see you." He smiles and wriggles free, taking Colin by the hand into the living room. Christa gave him a new video game, Guitar Hero, and he can't wait to play it with his buddy, Colin.

"Is she bringing anyone?" Elaine whispers and scans my face for a reaction.

"She didn't say, but I can't imagine she'd bring her *here*." I try to keep my voice from rising.

"How are you managing?" Elaine asks, pouring two glasses of Chardonnay.

I stare into the glass like it's a crystal ball, holding the answers to mine—and Deshy's future. "In some ways my life is the same; I get up, get dressed and walk Deshy to the bus stop. I do all the things around the house that I did before. The nights are the worst, though; sleeping alone and trying not to think about the two of them together."

Elaine takes a sip of wine and says, "When Tom and I separated, I tried to be stoic. I mistakenly thought I could keep my life from spinning out of control with sheer willpower. That was ridiculous, of course. At my Al-Anon meetings I learned that it's alright to let your guard down…to show that you're feeling the loss, too. If I'd done that, especially with Stephanie, things may have been different between us." It's like I'm not even sitting here. She continues. "I think she somehow blamed me for the break-up. She never let go of her resentment about the divorce. Maybe she thought I drove Tom away. I guess I'll never know." Elaine's voice trails off. We sit in silence for a few moments.

"I'm pretty open about it," I say. "I tell Deshy that no matter what's happened between Christa and me, it's not his fault. I make sure he knows that cleaning his room or eating all his veggies won't result in Christa coming back. Once he said, 'You should make her favorite—enchiladas—and she'll come right home.' If only it was that simple."

"Listen to us," Elaine says, "It's Thanksgiving. We're supposed to be thankful for what's most important to us—friends and family. In the end that's all that really matters, isn't it?"

We sip our wine, mulling over our histories of loss.

Christa

Mercedes doesn't "do" Thanksgiving. She was born in Spain, a foreign-service brat whose family moved a lot when she was growing up. The perfect American family, Mom, Dad, and two blonde-haired children gathered around a bountiful Thanksgiving table with snowy linens, good china, and a perfectly browned turkey on a platter—that's not her reality. Is it anyone's, I wonder, or was it invented by Normal Rockwell? It was a scene that my parents and my friends' parents tried to recreate, and always fell short. Mercedes will be dining with some Latina friends at an upscale fusion cuisine place without a pumpkin pie in sight.

I'd love to kick back and wear jeans and a comfy sweater today. But I know Trish will go to a lot of trouble making sure everything's nice, so I'll respect her effort and wear slacks and a blouse.

I'm always the one in charge of bringing the easy stuff to Thanksgiving dinner. This year Trish asked for dinner rolls and cranberry sauce, "Not from a crack-open tube or a can, please." No problem; I stopped at a gourmet grocery on my way home from work last night and got cranberry-orange relish and the last artisanal dinner rolls.

Trish's place is homey and inviting and smells fantastic. Deshy runs to me and throws his arms around my neck. I scoop him up and whirl him around. "I love you so much," I tell him and smother him with kisses. He giggles and squirms and the instant I set him down, he gallops back to Colin and their video games. Colin's shot up like a weed. He's at that awkward pre-adolescent phase—not a little kid any longer but not an adult either. How old is he now...twelve?

"Hi Aunt Christa," he says shyly. A hug or kiss might embarrass him, so we politely shake hands instead. It's awkward, but inevitable. Things change. Kids grow up.

Trish is in the kitchen basting the turkey. She looks sweet and feminine in a dress that skims her petite frame. I hand her a bouquet of multi-colored blooms and try to hug her, but she stiffens and pulls away.

"You look great," I say, reaching for a vase. She busies herself arranging the flowers. She's not making this easy...but why would she? I'm the one who left.

Elaine and I make small talk about the weather and how big the boys have grown, careful not to mention anything that might upset Trish—like Mercedes and me. Best not to talk about it, but Elaine remarks that I look happy—and relaxed.

Trish and I never say grace before meals, but it is Thanksgiving, so I improvise, "Here's to sharing our bounty with those near and dear to us."

"Here, Here!" Everyone clinks glasses.

"Let's eat!" Colin yells, and I have to admit it's the best idea I've heard.

After we've lingered over pie and coffee, cleared the table, divvied up the leftovers, and said good-by to Elaine and Colin, it's just the three of us. I bring two mugs of pumpkin spice coffee to the tiny living room and Trish tells Deshy to turn off the television. "This is our time together," she tells him.

Trish brings out *Cranberry Thanksgiving*, the story book we've read to him every year, even before he could sit and listen through the whole thing.

"Christa, Christa! I want Christa to read it!" he shouts. And so I read the story of Grandmother's cranberry bread and the stolen recipe, and for a little while we're a family again.

Deshy yawns and rubs his eyes. "Read it again, okay?"

"It's time to go to sleep, big guy," I tell him, happy for the chance to tuck him into bed.

"But I'm not tired," he says, stifling a yawn.

I take his hand and walk him down the hall. He brushes his teeth and puts on his pajamas. I tuck his Spider Man comforter around him and give him a good-night kiss and hug. "Never forget how much I love you." I tell him before I close the door.

The house is quiet. While Trish goes to kiss Deshy goodnight, I pour two glasses of wine hoping that she's in the mood to talk.

I hand her a glass and sit next to her on the sofa. "I miss the good times we had together, Trish, before..."

For a long moment, she stares at the wine. When she looks up her sable eyes are liquid.

"You've got Mercedes. That's who you wanted, and now you've got her."

"That night at the gallery, I was blind-sided, like you, and everybody else. I had no time to think, and Mercedes took advantage of that. She met a need that was missing in our relationship, the need to touch and to be touched. Something deeper is going on when two people who love each other aren't having sex."

"I tried, Christa. Don't say I haven't tried. I practically begged you to have sex with me…that day."

"That was the one time and only when I had an appointment waiting for me at the office. And you knew that."

We sit, listening to the stillness, not meeting each other's gaze.

"There's something I haven't told you," Trish whispers, wringing her hands. "Sex for me has so much baggage." She shakes her head and stares at the flames in the fireplace. "It's not about you, it's just that this is so hard, Christa." Another long silence. "I thought I could live my life like it never happened. I was just a kid, and he was my uncle…"

Good God, why didn't I see it? In the beginning, there was the novelty of our new relationship, such a relief to hold and be held, the warmth of her skin next to mine, becoming part of a couple without all the Mercedes drama. I admit I needed rescuing when Trish came into my life. My "Mercedes" wounds were still tender, so being with Trish made it easy to overlook the fiery passion that was missing. Living over a thousand miles apart inspired all kinds of fantasies, fueled by phone calls three or four times a week; of course we were all over each other when I flew in for a long weekend, and it was only after we were living together, fully available to each other, that our desire cooled—Trish's, really. And things changed even more when we brought Deshy home.

I never wanted to see it, so of course I didn't. I just kept denying we had a serious problem, that any yearning we'd ever had might have been temporary. How could I have thought things would change, just because I wanted them to?

Trish's voice interrupts my reverie. She's struggling with the words, and how well I know that struggle. I see it so often with my clients, but never before with Trish.

"So," she takes a long, resolute breath. "I have a hard time trusting people. I wonder if I even know how. Trusting someone physically, even trusting myself, surrendering to the feelings and sensations…there've been times when I wanted you so badly, but I just couldn't let go of the past and reach out to you." She's about to cry. "Always with the physical part…" she manages, "I couldn't keep that piece of a relationship going, and I guess it was inevitable that it would end badly, with so much hurt and disappointment. I mean, what did I think would happen? I hoped it would be different with you—with us." Tears spill over and run down her cheeks.

"Trish, did you ever talk to anyone about this? That must have been so awful for you." I take her hand and put my arm around her, even though I know it's not a good idea. We're not together any more, but I still care about her.

Her shoulders slump, and with what appears to be her last ounce of energy, she says, "You never answered my question about your bike trip. Were you with someone?"

Trish is so vulnerable right now. Everything depends on what I say next. I take a deep breath, still holding her, and stare down at my hand resting over hers.

"Oh, Trish, I never thought we'd end up like this. I thought we'd always be together—happy—and raising our son. But, yes, there was someone." Trish stiffens and pulls away from me, pain etched in her dark eyes. "I never planned for it to happen.

I couldn't sleep even though I was exhausted, and I ran into him by the bathroom, and he invited me into his tent, and..."

Trish stares at her lap, mute. To fill the void, I keep talking, and dig myself a deeper hole. "He held me when I needed to be held, reassured me and helped me make it through the night." The truth is that besides being sleep-deprived, I was horny and so was he. "It was purely physical," I tell her. "There was no emotional connection. We haven't contacted each other since the trip and I don't intend to."

"So you cheated on me—twice." Her eyes flash angrily then dim with sadness. "That's why you turned the tables, grilling me about who I slept with. This changes everything," Trish says softly, her sad eyes searching mine for a small shred of hope.

It starts after Halloween, the constant barrage of advertising promoting holiday bargains that distort the real meaning of Christmas; being with family and spending time with the people who matter to us. Elaine is walking a thin line, trying to please everyone. I'm invited to her place for Christmas, but will she invite Mercedes, too? It would be risking another scene, but I won't go if Mercedes isn't welcome. Since Trish's revelation about her uncle, and mine about Dave, Trish and I are at a stalemate, except to parent Deshy.

When I bring up Christmas plans to Mercedes, she catches me off-guard. "I thought we would travel for the holiday, just the two of us. I bought a string bikini that would be perfect on a Mediterranean beach. We could stay at my father's condo on the Costa Brava."

A week with Mercedes in Spain, how wildly romantic. There's just one problem: It would be my first Christmas away from Deshy. When I suggest to Trish that Mercedes and I take him to Spain for Christmas, she narrows her eyes and hisses, "Over my dead body."

Trish

Mercedes and Christa playing house in Spain...with Deshy? No way. Mercedes is so self-absorbed; I can only imagine her reaction to one of his sleep-deprived whining episodes. Mercedes wouldn't think twice about leaving him with a total stranger while she parties with Christa into the wee hours. On the upside, I know Christa loves Deshy; she'd see the real Mercedes, the person beneath the glitz and glam, and I'm guessing it's not pretty. Well, that's neither here nor there; I'm not about to sacrifice my son to prove a point. Christa can celebrate Christmas here with Deshy, or she can fly to Spain without him.

On the other hand, Christa could take him without my consent, but she risks not having me here when she returns. She'd have to find a full-time nanny and domestic. I wonder; is she willing to take that chance? Just how strong is that woman's hold over Christa? But then she could legally take him out of the country, and I might never see my son again. Christa and Mercedes hold all the cards. Christa's his adoptive mother, the one whose name is on his birth certificate, and she has all control over him. Even if I got a lawyer, they'd wear me down, outspending me, knowing it would be just a matter of time before they'd win. I can't allow Deshy to get on that plane!

Mercedes

Packing for our getaway is easy since I plan to spend a lot of time with Christa—naked in bed, or on the sofa, or the floor. And sunning together on the beach, or walking with the incoming tide at our ankles, holding hands as the light fades.

"You'll come to know why I love Spain so much," I tell her a few days before Christmas. We're having a quiet meal at my home, not dining out as we often do. I love making Spanish dishes for her—fresh scallops, sea bass, lobster and mussels—so expensive to have flown to Santa Fe. A rare treat; her favorite.

"In the evening, everybody goes to neighborhood cafés for tapas, and then later, much later, the flamenco dancing starts. The Spanish culture is rich and unhurried, where everyone eats and drinks and socializes over long meals. Here, everyone gulps their food, and goes back to work." I pause for effect. "Where is the enjoyment? Where's the pleasure?"

Christa pushes the food around her plate, not meeting my gaze.

"What's wrong?" I demand. "Don't tell me you've changed your mind! I've already bought the tickets."

"Deshy and I have never been apart at Christmas. I love watching him open his presents and I'd miss it." Christa finally looks at me, her eyes full of doubt. "I don't know if I can do this."

"Deshy will be with Trish. So will Elaine and her grandson. You can open presents with him before we go, or after we get back. I have a million divorced friends who do it that way."

"Well, I don't—and I don't see him enough as it is."

"Okay, let's bring him along." It's a hollow offer. *Who needs a kid underfoot? He'd cling to Christa day and night, want McDonald's hamburgers, and go to bed at sundown in a country where people don't even eat dinner until ten!*

"Trish won't allow it."

Thank God *I* don't have to be the villain. All I want is to spirit Christa off to a romantic getaway with no intrusions; just the two of us rising early to buy the catch of the day from the fishermen on the beach, shopping for fresh fruit and vegetables at the stalls in the mercado, cooking together and eating when we're hungry, making love on a whim with no interruptions, lying on the beach, eating at a tapas bar; then dancing together in the evening, so much more intimate than dancing in a crowd at a wedding. This must be what falling in love feels like. I want to share everything with her.

Christa

This trip means so much to Mercedes; she'll be heartbroken if we don't go to Spain. I'm torn between my lover and my son; not seeing him open his gifts on Christmas morning would be more than I could handle. Yet what about opening gifts with Mercedes? I'd hoped that our first Christmas would mean decorating a small tree with her collection of antique ornaments while we sipped wine and listened to traditional Christmas carols. I would arrange my Christmas Village around its base with the gas station like my father's placed in the center of the town.

We could have that on the Mediterranean, just the two of us, for Christmas and the rest of the holiday season.

Elaine

It's noon on Christmas Eve. Christa calls and asks if she can bring Mercedes to dinner tomorrow. Christa says Trish left her no choice; it was either Christmas in Santa Fe with Deshy or in Spain without him.

"Would you mind terribly?" She says, knowing full well I won't refuse.

"Oh, well, sure." It's all I can manage. I might need to hire a security guard—frisk everyone at the door. What about presents? This is super awkward. Trish, Christa and I have always exchanged gifts. Am I supposed to buy something for Mercedes? What would I get her, a rhinestone studded thong? Eeewww!

The more I fret about the holiday, the faster it comes. I've got to stop worrying about who'll sit where at dinner and if there's at least one gift for everyone, Mercedes included. *Let it go, Elaine*, I tell myself. Besides, it's too late to rush out and shop.

Roxy will arrive in Santa Fe later this afternoon. I'm thrilled that she's coming home. Not that Santa Fe was ever her home. Relocating here was my choice; a chance for a fresh start. Roxy was a senior in high school and refused to come out here with me. She finished the school year living at her best friend Katelyn's house. I don't think she ever forgave me, but she's grown into an independent woman and I'd like to think I had something to do with that.

I'm thankful for Trish's help with cooking, wrapping gifts, and last minute trips to the grocery store. I insist that she and Deshy spend the night—a Christmas Eve sleep-over. Deshy's worried about Santa passing over his house if no one's home, but Trish assures him that Santa knows he's at his Aunt Elaine's and will bring his presents here on Christmas morning. I'm so excited about waking up to presents with the people I love most in the world. I still have a knot in my gut about hosting Mercedes and Christa; at the least it'll make for some interesting dinner conversation. I try to squelch my anxiety, but it's like flattening a risen loaf of bread—impossible.

A car pulls up the drive. It's Roxy. She looks like a wilted flower from the flight and drive, but when I wrap my arms around her she perks up. My heart is about to burst with love for Roxy and everyone who's gathering here in my house. Tonight we'll bake cookies and have hot chocolate with marshmallows.

Then we'll walk to the Cathedral of St. Francis for Mass, and light votive candles for Stephanie and Liam.

Roxy

"Hi Mom, it's great to see you, too." I say. We hug and rock, nearly toppling over. I inhale Mom's floral moisturizer, the one she's used for years. I can still see the bottle on the bathroom counter. We laugh as if there's never been distance between us—and then we cry tears of sheer joy. It feels like a true homecoming.

Trish is here, too. Deshy's hiding behind her skirt. Trish in a skirt? Now that's something! It's impossible not to run my fingers through his silky hair. "Hi, Deshy. I heard you were pretty sick for a while." He grins shyly.

Colin hangs back. He's more like a little brother to me than a nephew, one I rarely see. He's really growing up; his face is thinner and his hair is longer. He's at that oh-so-awkward age I remember well; one minute confident and ready to test limits, the next retreating back to just being a kid. I start to hug him and when I feel his shoulder muscles tense up I decide to pat him on the back instead.

"Hi Roxy," he says.

So what happened to *Aunt* Roxy?

Mom's fluttering around the kitchen, happy as a mother bird with all her chicks in tow. She sets out the ingredients for sugar cookies; flour, sugar, eggs, butter, vanilla. Mom's doing cookies and Trish will prepare the main course.

"How can I help?" I ask.

"Grab that baking dish and spray some oil on it, will you Rox?" Trish says.

Everything's hustle and bustle. Mom mixes the cookie dough with a wooden spoon and sets the bowl in the refrigerator to chill;

Trish fills tortillas with spicy shredded chicken; Colin and Deshy play a video game in the living room. I take it all in, this family I haven't seen in far too long. It was snowing when I boarded the plane in Chicago. It snowed here, too…last time. A few flakes would be nice, more like home. I try not to feel like an outsider.

Three women in one small kitchen with limited counter space is usually a recipe for disaster, but we find a rhythm, weaving around each other, talking, catching up on the news. Suddenly we're laughing, standing in a clump all trying to get into the same cabinet.

"I'll make the salad," I offer, clearing a space. The jumble of aromas, spicy cumin and cilantro intermingled with sweet cookie dough, reminds me that I haven't eaten since early this morning. Cheese browns to a crispy top on the enchiladas baking in the oven. Mmmm, home- made Mexican food. Almost as good as Chicago deep-dish pizza.

Mom rolls out the sugar cookie dough. She holds up a draw-string bag like a trophy. It's the cookie-cutters—the same ones Stephanie and I fought over when we were little.

"I want the star," I'd say.

"You get the gingerbread man," Stephanie would boss me.

"Mom, Stephanie won't give me the star."

"Girls, you need to take turns."

Funny, I don't remember Dad being around for that. He was probably at the corner tavern with his drinking buddies. It was always just me, Mom, and Stephanie. God, I wish my sister was here now—arguing, laughing. I'd hug her so hard I'd never let go.

Later, Trish calls the boys into the kitchen to decorate the still-warm cookies. "Wash your hands, guys," she reminds them. Deshy grabs a handful of red candies and squishes them into the cookies. Colin gives the gingerbread men candy eyes and noses. Deshy shakes red and green sprinkles over them. Sugar sprinkles end up all over the counter top and the floor, but it doesn't matter—not on Christmas Eve afternoon.

Trish

Colin inhales my supremely delectable, cheesy, gooey, world renowned enchiladas.

"These are the best!" he shouts, between mouthfuls. I'm happy about that, but in the midst of all the holiday cheer, there's an empty place where Christa should be. I decide I'm not going to dwell on missing her and spoil this lovely evening. She'll be here tomorrow—with Mercedes. I hope those two will manage to keep their hands off each other, not just for my sake, but for Deshy's, too. I can't even begin to imagine how I'd explain their public display of affection to him.

I wonder what extravagant gift they'll buy for him. Mercedes has a say in what my little boy gets for Christmas, isn't *that* something! A red-hot mama who isn't maternal in the least, selecting a gift for a child she hardly knows, doesn't love, doesn't even like, and probably wishes didn't exist! Unbelievable!

Mercedes doesn't have a clue about the flaming hoops Christa and I jumped through to adopt Deshy. We were a team, racing over an obstacle course fraught with pitfalls to get our son, a child we would love forever, nurture to adulthood, and provide every advantage, thanks to my at-home care and Christa's income. She and I were never as close as when we were mutually obsessed with our goal. It was us against the world. Together we withstood the flight from Beijing—twelve hours with a squalling infant, a baby with a cleft lip that made it almost impossible for him to suck. Poor Deshy was starving, and we were clueless new mothers. We'd had a few hospital classes to give us the basics on how to care for him, but Deshy wasn't just any baby. We quickly realized we were in over our heads. Finally, a compassionate flight attendant took the bottle and made the hole in the nipple bigger, and that did the trick. I squeezed Christa's hand and nearly cried with relief when I saw him sucking from the bottle.

Deshy's surgery was the next hurdle. Christa wanted him to have it immediately, but the specialist insisted that we wait until he was ten weeks old, weighed at least ten pounds, and had hemoglobin of ten. So we waited. After the surgery, we brought our little guy home with a list of instructions and supplies; cotton swabs, peroxide, and antibiotic ointment. The nurse showed us how to swaddle him, keeping him still long enough for me to clean the stitches with peroxide and apply the antibiotic ointment on his lip. He'd try licking it off, which made him cry harder, poor baby. I was overwhelmed, questioning everything I did. Was I cleaning the incision properly? Applying enough ointment? Gentle enough? Thorough enough?

The first week was the worst, but once we settled into a routine it got easier. I felt more confident every day. By the time his incision healed, we were cleft lip repair experts. We were relieved when he quickly gained weight.

I never could have done it without Christa. When I look at Deshy now, my heart does a flip. He's perfect. I can only imagine how smart and handsome he'll be in a few years.

Elaine

Roxy pushes her chair away from the table, her hand on her tummy. "Everything was delicious. Good thing I don't eat like this all the time—I'd be as big as a house."

"Thank Trish's fine cooking," I say, adding, "Colin, please help clear the table so we can have dessert." We'll have fresh-baked cookies, hot cocoa and cinnamon-spice coffee, and then head out for our walk to the Cathedral.

"Deshy, you help, too." Trish says. "One plate at a time, just like I taught you."

I watch as Deshy carefully brings his empty plate to the kitchen, his forehead furrowed in concentration. He is such a sweetie. I remember how getting Stephanie and Roxy to clear the table was always a battle. Neither one wanted to do one scrap of work more than the other. I'll admit that I was often so tired and overwhelmed worrying about Tom that I often fell short in the discipline department. All of that responsibility landed squarely on my shoulders since he wasn't around to enforce the house rules. When he wasn't home, I fretted in anticipation, wondering if he'd be drunk or how much money he'd have left from his paycheck. I wasn't up to listening to the girls bickering, so I'd clear the table myself. Later I realized that I wasn't helping by doing that. Going to Al-Anon meetings, like Alcoholics Anonymous only for families of alcoholics, taught me to live one day at a time and admit I was powerless over my crazy life. Those Tuesday night meetings in the church basement, with an urn of coffee brewing in the kitchen, were the only glimmer of sanity in my week.

Tonight we'll go to Mass, and afterward Colin will light candles for his mother and father. I wonder if he remembers her fire-red hair or her full-of-life personality. He was only a toddler when she died. A single photograph, one picture that shows little Colin wedged between Stephanie and Liam, is all he has. That, and the hazy, fragmented memories of a three-year-old.

Roxy

When Colin was five I remember walking together to the Cathedral of St. Francis on Christmas Eve and chasing him all over the plaza. He ran in and out of the crowd, grabbing candy canes and cookies from street vendors. The kid is high energy, that's for sure. The story that Mom and Christa tell about that night is legend now. A stranger with scars on his face stared at Colin as he dropped coins in the donation box at the back of the church. It was so weird that it scared the hell out of them. When Mom got the call later that night that Liam had passed away, she calculated he had died at the time the stranger was watching Colin in church, and was convinced that the two events were somehow connected.

Colin and Deshy are already out the door, but we're not ready to go just yet. Mom's still putting plastic wrap over leftovers.

The phone rings.

"It's probably Grandma Helen," Mom says. "Walk slow, I'll catch up."

I go off with Colin and Deshy. Trish stays behind with Mom.

"Hold up," I call to the boys and power walk toward them. My breath is cotton candy puffs in the chilly air.

After what seems like a long time, Mom and Trish join us. Trish is dabbing sad eyes with a tissue. Mom's lips are drawn into a tight frown.

"What's wrong? Is it Grandma?" I ask.

"Grandma's fine. Everyone's fine. I'll tell you later. We'd better hurry." Mom's clipped tone tells me to back off.

The sidewalks are lined with *farolitos*, flickering candles in white paper bags anchored with sand. They illuminate our way to the Cathedral. They're as magical now as the first time I saw them. Neighbors gather around small bonfires in courtyards and call out holiday greetings to us as we hurry along our way. Our breath steams in the chilly night air.

The church is half-full when we arrive. The altar is lavishly decorated with many pots of red poinsettias. Christmas carols drift down from the choir loft to the pews, soft as snowflakes, dusting worshipers with melodies of comfort and joy.

The altar servers walk slowly up the main aisle, a procession of angelic-looking school children in white robes cinched at tiny waistlines. The priest follows, in satin vestments trimmed in golden threads. He proceeds slowly, rocking the smoking censer back and forth. The mystical scent of incense permeates the church and stings our nostrils.

"In the name of the Father and of the Son and of the Holy Ghost."

"Amen." We intone.

As Mass begins, Deshy stretches out on the pew and falls asleep. The huge meal, the candlelight, the closeness, and the heavy fragrance of incense have me wishing I could catch a nap, too. This is the only day of the year that I attend Mass, and I struggle to stay awake.

At the end of the service, after the last verse of "Joy to the World" is sung, Colin walks solemnly to a side alcove and lights two votive candles, for his mother and father. No votive lighting for Grandma Helen eases my mind about that long phone call, but Mom's wearing her concerned look. Something's up. Trish remains silent as she carries Deshy, still fast asleep.

Christmas morning comes early with an excited five-year-old in the house.

"He came! He came!" Deshy's shouts and the flap of his bare feet across the wood floor awakens me. It's not even seven o'clock. I resist the urge to pull the covers over my head.

"Did you see him, Col? Did you?" Colin's sprawled on the sofa, barely awake.

"I didn't see him, Big D. But look, he ate the cookies and drank the milk you left for him." Colin hoists himself up on his elbows and nods toward the empty plate and glass on the coffee table. Deshy glances at them and goes straight to the presents under the tree. He grabs the ones with his name and stacks them in a precarious tower.

Mom calls from the hall: "Don't open anything yet! I can't function without coffee."

"Do I have to?" Deshy whines and looks to Trish. She nods in agreement. Its Christmas morning. It should be totally festive. But somehow it's not, and I'm thinking it has something to do with that mysterious phone call last night.

Still in our pajamas, Mom, Trish and I clutch our empty mugs and wait for the coffee to brew. The aroma is heavenly.

"Mom, you've still got the red reindeer mug I gave you."

"Of course, honey, it's my favorite."

"You're really going to like what I bought you this year." I say, trying not to glance at her bathrobe, raggedy as frayed jeans, but not as hip. In the living room, the boys have removed all the gifts from under the Christmas tree and placed them in separate piles according to the tags. Somebody has plugged in the lights, and a thousand little dots glow like fireflies on the branches.

"Deshy's the youngest so he gets to go first." Mom says with a tight smile. Trish is pale and preoccupied, almost unaware that Deshy's about to open his gifts. Whatever's spooked them, it's huge.

Suddenly Trish snaps to attention. "I almost forgot, we always take…every year there's a picture of Deshy opening his presents. Roxy, would you, please?" Trish hands me her camera and poses stiffly next to Deshy.

I snap away until he's opened the last gift, a Jedi Starfighter Lego set. Colin gives it two thumbs up and offers to help him put it together later.

Next, Colin attacks the wrappings of his big gift. "It's a PlayStation!" He's over the moon. Quickly, he rips the paper off the game cartridges; Guitar Hero and Spider Man. "Thanks, Mom, I mean Santa." He winks and glances toward Deshy who's scattering Lego pieces like confetti.

Now it's my turn. Inside a beautifully wrapped package is a cashmere sweater the color of raspberry sherbet, with a matching scarf and hat. I thank Mom with hugs and a kiss.

Trish opens her gift from Mom; it's cashmere gloves, a hat, and scarf—apricot this time.

Finally, Mom opens my gift and her tears flow like water from a spigot. It's not that big of a deal—one trip to Macy's and there it was. I guess it's a Mom thing.

"Roxy, sweetie, I love it. How did you know?" She wraps the pink fleece robe around her.

"You might have mentioned it." I say.

Deshy looks up from his Lego project. He's as happy as I've ever seen him until…

"I still have one more," he says. "From Mommy Christa." His eyes darken like a brewing storm. "Where is she? Where's my Christa?" he asks Trish.

Good question. Mom makes the Sign of the Cross and glances heavenward.

"Come here, baby." Trish sighs and gathers Deshy in her arms. "Christa was supposed to be here today, but she changed her plans." She buries her face in his hair.

"Why? Why isn't she coming?" His voice is high and whiny. He pulls away from Trish. "I want her. I want my Christa!" He howls and stomps on the Lego blocks on the floor.

It's painful to watch, but there's nothing we can do to soothe him. This is just the first of many heartbreaks and disappointments. My parents split up when I was about his age. It doesn't matter that he has two moms. It doesn't hurt any less. I want to tell him that I know how he feels, but it won't lessen his pain.

Trish speaks to him with a mother's soothing voice. "I know you want her, sweetheart. I want her, too."

Crap, now they're both crying, and Mom's crying, and I'm crying, too.

"But why? Why isn't she coming?" He manages, between hiccups and sobs.

"I don't know, honey, I really don't." She seems as bewildered by Christa's absence as Deshy is devastated. It's heartbreaking.

"Where *is* Christa?" I whisper to Mom.

"In Spain—with Mercedes. That's what last night's call was about." Mom shakes her head, as if she can't understand how Christa could have done such a thing.

I should have stayed in Chicago. This is turning into a real bummer, like that Christmas when little Colin spilled hot cocoa and smashed pieces from Christa's cherished Christmas village. What is it with this family and Christmas?

Colin

As soon as Deshy stops crying I'm right there at his side. Nobody should be sad on Christmas, especially a little kid who still believes in Santa, the Easter Bunny and the Tooth Fairy.

"Come on, Big D, let's put your Starfighter together." I wave him over to the pile of plastic blocks on the floor. "We'll have battles against the Empire." At first he won't leave Trish's side. But after she gives him a squeeze and a nod, he gets down on the floor with me and a gazillion Lego pieces. I show him how to put the battleship together using the pictures in the directions. That's how I did it before I knew how to read. He's not saying much, but at least he's not crying anymore. It sucks to be the one left behind. I know, sometimes it was just me and Granma at Christmas. My Ma died in a crash and my Da was in the hospital for a long time and then he died, too. It left a big hole in my heart. It still hurts, especially when I see kids having fun with their parents, but I try not to think about it. Anyway, it's kind of worse for Deshy right now. My parents didn't have a choice about leaving me. Christa did, though.

Elaine

Christmas carols on the radio promise peace on earth, but they sound like hollow clichés. I turn the volume down and slide a pan of cinnamon rolls in the oven. No matter what, we've still got to eat.

"We'll get through this," I tell Trish. She's watching the boys playing on the floor, but her thoughts are half a world away.

Trish

Christmas was exhausting. After the morning's drama, I put on my 'happy face,' trying to salvage what was left of the day. After dinner, Deshy was over-tired and I was completely drained, unable to keep up the charade. It was a relief to load up the car and head home.

Finally, we're in bed, snuggled under a blanket and watching "The Christmas Story." Before I can say 'Bah Humbug,' Deshy's asleep. As I tuck the blankets around his shoulders, I feel like the only kid in the class that didn't get a birthday invitation. We've been forgotten, pushed to the side, ignored.

I curl up on the sofa; torn between hurt, anger, and, let's face it, jealousy—a bitter taste that sours any happy memories of Christa and me. While Christa and Mercedes are together in some posh Spanish love-nest having hot, juicy non-stop sex, I'm alone with a glass of wine on Christmas.

The phone rings. "Did I wake you? I'm so sorry for the last-minute change of plans." Christa's apology is a needling jab to my raw heart. No doubt she's rehearsed her speech. "It seemed better for everyone if Mercedes and I weren't there. I didn't want to ruin it for everyone."

"How selfless of you." My tone is icy. I'm trembling with rage. What nerve! She ruined Christmas and now she calls to chat about it?

"Has Deshy asked for me?"

"Of course he did—he cried and cried for you, for God sake! You're his mother, too. It's Christmas, isn't it?" I'm talking faster, louder, despite my best intentions. "How could you do this? And at the last minute! He's devastated, Christa."

"Please, let's try to be civil about this." It's that professional monotone, the one that drives me absolutely crazy.

"You want civil? Civil went out the window when you and that bitch stepped on the plane."

"Let's face it, Trish, I'd be damned either way. Mercedes and me at Elaine's? It would have been awkward as hell."

"You're already damned as far as I'm concerned." I suck a mouthful of air and struggle to keep it together.

"Can I talk to him, please?" she asks. Now I'm the one in control.

"He's asleep." I answer tersely.

"Please, Trish, he needs to know I haven't abandoned him. I just want to tell him I love him and that I'll be home soon."

Did her voice just crack a little? She's got a point. For Deshy's sake I get up and hold the handset next to his ear. He doesn't awaken, he just moans and turns over.

"He probably didn't hear you. He's sound asleep. It's been a tough day. He was heart-broken when he found out that you weren't coming. He cried so hard, and for so long. I'm not waking him up so he can go through that again."

Silence, then, "Thanks for trying. It means a lot. Maybe he heard me in his sleep." After a moment she says, "I should have stayed at home."

I hear Mercedes in the background. She's asking Christa who's on the phone at this hour. *Duh, who does she think it is, Santa Claus? Stupid bitch!*

Christa

"What's wrong, Love?" Mercedes says. "You were so festive last night, but now, not so much." She hands me my morning espresso. With a knowing smile, she brushes against my hip. That and a spectacular view of the Mediterranean shore fail to move me.

"You have no idea how guilty I feel being here. I should be home in Santa Fe with Deshy." I stare out at the waves lapping at the sandy beach in hypnotic rhythm. The day's first sun-worshipers are laying striped beach towels on the sand. It's a breathtaking sight, yet I couldn't care less.

"Not this again," Mercedes sighs, irritated. "We've been through it all before. Really, Christa, are you sure you're not

Catholic? You certainly have the guilt thing down pat. It takes all the joy out of life. Years of therapy finally cured me of feeling guilty for being happy. I love loving you. Why can't you admit that you love me, too, and just embrace it?"

Oh, my God, if only I could! She doesn't understand how torn I feel. "I called to talk to Deshy, and he was already asleep. It's Christmas. He's just a little kid." Tears trickle down my face onto my tank top.

I cry noiselessly, staring beyond the morning joggers on the beach to the hazy communion of sea and sky. Palm trees rustle, seabirds squawk, the waves rush and retreat. An old man and woman plod along the sand, hand in hand. A sharp knot of pain seizes me. Can two people live happily ever after? My parents stayed together, not lovingly, but committed to each other.

Once I thought I wanted someone good, someone solid, to live out my life. I'd hoped it would be Trish, so down-to-earth, predictable—and safe. But I realized that safe wasn't enough, and since then I've felt lonelier than ever. No relationship has ever been enough. I just kept hoping for The One.

With Mercedes I feel alive and open to every possibility. But that lingering fear still remains; that she'll abandon me again.

"We could adopt a child, Christa, if that's what you want," Mercedes says, this time, softly. It's a startling offer that jars me from my thoughts. And it appears to be genuine; her expression is questioning, but serious.

"Look, it's not that easy. You can't substitute one little boy for another and think everything will be perfect, our own little fairy-tale family. You don't even *like* kids!" I put my coffee cup down and turn away, feeling suddenly chilled.

"I want you to be happy, so if that's what it takes…" Mercedes' shoulders slump. She's disappointed that I'm not buying into her outrageous offer.

"I would never do that—just to keep us together. It's insane." I storm past her.

"So now I'm insane?" She fires back at me. "You're always this way after you talk to mousy little Trish."

I swivel around and confront her, something I should have done months ago, at the gallery, right after she kissed me.

"I already have a child, and I'm letting him down every time I'm away from him. So much of my time is spent shuttling back and forth between my house and your condo and Trish's place. It seems like I'm with him so little as it is. I'm missing out on so much. Every time I see him he's doing or saying something new. Now you're saying I should have another?" *Mercedes can't possibly understand .She's never experienced the bond between a mother and her child.*

I storm to the bedroom and begin tossing clothes into my suitcase.

"What are you doing?" She's blocking the doorway, her hands planted on her hips.

"Packing!" I march past her to collect my toothbrush and cosmetic bag from the bathroom.

Her eyes flash. "Fine! Just leave! Get the hell out of here and go back to Trish if you're so enamored of the life you had with her." Her voice quiets and color rises in her cheeks. "How good was that?"

My gut clenches. *It's over? She's kicking me out?*

She watches me gather my things and stuff them into my suitcase. "Where will you go?" She says, concerned.

"Home." I stare past her. "I'll wait at the airport for the first flight out."

"Fine." She moves away from the door and I'm out of there. When the elevator opens in the lobby the doorman glances at my suitcase and whistles for a taxi. He knows me as Senorita

Thompson, a 'friend' of Mercedes on the third floor. I wonder how many 'friends' she's brought here, to her little love nest.

Exhaustion and emptiness overtake me. I have no real home anymore. I'll be waiting at the airport before I even begin the long flight back to the states. My yearning for Mercedes, guilt about missing Christmas with Deshy, and dread of the inevitable confrontation with Trish pushes me over the edge. I dissolve into tears.

"Can I call someone for you? Senorita Martinez, yes?" The doorman asks.

"No!" I shout, sending him scuttling back to his post.

I sit in the lobby, hunched over in self-pity, crying and half hoping the elevator door opens and Mercedes comes to me.

Admit it, Christa, your life is a mess. You can't blame it all on Mercedes, either. My past has been a pattern of highs and lows—a string of disappointing relationships, and then that low-life investment banker who claimed to be divorced— but wasn't; the hope I felt meeting Trish and starting fresh in Santa Fe; the complete and utter love I felt toward Deshy; watching helplessly while my relationship with Trish disintegrated; and the elation at a second chance with Mercedes. Now this, my worst fear; Mercedes abandons me again.

The sound of screeching brakes cuts my pity party short. A taxi pulls up to the curb.

"Where to?" the driver asks.

"The airport."

As we speed away, I slump back in the seat, a bubbling stew of emotions; guilt, humiliation, loss, confusion. Mostly fear that Mercedes might be imagining her next liaison. She won't be alone for long, of that I'm certain. Why can't I just accept that I want her? She offered what she thought *I* wanted, a child to replace Deshy. She put my needs before hers, and even though her idea was misguided, it showed how much she wanted to make me happy and keep us together. I was too caught up in myself to see it.

For all I've changed—coming out and living with Trish—am I still that straight-laced Lutheran girl from Ohio, too repressed to acknowledge my sexuality even to myself? It hits me like a thunderbolt: I've been thrown out by the person who is the absolute best for me—my true soul mate, Mercedes. Is it too late? Will she take me back?

"Stop!" I call to the driver. I see his startled look in the rear view mirror.

"Take me back to where you picked me up."

He shakes his head and slams on the brakes. The cab swerves and comes within inches of a light pole.

I sink deeper into the seat, completely spent, and hoping against hope she'll take me back.

Mercedes

Oh, Christa, mi amor, you never gave us a chance. She's right, of course; I don't like children. I assumed if we adopted a kid, we'd hire a nanny to do all the messy stuff. People do it all the time, and God knows there are plenty of children in need of a good home. I imagined a Hispanic child, of course. With Christa and me, two professional parents, he'd have tremendous opportunity. Does that make me "insane?"

Enough is enough. How long was I supposed to listen to her guilt spoil our holiday—our lives together? I get it, she's conflicted, but she has to get over it and choose, just as I did with her.

If only Christa and I were together, really together, not doing all this shuttling back and forth. What is it she wants? I'd never ask her to give up Deshy, of course not. That's a given. I know better than to get between a mother and her child, but I offered everything to her, my whole self, with a love I've never felt for anyone before. I have to have that same commitment in return…and I won't wait forever.

The walls of the condo are closing in around me. I've got to get out of here.

"My shoulders and neck hold all my tension," I tell the petite Asian masseuse at The Senses Spa down the street. A eucalyptus candle perfumes the intimate space. Calming music plays softly. Why mope around the condo? What would that accomplish? Face down on the table, nude except for my panties, I feel my muscles relax while she kneads jasmine scented oil into my back and shoulders. How long was I supposed to listen to her guilt spoil our holiday—our lives together? I get it, she's conflicted, but she has to get over it and choose, just as I did with her.

After showering at the spa I decide to visit the nearby botanical gardens. My parents took me there as a child and it left an impression on me; the craggy landscape overlooking the deep blue Mediterranean. Better than lying around the condo brooding about Christa.

A stone pathway winds through the gardens. I'm lost in the memory of my parents calling to me as I run far ahead of them. Although I was their only child, they weren't overprotective. They gave me plenty of freedom and when I brought my first serious girlfriend home in college, it wasn't a big deal. I think they half expected it.

Ancient olive trees shade the walkway leading to a wrought-iron bench near the precipice overlooking the sea. Quickly, I take a few photos of the landscape to take home and paint. I can look forward to that, at least. I close my eyes and listen to the muffled sound of the waves crashing against the rocks far below. I inhale salty air. I'm suddenly chilled by a sudden ocean gust. If only Christa was here beside me.

Christa

The cab pulls away and I'm left standing at the curb in front of the condo. Should I go upstairs and tell Mercedes I'm sorry for carrying on about Deshy and ruining our holiday? Should I phone her? I'd never seen her as angry as when she yelled at me to leave. No one's ever done that. The midday sun is relentless. I have nowhere else to go.

When I step into the lobby the doorman is at my side, taking my suitcase and calling the elevator. I knock on the condo door and wait, but she doesn't answer. Naively, I'd fanaticized that Mercedes would be here welcoming me with open arms. I've no choice but to stay and wait. She's got to return—sooner or later.

Mercedes

I linger over lunch at a quiet café nursing a glass of wine. A distinguished looking gentleman asks if he can join me. "I'm waiting for someone," I tell him. And it's true.

Late in the afternoon I return to the condo, tired and lonely. My feet ache from walking with nowhere to go. I'm missing Christa and regretting, so regretting, throwing her out.

She could very well be half way across the Atlantic by now, on her way to a happy reunion with Deshy—and Trish.

The elevator door opens at the third floor and there in front of my apartment door is Christa, sound asleep with her head resting on her suitcase, a sweater draped over her shoulders, and her knees drawn up to her elbows. I brush her hair away and gently kiss her forehead. She slowly opens her eyes, startled at first to awaken in the hallway. I offer my hand and help her to her feet. Christa wraps her arms around me and rests her head on my shoulder.

"I love you, Mercedes," she whispers. "I never stopped loving you, not from the first moment I saw you."

I unlock the door and close it gently behind us.

PART III

Stuart

Elaine will see the area code and know it's from Chicago. But a call out of the blue from her brother-in-law means the news can't be good. She cuts to the chase.

"Stuart? Is everyone all right?" Her voice is strained.

"Denise is fine." I say.

"It's Mom then."

"Helen's fine too, actually, but…"

"But what, Stuart?" Elaine demands. "You haven't called for small talk. What's wrong?"

"We—Denise and I—thought you should know that your mother's been busy at her senior group lately. She's learned how to use the Internet. She's got an e-mail address now, silverfox@aol.com, and it's opened up a whole new world for her. In fact, she has a new online friend."

"What kind of friend, Stuart?"

"She met him on a website for seniors. 'Goldengeezer,' he calls himself. He says his wife died of cancer six years ago. In his photo he looks a lot younger than Helen, if that's really him."

"Good lord, a scam artist. Stuart, you're an attorney, isn't there something we can do legally? Doesn't anyone keep tabs on these things?"

"No one, Elaine. Not unless there's an actual crime committed, and so far there hasn't been. Denise was over at your mother's the other day and got an eyeful of Goldengeezer's latest Instant Message while Helen was in the kitchen making tea. He asked your mother, "What are you wearing?" Denise wrote back, "Who the hell are you and why are you asking my mother what she's wearing?"

"I've heard enough, Stuart. Colin and I are getting on the next plane."

"Well, that's part of the problem. Helen's booked a flight to Pensacola next week so she can meet this guy."

"Stuart, you cannot let her get on that plane!"

"I can't stop her, Elaine. Your mother's independent and in control of her faculties."

Elaine

"Let me talk to my sister." I hear muffled voices, and then Denise gets on the line.

"This was better coming from Stuart. He's always calm and collected," she says.

"Well, I am not calm, Denise."

"Elaine, honey, we didn't want to worry you. You've got enough on your plate what with raising the boy and all."

"When were you going to tell me, Denise? After they got married by an Elvis impersonator at an all-night wedding chapel in Vegas?"

"Please, Elaine, this is just what I didn't want—getting you all upset."

"Surely, you don't approve of this relationship. And don't tell me what's good for me." I feel pressure building behind my eyes—a migraine is brewing. "What are you planning to do about this, Denise?" We can go round and round like this without ever solving the problem.

"She's your mother, too." Denise says. Like I don't know it?

"What's that supposed to mean? You're *there*, Denise. I'm *here* dealing with soccer practice, and car pools, adolescent angst and endless homework. …you have no idea what goes into being a soccer mom." Obviously she doesn't because she quickly changes the subject.

"There's a private investigator at Stuart's firm. He's asked him to check out this guy, Max, see if he has a criminal record. Nothing's turned up."

"I've seen this sort of thing on TV. A smooth-talking hustler swindles lonely widows out of their life savings. I feel so helpless—so far away." My stomach is churning, acid is blasting up my throat, and my vision is getting blurry. It's the beginning of a migraine, for certain.

"Denise, I'll have to call you back. All this is just too much. It's making me sick, literally. I feel a migraine coming on and my gut is in a knot." It's time for some extra strength pain killers to nip this in the bud before I'm forced to bed for hours with a cold cloth over my forehead.

No way am I letting Mom get on a plane and rush into the arms of some creepy-geezer. Just because there's no criminal record on this guy could mean that the authorities haven't caught up with him yet. He's probably not even using his real name.

Whatever has possessed Mom, I can't imagine. She's always trusted known entities, like the Good Housekeeping Seal of Approval. I refuse to stand by and watch while her heart is broken and her bank account emptied. Not for myself, but for my Dad. He worked his entire life to provide for us, climbing the ladder, literally, at the electric company from a lineman in a bucket truck to a middle manager in a shirt and tie. I remember how Mom sweated over those shirts; putting bluing in the wash and starching the collars and cuffs. After she ironed them she put them on wire hangers and hung them over the bedroom door. Denise and I knew better than to disturb those shirts after all her work. Damn it, no con-man angling for a silver-haired widow with a pension is going to weasel his way into Mom's affection.

Colin hasn't seen his great-grandma Helen in ages, so this is a perfect reason for a visit to Chicago. Maybe seeing Colin will remind her that she's an eighty-year-old great-grandmother, not a love-struck teen-ager.

If Helen insists on flying to Florida to meet this guy, she's not going alone. We'll go with her. The thought of Colin meeting her new 'friend' might be enough for her to call it off. I haven't seen my mother in a while, either, and each time we're together I realize it could be the last.

I love Helen's home-cooked meals and motherly advice, even though it's sometimes misguided. She thinks no woman is complete without a man. Now the tables are turned; I'll be the one doling out advice. I'm not only dealing with Colin and his attention issues, but also an elderly mother who thinks she's in love. This is what being sandwiched between two generations feels like. It's a tight squeeze with no room to breathe.

I don't need this. Not now, not ever.

Helen

Finally, after months of phone calls and greeting cards, my daughter and my great-grandson are finally here, standing in my front hall. Denise spilled the beans before they arrived. Elaine's on the warpath over my trip to Florida to meet Max.

"Colin, how you've grown! My goodness, you're as tall as me." I kiss him and hold him close until he stiffens and I know to let go. They grow up so fast. "And Elaine, look at you." I hug her and then step back to assess my youngest child. "You look tired, dear." She looks even thinner than I remember. It must be all that running around she does with the boy, and no one to help her.

"Well, come in you two. Don't just stand there in the hall." I shepherd them into the living room. In a wink, I have a plate of homemade peanut butter cookies, a glass of milk and a dish of peppermint candy on the coffee table.

"Granma, do you have PlayStation?" Colin asks between bites.

I look to Elaine. "PlayStation, what's that? A new toy?"

"No Mom, it's an electronic game you play on the television set."

"My friends tell me all their grandkids want these days are video games. I have a great board game, though—Sorry. Remember, Elaine, how you used to love playing that game with your sister? You'd send Denise back to Start and she'd have a fit." I watch Elaine's face light up for a brief moment then fade. "When you girls got home from school it was milk and cookies in front of the television set. You watched Garfield Goose and Ray Rayner. Life was a lot simpler then. You and Denise played hide and seek after dinner until the street lights came on and no one blinked an eye. Now it's electronic games and organized sports. Not the way it used to be."

"What are you cooking, Mom? It smells delicious."

I made your favorite, Sweetheart. How often do I get to cook for you and Colin?"

After the meal Elaine pushes away from the table. "I feel like I've gained five pounds from your meatloaf and mashed potatoes. The gravy was delicious, too. One envelope of instant potatoes is enough for Colin and me, but they don't come close to the real thing."

"I should think not! A package of potato flakes—dear Lord, no wonder you're so thin. There's nothing like good old-fashioned home cooking. Remember when I came out to Santa Fe and cooked for you and Colin every day; old-fashioned suppers like pot roast with carrots and potatoes? Roast chicken? Beef stew?

"I love your beef stew, Grandma Helen," Colin chimes in.

"Colin's right, Mom. You are the best cook ever. Colin and I will get the dishes, right, Col? That's his job at home."

After the kitchen is clean, Colin settles in the guest bedroom to watch TV and Elaine and I munch on the last of the cookies and sip chamomile tea in the kitchen.

"Elaine, I'm thrilled that you and Colin are here, but your sister told me why you've flown halfway across the country. It hurts to think that the only reason you came is because you think I need a chaperone to fly to Florida. I'm still capable of making decisions on my own, Laney. Don't forget that.

Elaine

I cover Helen's gnarled fingers with my hand. Her skin is tissue-thin, threaded with ropy blue veins just beneath the surface.

"We love you, Mom. And we miss you." I squeeze her hand. "I'm worried about you, though. You're ready to get on a plane, alone, and fly down to Florida to get together with a stranger. That's all he is…a stranger you met on the Internet. People put all sorts of stuff on the Net. That photo you showed me—it was probably taken twenty years ago."

"Elaine, Sweetheart, you have no idea what's it's like to be old and alone." She slides her hand out from under mine and stares down at her lap, her head bent. "You have Colin. He's your reason to get out of bed every morning. I have no one. Denise doesn't need me. Now you think I'm some doddering old fool."

"What do you hope this man can give you, Mom? Anything like the wonderful years Dad gave to you— to us? Like when he drove us all the way to the Grand Canyon, and when he took us apple picking in the country every fall. We'd bring back a bushel of the best ones. You'd roll out the dough for pies and strudels and Dad would help us peel an entire bushel of apples. He showed Denise and I how to do it so there was one continuous peel.

He helped us carve pumpkins for Halloween. I liked a fat, round one and Denise wanted a tall, skinny one. The face on hers always looked scary."

Helen lifts her chin, a far-away look in her eyes. "No one could ever take Harry's place. He was one in a million, your father." Tears stain her face. "But he's been gone for so long. I'm lonely, Elaine. I'd love to have someone to cook for, watch television and play cards with, and mostly just share a good laugh. Someone who makes me feel special like your father did and someone to cuddle next to at night. Is that asking too much?"

I slip my arm around her. She leans into me and rests her head on my shoulder. "You can't possibly understand," she says.

"I can try. I feel lonely, too, sometimes. But I don't think that hooking up with some man you barely know is the answer. Think about it tonight. If you decide that's what you want, Colin and I will go to Florida with you."

Denise

Everything comes to a screeching halt because my little sister decides to get on a plane, with Colin in tow, and take charge, as if Stuart and I aren't capable of dealing with this situation. What am I supposed to do, ground my mother? Take away her computer and phone? She's still independent and mentally alert, capable of making her own decisions. Even though I'm not thrilled about the idea of her and Max, I can't stop her. What's next, no television for a month? Forget those Golden Girls reruns, Mom, you've been a bad girl!

The next day Elaine drops Mom and Colin at the movies and now she's plopped down at my kitchen table, jaw clenched and primed for a fight. I was on my way out the door and now I'm stuck, a captive audience to Elaine's rant about senior citizens meeting online. I glance at my watch. Looks like my errands will have to wait. I sigh and put on a pot of coffee. This could take a while.

Elaine starts right in, her face flushed with anger, her eyes blazing. "Did you know, Denise, that our mother is planning to fly down to Pensacola tomorrow—alone? *I* tried to convince her not to go We'll have to wait and see."

"Mom feels that Max fills the emptiness in her life," I explain, cool as a cucumber on the outside, but boiling mad inside at Elaine's lack of compassion for Mom's loneliness. "Surely, you can understand her need for companionship."

"A man she barely knows." Elaine says and gets up to pour herself a cup of coffee.

"So she'll get to know him, and maybe…"

Elaine, so thin and exhausted looking, leans across the table with slit eyes, her face inches from mine. "…maybe he's a sweet talking con man who'll make her think she's irresistible before he empties her bank account and leaves her heartbroken, that's what!" She slams her cup down on the table. Hot coffee spatters the table and her hand. I don't offer to help her.

"You really don't know that, Elaine." I rub my aching neck, and get up to pour myself a cup.

"One thing I do know—she's not getting on that plane alone and if *you* were the least bit concerned *you* wouldn't let her either!" She huffs and crosses her arms over her chest.

"Just shut up, Elaine!" Suddenly I jump to my feet nearly knocking over the chair—surprising myself at this unexpected outburst. "Where the hell do you get off saying that I'm not concerned? Of course I'm concerned. I'm the one who called you, remember? How in God's name did Mom and I manage without your unsolicited advice after you moved to Santa Fe? But we did, thank you very much, and I even managed to forget about you from time to time! Still do."

"Calm yourself, Denise. I only know what I'm told. Mom didn't share the news of her new relationship with me."

"Mom couldn't get on a plane fast enough to help you out when you up and moved to Santa Fe. She's never done anything like that for me."

"Because, Denise, you never need any help. You're always so competent and in control."

"I'm supposed to apologize for that?"

"And bedsides," Elaine finishes, her eyes glittering in triumph, "you have Stuart."

"What's that supposed to mean? Just because we've stayed married all these years doesn't mean we haven't had problems. Believe me. Marriage isn't a magic bullet that cures all problems."

Elaine continues as if she hasn't heard me.

"You have no idea how hard it was to raise my girls alone. You couldn't possibly understand what a mother goes through; let alone how it feels to lose a child."

"You were always the wild one, Elaine, staying out late and worrying Mom and Dad half to death. The apple doesn't fall far from the tree. No wonder Stephanie…"

"No wonder what, Denise? Are you saying that I'm somehow responsible for Stephanie's death? Out with it! What else has been eating away at you all these years?"

"You've always been impossible, Elaine. There I was at Stephanie's wake, trying to explain to Mom why you broke down when your embarrassingly young boyfriend showed up, and you practically fell into his arms. You were nearly hysterical."

Elaine

"For the love of God, Denise, I'd lost my daughter. Yes, I cried, I grieved, I showed emotion. Something that seems difficult for you, big sister."

"Carrying on with that man was wrong, Elaine—a woman your age—it sent the wrong message to Roxy."

"And I don't regret it, not for a minute. Besides, that thing with Jeff was a hundred years ago and it had nothing to do with Stephanie."

Denise's face puffs with resentment. "We were not raised that way, Elaine, and you know it!"

I grab the car keys off the counter. The movie will be over soon. Thank God Mom and Colin weren't here to see this. I had no idea Denise was harboring all this resentment from years ago. A big sister cleans up her little sister's messes. That's what they do—like how Denise got really good at forging Mom's signature on my detention slips. And how she'd unlock the front door for me when I was out past curfew so I didn't wake Mom and Dad. Denise should have had more fun when she was younger while she still could have. Maybe that's why she's so angry now.

At the door, I turn to deliver one last zinger:

"I don't know how Stuart's put up with you all these years, Denise. You are such a prude. You need to get drunk and get laid. Sorry, Sis, that's my professional nurse's opinion." Before she can reply, I'm out the door and in the car. The engine roars to life and I take a few deep breaths to steady myself.

After a restless night, I knock softly on the bathroom door, waiting for Helen to emerge. Colin's in the kitchen eating breakfast, dressed and ready to go to the airport.

"Mom, if you're going to do this, we've got to leave in the next ten minutes." Helen opens the door a crack and waves me into the bathroom. "You're not even dressed."

"Shh, I don't want Colin to know what an old I fool I am."

"You're not a fool, Mom. You're just lonely."

"I barely slept a wink last night thinking about what you said. You're right—I am lonely. But not lonely enough to move to hot, muggy Florida. And not lonely enough to have some man move in here with his boxer shorts, dirty cigarettes and nasal hair trimmer. I'll just tell him I had a surprise visit from my daughter and great-grandson. We can still be friends— online."

"He smokes?"

"I didn't want to tell you, dear. I knew that would be a deal-breaker."

I kiss her forehead. "I love you, Mom. I'd love you either way, but I'm glad you're not going to Florida."

Later, over coffee, I tell Mom that while we're here we should visit Stephanie's grave.

She smiles, her faded blue eyes brightening, "I'd love that, Elaine." We'll all say a prayer for our Stephanie."

"Then out to lunch, my treat, and maybe to a museum or the Aquarium. I'll be your chauffeur for the day. You won't have time be lonely as long as we're here. You'll probably be happy to see us leave, just so you can get some rest."

"Give me a few minutes to get myself together and put on my face." Helen says as I close the door.

"Guess what, Col? We're going to the Aquarium!"

"I thought we were going to Florida." he says as he munches another spoonful of Cap'n Crunch.

"Change of plans, buddy."

At Holy Sepulcher, we kneel at Stephanie's headstone. "Loving Daughter, Wife and Mother." We pray silently for a few moments. Colin lays a convenience store bouquet on his mother's grave and runs his hand across the cold granite marker. I brush a tear from the corner of my eye and squeeze Helen's hand.

Then it's on to the Aquarium, the Planetarium, and the Field Museum, all within walking distance on Chicago's lakefront campus. Like any twelve-year-old boy, Colin is enthralled by the skeleton of Sue, the gigantic Tyrannosaurus Rex in the Great Hall of the Field Museum. We walk until we can't walk anymore, then we stop at a street-vendor's cart and snag lunch: Chicago-style hot dogs with neon green relish, yellow mustard, tomatoes and chopped onions. Catsup on a hotdog is practically illegal in Chicago.

Before Colin and I leave, I promise Mom I'll call and visit more often, but I know that it's easier said than done. Flights are expensive and school breaks and summer vacation are the only times that work. Maybe it's time for Helen to visit us, again. She clearly enjoys cooking and fussing over us, so that might be the way to go.

Back in Santa Fe, Colin and I quickly settle back into our routine. One morning, though, as he grabs his backpack and hurries to the door, he asks if he can bring a friend home after school.

"Sure," I call, but he's already out of earshot, running down the sidewalk to catch the bus before I can ask about his new friend.

I'm delighted, of course. It's often just the two of us and the cat padding around the house in the late afternoon. Sometimes he rides his bike until dinner time. When I ask him where he's been and what he's been doing, he shrugs and says, "Nothing, just riding around."

Colin's almost thirteen, but he still loves building things with Lego blocks. On any given day, forts, castles, fighter jets and galactic ships are spread across the living room floor. And he loves his video games. I limit the time he spends in front of television, or he'd never move off the sofa. It's ironic that kids with attention deficit can spend hours playing video games but have difficulty focusing on schoolwork for more than a few minutes. Their bodies might not be moving, but the high-octane brain activity keeps them rooted in one spot. I wish his school assignments were as stimulating.

We're not a traditional family, Colin and I, but two-parent families are becoming rarer and rarer. Colin's classmates have all types of family arrangements; two moms, two dads, a single parent, and grandparents raising their grandkids, like us. So I guess we're not all that different. Colin's special accommodations in the classroom do set him apart, though. He's allowed extra time to finish tests, and his teacher has to initial his assignment book every day to make sure he's written down his homework. There's a stigma no matter what kind of 'special' a kid is, especially for kids like Colin, who have to go to the nurse's office every day for medication.

I held off medicating him, but the effects of that were probably more negative than positive. It broke my heart to see him spend so much time alone. Besides being impulsive, ADHD kids have poor social skills; they can't decipher facial expressions or recognize social cues. No close friends meant low self-esteem. I made a list of the pros and cons of medication and decided that it wouldn't hurt to try, so fifth grade marked a turning point. Turns out I saw improvement almost immediately; his was less antsy and could sit and concentrate on his homework longer. Within a month or so his grades went up, and he didn't bring home as many discipline notices. He's in seventh grade now, but I still have to keep on him. Medication isn't a silver bullet, but it helps.

I set snacks out for Colin and his friend: granola bars, cheese sticks, pretzels, apples, peanut butter and crackers. They'll be hungry after a long day, so I put out lots of choices.

The front door opens. "I'm home," Colin yells. I'm in the courtyard, pretending to read a magazine. I resist the urge to rush inside and check out his new friend. Hovering is the kiss of death, I've heard. The sounds of the refrigerator door opening, glasses clinking, and wrappers crinkling drift outside. They've got their snack, so it's a good time to make my appearance.

What?! Colin's 'friend' is a girl! A really darling girl with shiny black hair, a flawless complexion, and dark brown eyes. A budding beauty.

"Mom, this is Anna Lucia," Colin says, popping a peanut butter slathered apple wedge into his mouth. She smiles shyly.

"It's nice to meet you," I say, having only partly recovered from the surprise. "Anna Lucia—that's a beautiful name."

The girl smiles and looks to Colin.

"Anna doesn't talk that much. She's new and kids make fun of her sometimes, so mostly she doesn't talk to the other kids, except me. I understand her most of the time."

Anna's hands suddenly become animated and I realize she's signing. I didn't notice her hearing aids until now.

"She says, 'Thanks for the snacks. It's nice to meet you, too.'" Colin tells me.

"How do you know that, Colin?" I'm amazed.

"Sometimes Anna's special teacher comes and shows the class how to sign. It's easy, once you get the hang of it." Colin acts like it's no big deal. I wonder what else he hasn't told me about what goes on at school.

"Anna, do your parents know you're here? Maybe you should call home and let them know where you are."

Colin gives me a look. "It's all good, Mom. Her brother's coming for her at five."

Maybe I should go back outside. Do eighth graders need a chaperone? Oh, yeah, they do. This is *so* sudden but I can manage. I taught sex ed for years when I was a school nurse in Chicago. Still, I'm not ready for Colin having a girlfriend.

Colin

I have twenty math problems to do plus soccer practice, and I promised Anna I'd help her with her science project. I could blow off practice, but then coach will bench me. I hope Granma washed my soccer clothes.

Suddenly I realize Mrs. Munoz is calling my name. "Colin! Colin McElroy!"

Oh no, she looks pissed.

"How nice of you to join us, Mr. McElroy. Settle down, class. I'm sure we'd all like to hear from Colin. Please answer problem fifteen."

"I...I did it last night. I just, I just can't find it right now." I turn my backpack inside out but no homework paper appears.

Mrs. Munoz puts on her mean teacher face. "See me after class, Colin."

After the bell, she's sitting at her desk messing with a bunch of papers. Finally, she looks up and notices me standing there.

"Colin, did you take your medication this morning?"

"I think so."

"You don't know? Doesn't your grandmother give it to you before school?" Her face is all screwed up and red.

"Yeah, she puts it on the table next to my cereal."

"I'm really disappointed, Colin. This is your second missing assignment this week."

"I'll make it up." I just want to tear out the door. She whips a yellow pad from the drawer.

"Here's a pass. Go on ahead. You can't afford to miss a minute of class time."

Elaine

I hate to jump on him the minute he gets home. I'll let him have his snack first. He needs that. Then I'll break the bad news about the phone call from Mrs. Munoz.

"How was your day?"

"Fine." He dunks an Oreo in milk and stuffs it into his mouth.

"Anything happen?" It's best to hear his side first.

"No."

Today's run-in with Mrs. Munoz is just a blip on his radar, so routine that he hardly notices.

"Mrs. Munoz called. She said didn't have your homework."

Colin looks at me like this is the first he's heard of it. "But I did it. You helped me with it last night."

My sweet boy looks so beat down, like everyone's against him. He needs someone to build him up, not drag him down.

"That's what I told her, too. But it's like I keep telling you, unless the homework is handed in, it's like you never did it."

He concentrates on dunking another cookie.

We search the folders in his back pack, but there's no math homework paper. Maybe I need to get a fax machine and send the finished assignments directly to school the minute he completes them. I'm doing my part; making sure he takes his meds every morning, helping him with his homework every night, filing the finished work in his folder. Whatever happens between here and school, I just don't know. He's supposed to have something called "accommodations" in every subject, but that might be part of the problem.

It's time for me to meet with all his teachers and make sure everyone's aware of his Attention Deficit Disorder and doing what needs to be done. I know from working in a school system for years that it's the parent who raises a fuss that gets her child what he needs. I'm willing to make a stink to help Colin. A prayer to the Blessed Mother and Thomas Aquinas, patron saint of scholars, won't hurt, either. I make a vow that Colin and I will go to Mass every Sunday in return for his graduating from eighth grade. As an extra bonus, I throw in his Confirmation. If all our church-going pays off I'll have a big party and invite the Chicago relatives. What a great excuse for a family reunion!

Colin and I usually sleep in on Sundays, but not today. I linger in bed for a few more cozy moments while the sun casts shadows through the blinds before I put on my slippers and robe, and pad to the kitchen to make coffee. Callie weaves through my legs, reminding me that she's hungry. The aroma of brewing coffee, sunlight filtering through the window, and sweet silence are my morning comforts.

For today, and every Sunday to come, I am pledged to a promise. Colin and I will go to Mass. Period.

I'll wake him up after my first rejuvenating cup of coffee.

Colin

"We're going to church? Did somebody die? We only ever go on Christmas Eve when I light candles for my ma and da."

"From now on, we're going every Sunday," Granma says. "Come on, we don't want to be late. Wash your face and let's go. You can feed Callie when we get back."

She hands me a comb and we're out the door. The street is deserted except for an old man wearing a baseball cap out walking his dog. It's kind of nice, just me and Granma. The rest of Santa Fe is still asleep.

Denise

Sisters fight, that's normal, but I'm glad Elaine and I are over that thing with Mom. It helped that she decided at the last minute to not go to Florida. I have to admit, Elaine played a part in persuading her. The Prodigal Daughter returns and

Gets Things Done. *I'm* the one here, watching out for Mom every single day, though, the responsible one.

And here's the latest development that has Mom over the moon: Elaine is having a big blow-out for Colin's graduation. This time we'll all fly out to Santa Fe for the celebration. Colin's made his Confirmation, too. I have to hand it to my sister, she gets results.

Our plane touches down in Albuquerque and we head straight to Elaine's in a rental car: Roxy, Helen, Stuart and me. The party's just getting started when we arrive. Elaine greets us at the door wearing a floral dress and shepherds us inside. She's balancing a tray of soft drinks and snacks for Colin and his friends in the courtyard. I notice a girl with shiny dark hair, a flawless mocha skin , and mile-long legs and arms.

"Who is she?" I ask Elaine.

"Anna Lucia, Colin's friend. She moved here last year. They're practically inseparable." Elaine says, grinning, as she empties a bag of chips into a bowl.

We watch from the kitchen as Colin and Anna put their heads together, exchange a few words, and laugh at their own private joke. I have to admit they're a handsome couple; Anna with her beautiful smile and deep brown eyes, and Colin, tan and muscled from playing sports. He brushes his copper-tinged hair out of his eyes. He's quite handsome.

"It's such a shame that Stephanie isn't here to see him growing up," Elaine says quietly, staring at them.

"Aren't you worried that they're so close—Colin and Anna?"

Elaine stops arranging cheese and crackers on a tray, looks proudly at her grandson, and then locks her gaze on me, eyes blazing.

"Is that the first thing you can say when you've just walked in the door? Look around—it's your first visit here, and it wouldn't hurt you to comment on the place, the back courtyard in full bloom with the cholla's pink flowers, the yucca stalks full of cascading white flowers—so lovely with the orange petals ringing the top of the barrel cactus next to it." She moves in closer, practically getting in my face, but she continues. "Have you ever seen anything like it? It was one of the first things I worked on when I moved here—and look how the light filters in."

Elaine's right. It is beautiful. I didn't know she was into gardening. "You really did a fabulous job, Sis. It's a lot to take in."

"So get your mind out of the gutter, Sis," Elaine says. "Anna Lucia is the least of my worries. In fact, she may be the best thing to happen to Colin in a while. He's really come out of his shell since they started hanging out." Elaine takes the cover off the slow cooker and stirs the pulled pork. A tangy aroma wafts up from the crock. "Besides, teenagers travel in packs, so it's not like they're alone, and I'm always around when they're here."

"But you can't be with them every second of every day." I remind her.

Elaine's smile tightens into a thin line. "Denise, don't go there, I mean it. With what I've had to deal with, I'm just thankful he's made it this far and is moving on to high school." Her look morphs from determination to smug satisfaction as she grins cryptically.

"I was going to wait to announce this to everyone later, but since you're concerned about his future..." She stirs the pork for effect, keeping me in suspense. "He's getting a scholarship—for soccer. They have a strong team at Sacred Heart and they recruited him." Her smile widens, triumphant. "It's an honor and he worked hard for it. Just because he's naturally athletic doesn't mean he didn't put in long hours of practice. The scholarship won't pay for everything, but it will help."

"That's wonderful, Elaine!" Since Colin's mother died, my sister's life has been anything but easy. She's put her life on hold to raise Colin and she's got every right to be proud and claim bragging rights. "Stuart and I want to help with his education. We're Colin's godparents, after all. Even with his scholarship you'll need help with his clothes and supplies and all the incidentals. What's the phrase? *It takes a Village.*"

Elaine

My conservative sister's quoting Hillary Clinton. Now that's a switch—and a generous offer. "Thanks, Denise. You're right, I can't do it alone and I do want him to go to this school."

"Is Anna Lucia going there, too?"

"It's co-ed, but without a scholarship or a rich uncle, I doubt it. She'll be at Capitol High."

Denise

Colin's going to a Catholic high school. I'm sure his first crush will fade once he's around other girls. Still, he's a thirteen-year-old boy. I wonder if anybody's given him The Talk.

"Elaine, is Tom coming to the party?" He's the boy's grandfather; the one who should talk to him. Not that sex isn't out there 24/7 in movies, TV and online. He needs someone to teach him about respecting women, valuing their opinions and accepting that "no" means "no."

"Tom said he couldn't afford the airfare because child support for his little girl with Cheryl is bleeding him dry," Elaine says. "I've stopped expecting anything from Tom. That way I'm not disappointed when he doesn't step up."

"You'd think he'd make the effort." *But he won't. True to form, Tom isn't here. Not that he ever was there for my sister, or the two daughters they had together.*

Roxy

Mom's doing Colin's graduation up big; homemade pulled pork, coleslaw, potato salad, deviled eggs, and salad with candied walnuts and dried cranberries. She even splurged on a sheet cake decorated with green frosting to look like a soccer field. Obviously, a lot of thought and preparation went into this party.

She didn't do anything like this for me when I graduated from high school. Stephanie's death was still a raw wound. We were all in shock. Even in death, my sister overshadowed everything. Actually, she was always the main attraction. When she graduated from anything, even Minnow Level at YMCA swim lessons, it was a big deal. Fried chicken picnic parties in the park. Cakes with "Stephanie" plastered across them. When I hear Mom going on and on about her poor dead daughter, I bite my tongue. She was my big sister and I miss her, but Mom only remembers the good stuff. Little did she know that while Steph was supposed to be watching me, Big Sister was dragging me to whoever's basement was Party Central for the night.

Her biggest accomplishment in high school was bringing her grade point average up just enough so she could graduate. For Steph's party Mom had a lavish spread of fried chicken, Italian beef, pasta salad, brownies and cake. Word got around and I swear, Stephanie's entire class showed up. There weren't even leftovers to have the next day. And didn't Steph haul in the bucks! She immediately spent every penny on movies, music, crazy-cool outfits with matching nail polish for each, and enough cheap jewelry to open a store.

For my high school graduation Mom and Colin came in from Santa Fe, so at least there was that, but my 'big party' consisted of take-out KFC chicken at Grandma Helen's with my BFF Katelyn and her folks, who I was bunking with 'til college. Dad dropped by for a hot minute, but left with a lame-ass excuse about getting home to his new family. Aunt Denise and Uncle Stuart were there, too, with a generous check that I used toward college tuition. Grandma Helen was all about Colin, loving his every word in brogue-y three-year-old English, and buying him little outfits, with matching shoes and caps.

Looking back, we had some smiles even though we were still frozen with grief, afraid to take a deep breath for fear we'd break—shatter, even. I remember the strain of treading lightly around Colin, measuring every word for fear we'd say something to set him off on a crying jag for his mom and dad. Steph was the dead elephant in the room, but nobody talked about it, so it was just as well that Helen took Colin in the kitchen with her, and let him play there with his Matchbox cars and the blocks she'd bought for him.

Now it's Colin who's in the spotlight; the only grandchild and the only child of my dead sister. I love him to pieces, but to hear my Mom tell it, he's a poor little orphan snatched from the jaws of certain doom in Ireland. But she found out in a flash that he's a poor little orphan with plenty of baggage—like Attention Deficit Disorder.

It hasn't been easy for him, though, being raised by his grandmother. I don't begrudge him his moment in the sun. After all, I'm an adult, and his aunt, and both my parents are alive.

Christa

Roxy's certainly grown up. She used to be this Goth girl with raven-black hair, combat boots, and a dog collar with chrome spikes. Now she's a young professional, probably with a closet of J. Crew business suits and conservative pumps. And she's beautiful: honey-blond highlights, dark blue liner around those stunning grey eyes. I'm happy for her when she tells Elaine that her observation of manatees at the Shedd contributed, in a small way, to an article about endangered manatee habitats in Florida. The recognition is long overdue; she's been overshadowed by her sister for too long, and now her nephew.

Elaine is hanging on Roxy's every word, asking questions about marine biology like she's read a book about it for the occasion. I was worried about Roxy for a while; she was pretty much on her own when Elaine moved to Santa Fe. Given that she was always the 'forgotten child,' she could have gotten into alcohol and drugs. Instead she finished college, got an internship and then a paying job, working with marine mammals at the Shedd. I'm proud of her, too. But seeing Roxy again, all grown up, makes me feel out of the loop.

Speaking of 'out of the loop,' why is Trish all dressed up in a floral mini-dress I've never seen, sandals with heels, her hair's curled, and she's even wearing lipstick!—nothing she ever did when we were together. Is that where my child support money's been going?

A knock at the door interrupts Roxy in mid-sentence. My stomach, already clenching at the sight of this New, Improved Trish, does a flip when Elaine opens it and I see who it is— Mercedes. Who was *not* invited.

She breezes past me with the authority of a four-star general, her four-inch stilettos click-clacking on the hardwood floor. "Where is he?" she asks. I nod toward the courtyard and she strides confidently into the circle of young people gathered there. With a theatrical flourish she deposits a large shopping bag with an Apple logo at Colin's feet. The guests gather to witness the drama unfold. Elaine watches slack-jawed. Trish reaches for Deshy, drawing him close as if protecting him from The Dark Side, for God's sake. Colin and his friends fall silent. Roxy's moment in the limelight evaporates like rain on a hot sidewalk.

I have to hand it to Mercedes; if she was going for Shock and Awe she's certainly succeeded; the Apple bag, the tight white skirt and low-cut black top, and the *piece de resistance*, a white gardenia tucked behind her ear, channeling Billie Holiday; she looks great, and I know she means well, but it's a graduation party for a fourteen-year-old boy.

"I couldn't help myself," she gushes to no one in particular. "Christa told me about the family celebration, and I couldn't let Colin graduate without a little token from me."

Yes, I told her about the party, but I'd made it explicitly clear that she wasn't on the guest list.

Mercedes taps her toe, waiting for Colin to pick up the bag. When he doesn't, she snatches it by the handles and shoves it at him. "It's a MacBook!" she cries.

Colin rips into the bag.

"This is awesome!" he yells, grinning and hoisting the box with the Apple logo for his friends to see.

Elaine

Colin's at a loss. His social skills are limited at best, and accepting a gift of this magnitude from a sexy stranger is beyond his scope entirely.

"Colin, honey, let me introduce you," I say, trying to smooth over a truly uncomfortable moment. "This is Mercedes, Christa's...friend." Friend, partner, lover; who knows what's proper anymore.

"Thank you for the gift," Colin says stiffly.

Overcome with her own generosity, Mercedes enfolds my grandson in her embrace. His face is buried in her cleavage, a destination he seems in no hurry to extricate himself.

"Yes, thank you," I say, prying them apart. Colin's friends snicker. Anna Lucia glances from Mercedes' ample breasts to her own newly budding curves. Colin and his friends go off to his room to set up his new computer, followed by Deshy in hot pursuit. Roxy storms into the kitchen, upstaged and annoyed, and returns with a beer.

As Mercedes re-enters the living room, I fix a determined look at Christa that she correctly interprets as "Get her out of here!"

Trish

I'm so angry I'm shaking, though I thought I'd worked through my feelings toward Christa, but no way when it comes to Mercedes. I quickly set my glass of wine on a table. I don't trust myself around *that woman*. It's painful to see the two of them together, even in the same room, but I don't want to leave, either. Luckily, Deshy tagged along after Colin and his friends. I scan the room for Tristan who's been chatting with Stuart over by the kiva.

Oh, I am so hurt, and so pissed off, too. I put on a radiant smile and stride toward the two men; a woman on a mission. Before either man speaks I thread my arm around Tristan's waist and crane my neck to give him a kiss on his freshly shaved, citrusy cheek. He's clearly delighted and kisses me back—on the lips. After all, didn't we just have dinner at Andiamo's last Thursday? Conversation stops and all eyes are on this new drama. Christa stiffens and grabs the sofa as if she might topple over. Mercedes looks self-righteous for a hot second until she sees Christa's stunned expression. Elaine inhales audibly and takes a small step back, her eyes shooting daggers in my direction. I didn't start this drama, but it looks like Tristan and I have just stolen the spotlight back from Mercedes. Stuart mumbles something about freshening his drink and drifts away. Now it's just the two of us and I can't help turning to gloat at Christa, who's close to tears, her hand covering her mouth. *It hurts, doesn't it, Christa, when the person you thought loves you—doesn't?*

Elaine hesitates a long moment. Her face crumples and her shoulders sag. *Get over it Elaine! Tristan is a free agent—and so am I. Let's face it, he's attracted to someone younger and the fact that I'd never had sex with a man before didn't hurt, either.* Elaine stares a hard minute at Tristan and me before she pulls it together and returns to the business at hand—Mercedes' expensive gift to Colin.

"How very generous," she says, her tone clipped, "and for a boy you barely know."

Christa

I can't believe what I just saw. Yet they're standing there, Tristan's arm around Trish, the two of them deep in conversation as if they're alone in the room, and it feels like I've been punched in the gut. I can't let myself cry, though. I won't give Trish the satisfaction.

Enough is enough. As I turn away, I feel Mercedes' arm around me, and she says, "Come here, mi amor," and I do.

We go to the narrow courtyard just beyond the front door, which at least gives us some privacy—Elaine's casita is so damn small! For a while, we're holding each other, not speaking, and when my breathing calms, Mercedes draws back, taking my face in her hands.

"She's really hurt you," she whispers, "and I wish I could take that pain away. I can only hold you and love you."

"There's nothing I would rather do than to leave here right now with you, but I can't."

"Of course you can't, my darling, of course not. You must stay and be strong, and to hell with her. We'll go back into the party together."

Helen looks relieved to see us return. "Come and sit with me." She pats the seats next to her on the sofa. "It's so nice to see new faces and meet people. I know you, Christa, from poor Stephanie's wake, but I've never met you, dear," she says, turning to Mercedes with a smile.

Bless you, Helen! "Helen I'm so sorry. I should have introduced you earlier. This is my partner, Mercedes Martinez." Mercedes extends her hand, rewarding Helen's kindness with a heartfelt smile.

"How lovely to meet you, Mercedes. I love the gardenia. You know, years ago, I saw Billie Holiday in her prime, and she was grand, just grand, and I never forgot. How glad I am to see you wearing one."

"My father loved her too, and we used to listen to her records together. That's how I learned about her."

At last. My shoulders relax with relief that someone in here—*someone*—has included Mercedes and made her feel welcome.

"So, dear, tell me about this partnership—you're in business together?" Helen asks.

Mercedes and I exchange glances. "Mercedes and I are together…we're, um…a couple." I say, trying to be as delicate as possible.

"Oh, in my day we said "my special friend." She grasps each of our hands in hers and squeezes, a knowing smile on her lips. She gets it and I could kiss her for her kindness.

Roxy

"Who is she?" I hear someone whisper.

"Christa's bitch, I guess," I say under my breath, but loud enough that they both heard it. Mercedes shoots me a fiery look, then resumes her 'party' persona, but Christa's face droops, her mouth half-open in surprise. She's so hurt; if only I'd never said it. I had no idea Trish and Christa are history, and they're both with someone new. No matter, my loyalty is with Christa. She was the one who was there for my mother—and me—during Stephanie's wake and funeral. She was the one who gave me generous checks when I graduated from high school and college. She was Mom's friend in Chicago and she's her friend now. Ugh, if only I could take it back, but Christa heard it and she deserves an apology. It's just that for once I got the recognition that always seems to slip through my fingers—until Mercedes stepped in and took it all away.

Christa

The guests return to their conversations. Helen compliments Mercedes on her outfit. Nobody gets her a drink, so I go to the kitchen to get her a glass of wine.

I take a deep breath and hand the wine to Mercedes "Helen, I hate to interrupt, but I need a word." With that I take Mercedes by the arm and walk her back out front to the courtyard.

"Merc, this isn't my party, it's Elaine's for Colin, and she wanted to keep it small, for her family and a few of his friends."

"Those people you care so much about?" Her mouth forms a hard line. "And that one who called me your 'bitch' in front of everyone?"

"Mercedes, sweetheart, she had no right, no right at all to say that, and I'm as shocked as you are." I take her wine and put it on the window sill, moving closer to embrace her—if she'll let me. "I've known her since she was in middle school, and that's so unlike her. All I can think of is that she's always lived in someone else's shadow, first her sister, and now Colin. But that's no excuse for what she said, no matter how she felt." I touch her hair, glossy in the sun light, putting my arm around her, bringing her to me, and feel the stiffness in her shoulders.

"I'm so, so sorry" I whisper, and she relaxes into me. "And you and Trish in the same room? Just what Elaine wanted to avoid. You're lucky—we both are—she didn't douse you with her drink—again." *Maybe because she's on her best behavior for Tristan?*

"Well," Mercedes says, stepping back, her hand planted on her hip, "looks like your ex has moved on–and to a man. Christa, when are you going to let go?" Then her mood changes and her eyes flash like warning signals. "Not wanting me here, that was just so much crap!" She turns to look through the window at the assembled group of women, all gazing back— for what? Afraid they're going to miss something of this continuing saga? Mercedes raises her voice, alarming me. "You'll do anything to continue this farce, this lie of a family, complete with visitation rights every other weekend. How very modern of you! In the meantime, Trish raises your child. They lived in your house—for almost a year! You pay their rent, and buy him what he needs, whatever he wants, in fact!" She flings her hands in the air, her voice shrill now. "This party would have been the perfect opportunity to introduce me to these people..." Surprisingly, her voice trails off. Softly, she says, "I was hoping you would. But you're ashamed of me."

"Of course not. You're my love, Mercedes," and I turn to stare back at our audience inside. Turning back to Mercedes, I take her hands in mine and say, "It's one of those get-togethers that I need to, *want* to attend. I've seen Colin grow up, after all."

"So I'm good enough to fuck, but not good enough to be seen with you in public, with *your* people, is that it? I've taken you to parties and introduced you, proudly, as my lady; we went to gallery openings with other artists, to the opera. You've met my friends, my colleagues," she declares indignantly, though her fierce eyes soften with hurt and her lips are drawn into a frown, one I'd love to kiss away, but I don't dare. Behind me, I know full well the guests are watching and listening.

"This is supposed to be Colin's special day. Let's not spoil it for him."

"What about me? It's already spoiled for me."

I search for a graceful way to get Mercedes to leave, not for me, but for Elaine who's already had enough drama for one graduation party. "Listen, I'll tell them you've got another event to go to this afternoon, and had to leave early."

From the corner of my eye, I see the others still peering through the window at us. We must be quite a show, so the hell with it—no chaste kiss on the cheek! I draw her close and kiss her full on the lips, deep and long, and slide my hands over the curve of her ass—give them something juicy to gossip about! Afterward she smiles and walks regally to her red convertible. As the car roars down the street, her hair flowing behind her, she revs the engine. "Later," she mouths.

Everyone quickly scatters. Helen waves me over, "She's quite stunning. In my day women didn't kiss like that in public. But that was a long time ago and everything's different now."

"Yes, everything *is* different now." I say, more to myself than Helen.

Elaine

Whenever Christa, Trish, and Mercedes are in the same room sparks fly. Thank God I'm not sponging wine from the carpet or sweeping broken crockery off the floor! After all, this was supposed to be Colin's special day, not a front row seat to the ongoing saga of those three! And that ungrateful bitch—Trish! First she took advantage of my hospitality, living rent free in my house for a week. Then after a seemingly simple task of feeding Tristan's parrot, she came home late reeking of alcohol and wearing someone else's clothes! What was I supposed to think? Now she humiliates me in my own house with a public display of affection with my would-be boyfriend! I've had it with her!

I'm starving and I'm sure everyone else is, too. It's time to serve dinner. Roxy helps me arrange platters piled high with rolls for sandwiches, the crock pot filled to the brim with savory pulled pork, and bowls of pasta and green salads on the dining room table. Guests find a spot in the house or in the courtyard patio, balancing plates piled high with food. I refresh their drinks and grab a bite to eat before some new spectacle erupts.

Hours later, Colin says good-bye to most of his friends and Anna gets a ride home from her brother. Now it's just family—and Christa. Denise, and Roxy help with the left-overs and Christa washes the serving bowls and platters. Helen stares over Colin's shoulder while he tries to explain the wonders of his new computer.

I wish everyone could have stayed here for the night, but there's no way. My place is too small. Colin and I wave from the curb. I hate to see them go, especially Helen. Each time I'm with her I know it could be our last time together.

Christa takes an overstuffed bag to the trash, and I'm washing the coffee pot when Denise mumbles about my friends flaunting their lesbian affection, kissing, and with their hands all over each other—in broad daylight, for everyone to see. At this point I'm too tired to care. Roxy's subdued, resigned to the distance between us, geographic and emotional. No matter how well we get along while she's here, when it's time to leave she puts up a wall. It's as if she's thinking, *you're my mother and I love you, but you've got your life here and I've got mine back in Chicago*. Mothers and daughters…it's complicated.

Colin and the rest of his friends leave for another party and the house is quiet after all the drama of the day. Christa's outside picking up empty cans and paper plates in the late afternoon sun. A deep sadness washes over me like being slapped by a cold ocean wave. It takes my breath away when I realize that I am truly, deeply, alone. My family has all gone back to Chicago and I don't know when I'll see them again. Colin is growing up and after high school he'll be gone—perhaps to college or to work at a trade—or to Ireland where he'll be groomed to take over the Caseys' dairy farm.

Chuck and I had dinner together, nothing serious, and with his looks I'm sure he has his pick of younger, more attractive women. And after seeing Tristan and Trish together...

I'm leaning over the kitchen sink, clutching the countertop for support. A single tear drips onto the worn surface, followed by another and soon I'm sobbing outright, loud, unrestrained blubbering.

"Laney, honey, what happened? What's wrong?" Christa is at my side, but I'm in no condition to explain. She leads me to a chair in the dining room where everyone was eating and talking earlier, but now it's just the two of us. She pulls a chair up next to me and puts her arm around my shoulder and I cry onto the collar of her blouse. I cry and stop and cry and stop until I'm cried out. I wipe my nose on a crumpled napkin, straighten up, hiccup a few times, and smile weakly.

"What is it, Laney?" It's the first anyone's spoken in a while.

"I was just thinking. Remember when you 'came out' to me on Good Friday...at this very table...how many years ago? You were the one crying then and I was completely clueless."

Christa laughs quietly. "You were the first one I told."

I take Christa's hands in mine. "I'm sorry for being such a crybaby. It's just that by this time in my life I'd hoped to have someone, a partner to share growing old. It seems like everyone's found someone—everyone except me."

"You don't have to apologize to me. I'm a therapist, remember, and you're entitled to your feelings. You should let yourself to cry more often. You've got a lot on your plate and you've done a fine job raising Colin. I'm always here for you. You know that."

"Tristan's been a good friend to me, and I always hoped we would get together. You sensed that, didn't you? We were such a good match, and he always adored Colin. But now he's with

Trish…" I see the look of pain on Christa's face. "You're with Mercedes," I continue, "and I have no one."

Trish

Tristan wants to take Deshy with us next time we go out to dinner and I'm okay with it, but also a little uncertain. It's great that Tristan wants to get to know Deshy better, but where is this leading? Tristan is my window to his upscale world of design and glamorous clients. One of them, he tells me, requested a bidet specially designed for her cat! It's fascinating and beyond anything I've ever imagined. For a few hours I can relax and forget about being a mother, homemaker and part-time cashier at Whole Foods.

I choose a family friendly pizza restaurant and we plan to meet at six, not eight o'clock like our other dates. At home we usually eat at 5:30, so by the time we're seated, order, and are served, we could be dealing with a hungry, crabby five year-old. Deshy is usually well behaved, but I don't want to risk him melting down in front of Tristan.

While we wait for our pizza, Tristan and I sip red wine and Deshy is thrilled that I ordered root beer for him, a rare treat. He's busy munching crusty slices of garlic bread and happily sipping his root beer as Tristan tells me about plans to build his dream house, authentic Southwest with wood beam ceilings, tile floor and an enclosed courtyard. Plus, of course, all the latest appliances and bathroom fixtures. It sounds amazing and judging from what he's done with his casita, it will be fabulous. Then he says something that stops me cold.

"It could have a playroom for Deshy with murals on the walls, built-in shelves and bins for storage, kid-sized fixtures in the bathroom, plenty of sunlight in the morning and shade in the afternoon."

Is Tristan offering me a luxury home with every possible convenience? He's talked about wanting a son, but he's so much older than me—at least twenty years! And that's not the only problem. Is this what our dinner dates were all about—laying the groundwork for an "instant family" complete with the son he's always wanted? A panicked tightness radiates throughout my body as I struggle to catch my breath.

"Tristan, I've been upfront with you. You know I love women and I always have. I can't change who I am. Who I've always been."

"I'm not asking you to change," he says, hope etched in his eyes.

"I could never make you happy." I place my hand over his. "I love you—but not like that." I say, looking into his now sad eyes. "You are a sweet, sweet man—my first, and that's saying a lot." I manage a smile.

Tristan glances fondly at Deshy. "It's no secret that I've always wanted a son. I hoped, maybe, that after our night together and getting to know you..." He turns, gazing at me intensely, as though trying to read my thoughts.

"And how you kissed me at the party...that maybe it could work."

Where is this coming from? Did I ever talk about the future when we were drinking margaritas on his sofa—or after? Did I lead him on? I never meant to. That kiss at the party wasn't real, it was for show, and I never thought he'd take it to heart. Oh, my God—he sees me as a woman, a desirable woman, he's serious, and he wants me. Still...

"I'm so sorry, Tristan, but I never lied to you." I squeeze his hand just as Deshy spills his drink and I quickly mop his shirt and pants with paper napkins.

We finish eating in silence. Tristan walks us to our car. After I buckle Deshy into his seat he comes around to the driver's side and I kiss Tristan good-bye for the last time.

"I'm sorry." I whisper. He turns and walks away.

When I turn on the engine, I let it idle. Am I insane? What am I doing, turning down a once-in-a-lifetime offer? But if I thought I was trying to be someone I wasn't for Christa, it would be worse with Tristan, denying who I am at the most basic level. And what about Deshy? He'd get attached to this man only to lose him. That's if Christa would allow it, which she wouldn't. She'd take Deshy away in a heartbeat. No, in the end, it could never work.

Elaine

The aroma of sandalwood incense beckons me into Sophia's shop. The summer heat is giving way to a pleasant evening, and my artist friends are gathered in small groups, chatting about their latest projects. A haze of pungent marijuana smoke drifts above their heads.

Ingrid joins me, breathing deeply, closing her eyes and smiling.

I'm on my second glass of merlot when Chuck walks into the shop, all polished and pressed and smelling of fresh-cut balsam.

"Hello ladies," he says, gazing in my direction. "You look lovely tonight." Ingrid gets the hint and drifts off.

"It's good to see you, too." It's more than good, but I don't want to seem too eager. I'm nursing the sting of seeing Trish and Tristan together at Colin's party. It surprised me that I still had feelings for him. But here's Chuck, one handsome—and brainy—guy complimenting me and I'm not about to let past history get in the way.

"I hoped you'd be here." He says, his hands stuffed into his pockets. Well that's nice, but he knows where I live and he's got my phone number.

"It's not a mystery, where to find me." I say. I'm not usually so blunt, but what the heck, I'm not getting any younger or better looking. I guess he's still embarrassed at the way our last date ended, but it's time to get over it. Life is short and we're here, now.

He opens a slender leather portfolio, draws out a photo of a massive metal sculpture, and shows it to me. It's amazing and abstract, a herd of galloping horses maybe?

"Impressive," I say. "The color reminds me of the Picasso installation in Chicago's Daley Plaza. Did you use Corten steel?"

I'm rewarded with a dazzling smile. "Now I'm the one who's impressed." He says. "No one, outside of another sculptor, has ever made that connection. How did you know?"

"I remember when the statue in the plaza was unveiled. Chicagoans couldn't get enough of it. Everyone had an opinion about what it was supposed to be. Over the years it weathered to a rich, coppery brown, like yours." I laugh, amazed at this sudden gift from my mental archive.

Chuck and I talk about his work, and how I feel the need to return to my watercolor painting. It's a part of me that's been neglected. There's another part that's been neglected too: male companionship.

As the gathering at the shop draws to a close, Chuck offers to drive me home in his pick-up, but it's only a couple of blocks and it's a perfect evening to walk. Stars blink like twinkling lights across a black velvet sky. I invite him in for a nightcap. The reflection from the television screen glows through the front window. Colin must be awake. When I open the door it's obvious we've walked in on Colin and Anna entangled on the sofa. They pull apart, startled, and straighten their rumpled clothes.

I'm mortified, and caught completely off guard. Colin fidgets with the remote. Anna combs through her hair with her fingers. Chuck stares with acute interest at a table lamp. No one dares make eye contact. Oh, I could throttle that boy!

"Anna," I say, icily, "do you have a ride home?" Her older brother usually comes for her, but I'm in no mood to wait around. "Never mind, we'll walk you home ourselves." It will give me time to think and to find out what's been going on with these two.

Colin looks humiliated. "You're not going to go in and meet her parents, are you?"

"Not tonight, but I may need to in the future. Anna, do your parents know where you are?"

She shakes her head. Great.

Chuck stuffs his hands in his pockets, looking like he'd rather be anywhere but here. I'd hoped for time alone with him, but obviously that's not going to happen. When I try to say good-night, he surprises me by offering to go along on the walk. I guess he's taking it all in stride. Well, he's a college professor, so he's not shocked by Colin and Anna making out on the sofa. Maybe Chuck should be the one to sit down and talk to Colin—if he's even around after tonight.

Colin and Anna are soon striding half a block ahead of us. In the Plaza, the shops are closed. The evening is mild and clear, and a few couples are lingering over dessert and coffee at outdoor tables.

"I know it's none of my business," Chuck says, "but they're just kids with raging hormones. The fact that your grandson is interested in girls is totally normal. I wouldn't be too hard on him."

He's right; it is none of his business. He's got a point, though. I appreciate his candor and the fact that he's making an effort to be with me. He could have turned heel for the door at the first whiff of trouble. I pick up my pace and Chuck follows suit.

With his long legs, it's hardly an effort. As we walk, I wonder about life's twists and turns. What if Tom and I had stayed together and it was Tom here with me, walking our grandson and his girlfriend home? It's not Tom I miss, but someone to share my life, to snuggle with when the desert nights turn cold.

A few blocks past the shops and galleries of the Plaza the streets are littered with windswept paper and the houses are run-down. Anna turns to announce that her house is at the end of the block; a clapboard bungalow in need of a fresh coat of paint. Many Santa Fe houses have cactus gardens and decorative stone walkways. The patch of tromped clay in front of Anna's house boasts a couple of overturned bikes, broken lawn furniture, and a rusty barbeque grill. Beneath the porch light I can see earthen pots with tomato and pepper plants growing in them. As we get closer, a short, muscular man with dark hair fills the doorway. He's wearing jeans and a T-shirt. Are those tattoos on his beefy arms?

"Dad," Anna says as she hurries past him up the front steps.

"It's after ten. Get in the house," he commands tersely, moving only enough for Anna to slip past him into the dimly lit interior. He directs his attention to the three of us.

"Thank you for walking my daughter home. It's past her curfew." His tone is clipped. He pauses, focusing his gaze. "You're Colin." It's an accusation. Before Colin can respond, I interrupt, hoping to defuse what could be an ugly confrontation.

"Nice to meet you, Mr. Silva. I'm Elaine McElroy, Colin's grandmother—and this is my friend, Chuck. Anna Lucia is such a sweet girl. We've enjoyed getting to know her."

"She's not even fourteen. Do you know that?" He stands at high alert—his stocky legs apart, arms crossed over his broad chest. Make no mistake; we are not welcome here. "…and she'll be busy this summer helping her mother around the house." End of conversation. He closes the front door and the porch light goes out. We stand for a moment, taking this all in. I try to put myself in his position and I can understand his disapproval. But slamming the door on this relationship is not the answer. I know from experience that branding something 'forbidden' only makes it more enticing to an adolescent discovering what he thinks is love.

We're left standing under the streetlight, summarily dismissed by Anna Lucia's father. I wonder what her mother is like and if she's watching from inside. Does she also disapprove? We have no choice but to turn around and head home—in silence.

Unexpectedly, Chuck reaches for my hand and squeezes it. My shoulders relax a bit.

After a while I turn to Colin who's lagging behind. "I think it's best that you don't call Anna for a while." He continues looking down at the pavement, dropping back farther, but he's heard me, I'm sure. I spout clichés about meeting new people, making new friends, and all the old platitudes I swore I'd never say.

As we approach the Plaza I can't help saying what's really on my mind. "Her dad's got a point, you know. She isn't even fourteen and you're just barely. It's a good thing he didn't know that you two were home alone doing…what *were* you doing?" There, it's out in the open. No sense pretending Chuck and I didn't walk in on them.

He scowls at me, his jaw set. I haven't seen defiance like that since Stephanie and I'm not anxious to go there again. "Look, you were…"

"Were what? We weren't doing anything." His body stiffens and he waves me away dismissively, creating more space between us. Chuck has the good sense to remain silent.

"Please! Obviously we surprised you. Who knows what would have happened?"

"She's an uptight Catholic girl with strict parents. You saw her father." He stops, his face flushed with anger. "There's nothing to worry about, believe me." His lip curls sarcastically which only makes me worry more.

"It makes me angry that you thought you could sneak her over behind my back. I will always find out, Colin, believe me. Chuck follows my lead and we continue walking until I stop abruptly and turn once more.

"Look, Colin, this is the way it is," I use my Strict Parent voice to make it clear this is not negotiable. I've said it; I just hope he listens.

Colin heads for home and I'm left standing on the curb with Chuck.

"I'll call you," Chuck says when we get to his pick-up truck still parked by Sophia's now deserted shop. His kiss is searching, hopeful. "I got that prescription," he says sheepishly and breaks into a hopeful grin.

God bless this man, but right now I'm preoccupied with Colin and Anna. I don't want to shut the door on the possibility of getting together with Chuck, though.

I look into his eyes and smile.

"Colin's got soccer camp next week. I'll make dinner for us. Will Saturday night work for you?"

Colin

The ball hits the side of the house with a thud, bounces off the packed dirt and back into my mitt. I throw it again and again. I don't have to see it to know where it will land. I twist my wrist and the ball finds its way to the soft leather pouch every time.

I feel tight, bottled up, like I'll explode into a million pieces and disappear. I can imagine Granma and Anna crying over my empty coffin, Granma wishing she'd been nicer to me. I lose track of time. Granma sticks her head out the door and calls me inside.

"Now, Colin. It's late and you're keeping the whole neighborhood awake. This is no time to be playing ball."

"Okay! I'm coming!"

I wish I was anywhere in the whole wide world but here. Santa Fe is so boring and small. TV is stupid; we don't get the good cable shows like everybody else I know. I'd love to sneak a call to Anna, but Gram's watching every move, so that's out. I have no privacy—unless I'm locked in the bathroom.

Study hard. Get good grades. Do this. Don't do that. Blah, blah, blah.

Other kids don't work as hard as I do and get better grades. I study twice as hard for half the grade. It's not fair. Yeah, so I've got ADD. Like I don't know it—like I can forget? I wish I was popular—and smart. I wish I was in Ireland. That's where my dad was born. He grew up on the dairy farm and that's where my other grandparents live—the ones that sent me holy cards and books about saints and soccer jerseys that were too big when I was small and are too small now. It's not like I'd wear them anyhow—they're soccer shirts from teams no one's ever heard of around here. I wouldn't be caught dead in them, but it's nice that they think of me. Now they send money and Grams puts it in a savings account for me. I wish I could get my hands on some of it—I'd buy my own phone.

Granma says I lived in Ireland when I was little. I even had my own pony. I can barely remember. Sometimes if I concentrate really hard and close my eyes I can see the old farmhouse. There was a pot-belly stove in the kitchen. And everyone drank tea all the time.

A dairy farm in Ireland would be awesome—so much open space, all the animals. And best thing of all, nobody telling me what to do and who I can be friends with.

My breathing slows. My heart beats steady in my chest. It's that feeling just before I fall asleep. I close my eyes. A beautiful woman appears to be floating above my bed. Her hair is red and wavy and it swirls around her face like she's underwater. She's all shimmery and she talks to me without words. *I love you so much, Colin, and I'm sorry I can't be there with you, helping you grow up. Be a good boy and listen to Granma. She loves you, too.*

Her image begins to fade. "Wait," I call out to her. "Don't go." She's the part of my life that's missing, the part nobody else can fill. When she disappears, all the happiness is sucked out of my heart. But moments later, I feel deep comfort and peacefulness, like snuggling under a warm blanket on a cold night. The beautiful woman is my mother, who loves me, still.

When my alarm goes off, I lie with my eyes closed, trying to remember everything about last night. How she looked. What she said. How soft her voice was.

"Granma, my mom had red hair, right?" I say at breakfast.

She stops buttering the toast, a surprised look on her face. "Yes, why?"

"I saw her last night. Maybe it was a dream, but it felt like she was really there."

Granma smiles, a far-away look in her eyes, "She was beautiful, your mother."

The peaceful feeling stays with me for days, warm like my mother's arms around me.

Elaine

"Do you have all your gear ready for camp—clean jerseys, cleats, shin guards?"

Colin's set to leave for soccer camp at St. John's College—ironically, the same college where Chuck teaches. I'm dropping him off tonight.

I have an entire week in June to myself, a good time to clean up the garden and enjoy a walk in the cool mornings. Best of all, though, Chuck is coming to dinner on Saturday!

During the week I shop for a new outfit, plan a gourmet meal, and spruce up the house with some new bed linens. Chuck's never seen me in a dress, only long skirts and peasant blouses. He'll actually see my legs!

I decide on beef bourguignon for dinner. It's basically beef stew with vegetables. How hard can it be? That and a tossed green salad and baguette will be a welcome change from burgers and mac and cheese. I can do this! No holds barred—I'm going all out to impress Chuck and hopefully the evening will end in a way that's mutually satisfying.

But on Saturday morning at the market, with the recipe in hand, I realize that I should have started collecting the ingredients sooner; dry-cured center cut Applewood bacon, kosher salt, Cognac, a bottle of Pinot Noir, fresh thyme and mushrooms! My quest for top shelf ingredients takes me to three gourmet groceries for the bacon alone, not to mention the wine shop and the florist.

At home I waste no time searing the beef cubes in the olive oil and browning the carrots and onions. While the stew is simmering I tidy the house one last time and draw a bath with scented crystals. I luxuriate in the tub, fantasizing about Chuck and me on my new Egyptian cotton sheets.

The sheets! I almost forgot the new sheets. It's been so long I've forgotten the protocol. Come to think of it, since moving here I haven't had anyone in my bed. I'm stunned when I do the math and realize that it's been twelve, long, celibate years! Tonight is critical.

Right from the start, Chuck is a perfect gentleman. He comes with flowers and a bottle of Cabernet Sauvignon. It's a good thing, too, because one of the two bottles of red that I bought went into the beef bourguignon.

We take our time and savor the flavors of the stew; thyme, garlic, bacon. The bread is crusty on the outside and yeasty soft on the inside. The wine is expensive and without any expertise in the subject, I can taste the undercurrents of plum, current and dark chocolate, as the label suggests. Not bad for a fine wine newbie.

Chuck is knowledgeable in so many subjects; wine, art, architecture, and physics, of course, which he teaches. I can't help but wonder what he sees in me. I'm an artist, after all, like him, even though I haven't completed anything new in a while. He's seen my water color paintings. He must be attracted to grounded, earthy women. I'm certainly not going anywhere.

The evening progresses from the dining table to the sofa and from the sofa to the bedroom. When we're both lying naked in the bed he caresses every inch of my body from head to toe, and kisses me as if I were his priceless treasure. I'm so grateful for his unhurried tenderness that my tears spill over onto his cheek.

"What's wrong?" Concern is evident in his beautiful eyes.

"Nothing's wrong. Everything's right. Please, don't stop."

Soon we're wrapped around each other and those twelve long years melt away. I feel what it's like to be held and cherished by someone I truly respect and could grow to—dare I even think it— love.

What a delight to awaken to a warm and fully occupied bed. While Chuck sleeps, I quietly pad to the kitchen to make coffee and breakfast for my man! Yes, I realize that calling him 'my man' is premature, but positive thinking might help turn my dream of love and companionship into reality. It can't hurt.

We linger over coffee, scrambled eggs and a coffee cake I made yesterday in anticipation of Chuck and I having breakfast together. He holds the mug in both hands, smiling contentedly. "I miss this," he says, before raising it to his lips.

"Mornings are the best," I say, returning his smile.

Later that week I see Trish at Target. At first I'm not sure she's seen me so I walk over to her. She looks up from her list and sees me approaching, wondering, I'm sure, if there's going to be a confrontation about Tristan, right here among the housewares. But when I smile and ask how Deshy's doing at school, she relaxes. "He's really coming out of his shell. I'm so proud of him."

I take the opportunity to brag about Colin's scholarship and that he's away at soccer camp for the week. Then I casually mention that I made a fabulous dinner for Chuck the other night and stop short of telling her he spent the night.

"I'm so glad for you. You look happy, Elaine. Happier than I've seen you in a long time," and she seems sincere.

Staying angry at Trish is difficult, and even though I still harbor a nugget of resentment, okay jealousy over Tristan, I'm ready to let it go. There've been times I, wanted to call her and gripe about the pit-falls of raising a teen-age boy—the endless laundry and his ravenous appetite— when I stop and remember that I'm holding a grudge. Life is short and holding onto past wrongs, real or imagined, is just too exhausting.

Colin

"McElroy, I need ten bags of topsoil and twelve of river rock," Luis hollers as he mops his face with a bandanna. He's the foreman on my summer job. "Load it up." He points to the beat-up pick-up truck with Desert View Landscaping on the door. I hoist a bag over each shoulder and slide it onto the bed.

"Come on, amigo," Luis calls. "I haven't got all day." He sits in the truck with the door flung open. It's easily a hundred degrees. The sun blazes with no relief. The bags are heavy, but my biceps and pecs are getting good definition. It's all good. I'll be buff when soccer starts. Besides, I'd rather be working outdoors than in a fast food joint flipping burgers.

Christa did me a big favor getting me this job. The pay is good and I finally got the cell phone I needed. Now I can call Anna without Grams being all up in my face. Desert View Landscaping does her place and a lot of others in her neighborhood. Yesterday a lady at one of the houses was staring at me when I peeled off my shirt. She brought glasses of ice water out for Luis and me. He kept hassling me, saying she was hot for my body. Whatever. She worked out, I could tell, but when she handed me the glass I saw the wrinkles around her eyes. 'Cougar.' That's what Luis called her. Anyway, Anna is ten times hotter.

After work Grams tells me to jump in the shower and reminds me to throw my clothes in the hamper, not on the floor. "And don't forget to put on deodorant." *Jeez, like I don't know to put on deodorant?* "What do you want for dinner? BLTs... grilled cheese...burgers?" She calls through the door.

"Anything. I'm starving. How about burgers? Mac and cheese, too. It there watermelon left?" I yell back.

Elaine

He's starving, as usual. I had no idea teen-age boys could eat so much. Every morning I pack two sandwiches, chips and some fruit in his Igloo, plus a candy bar for a snack, plus ice in his insulated mug for cold water in the heat of the day. All that after a breakfast of pancakes and bacon and sometimes a bowl of cereal, too.

Stephanie and Roxy never devoured food like he does, but then they never worked outside doing heavy lifting. I'm not complaining. I love cooking for him; watching him inhale hamburgers and pan-fried potatoes after a hard day. With all the calories he burns, he can pretty much eat whatever he wants.

Colin at work—my grandson is growing up! He's got an athlete's build. I wish I could convince him to cherish his health, his youth and his freedom. He'd just roll his eyes like teen-agers do and look at me like I'm clueless. Thank God he's staying out of trouble, though. And no angry calls from Anna's father. I hope it stays that way.

Colin

Now that I've got my own phone, I can call Anna whenever I want without Grams hearing every word.

"You guys can come over whenever you want," Anna's girlfriend, Flor, tells us, so now we meet in her basement. There's an old TV there with a coat hanger antenna and a smelly, beat-up sofa.

"It's so romantic, like Romeo and Juliet," Anna says.

She loves romantic stuff.

Flor's mom and dad work split shifts; when one parent is at work the other is asleep. As long as the music's not too loud Flor says it's okay.

Most nights, though, I'm so tired after work that I'm at home passed out on the sofa.

"Colin, you haven't moved from that spot all evening." Gram says.

And your point is?

A week before school starts Grams takes me shopping for new clothes. Sacred Heart High School has a dress code; no T-shirts, sandals or jeans. Not that I'd be caught dead in sandals, so it's not a problem. But T-shirts and jeans are all I ever wear. She has this image of me all preppy in a pink polo shirt and matching socks, khakis, and deck shoes, so I have to set her straight. Polo shirts minus the logo are okay. Dockers are okay. But that's where I draw the line. If the guys on the crew saw me in my new khakis and polo shirts they'd fall over laughing and never let me forget it.

"McElroy…Colin?" It's my new homeroom teacher, Mr. Garcia. If you saw him in the hallway, you'd think he was one of the kids. The guy shows up with bed-head hair and khakis two sizes too big. The denim shirt is okay, though, and I like that he leaves the top button undone and the tie loose.

He calls my name again. I raise my hand, and everybody turns to look so I slump farther down into the seat. By lunchtime it's clear that most of the kids here know each other from their private schools. I'm a total outsider. Grams and I went to orientation night and did the tour, but I still don't know where all my classes are. And I don't have any friends here.

Now that I'm at Sacred Heart and Anna's at Capitol High, it's like we're on different planets. At Sacred Heart the popular kids wear the latest, most expensive Nikes, shoes I can only dream about. Their fathers are doctors or lawyers and their mothers look like they could be on the cover of a fashion magazine. Oh, and the parents give their kids a car the minute they get their learner's permit; a new car, not a used one. If I'm lucky, Grams might eventually let me drive her beat-up Toyota *after* I get my license.

I'm more like the kids at Capitol High. All the parents have to work and the kids don't wear fancy clothes or have a car, unless it's a clunker. Grams keeps reminding me how lucky I am, and the guys on my soccer team, the Stallions, are okay, but I don't get invited to their parties. Mostly they ignore me, except for this one kid—Jake. He's the star midfielder on the team and he never misses a chance to remind me that I'm on scholarship. Like when we had a candy bar fundraiser, he made a big deal of announcing in the locker room, "Us guys have to sell candy so that Colin can go to school here. Right, Colin?" I kept my mouth shut, but I wanted to punch him in the worst way.

Anna and I make plans to meet at Sacred Heart's homecoming game. I'm talking to some guys on my soccer team when I see her at the concession stand with a bunch of her girlfriends. Anna and her group look older and sexier, the kind of girls the guys at my school call 'easy' cuz they wear tight, low-rise jeans and dark eye-liner and lots of lip gloss. Ann's hair is loose tonight, not pulled back like she usually wears it. She's a babe. My friends on the soccer team notice, too.

I step away from my teammates and go up to her. "Hey, Anna, how's it going?" Her girlfriends giggle and close ranks behind her.

"What's up?" She says. I love it when she smiles at me. It makes me feel special and proud, and I hope the other guys are jealous.

"Nothing. Where are you sitting?" She nods in the direction of the bleachers.

"Did you hear?" she says. She's excited, talking louder than usual.

"Hear what?"

"Flor's getting a 'D' in English. She's grounded. We can't hang out there anymore."

Shit. Now what? We can't go to Anna's house and we can't go to mine, either.

Suddenly Jake's standing across from me, eyeing Anna.

"Hey, McElroy! Looks like you'll have to find somewhere else to screw that sweet piece of ass." He says.

"Shut up Jake." I shout. "Shut the fuck up!"

Anna's friends gather around her in a tight knot.

But Jake doesn't stop. "Mmm good. Don't wanna let that go to waste, do we, Colin my man? I hear she totally puts out, even if she is, like, retarded."

I see Jake's mouth moving in slow motion. I can't hear the words anymore. His face is all screwed up. I'm gasping for air—short, shallow breaths. My neck is prickly and hot.

"Shut up, Jake. I mean it!" I shout and lunge toward him. I'm driven by a force I can't name and don't recognize. It's propelling me forward— head down—charging— aiming dead-on for Jake. A howl erupts from deep within as I plunge toward him. All I see is Jake's red jersey with *Sacred Heart Stallions* across his chest. I drive into him. He deflates—humph—and falls backward. His skull bounces off the pavement with a sickening thump, like a cracked melon. I'm over him, pounding him with my clenched fists. Tears stream down my cheeks.

He's screaming and covering his face, but I don't stop. I can't. I keep hammering him. Every nerve pulsates. The adrenaline rush reduces everything to a blur. Kids are screaming. I'm underwater—in slow motion. Without warning, Coach rips me off Jake and puts me in a chokehold. My chest is heaving and I realize I'm crying.

Guys rush over to help Jake. Blood is gushing from his nose and there's a gash over his eye. It's bad.

Jake screams at me as he struggles to his feet. "You bastard. My father's gonna sue your sorry ass. You are history, punk. You can forget being on this team—forget about going to Sacred Heart. You and your dumb-ass grandma won't even be able to afford that dump of a house where you live, when my father's done with you."

"That's enough, Jake," coach says. He yanks me toward the school building.

"In the office, now! Both of you!"

Elaine

I'm overcome with dread at the phone call. Sacred Heart was supposed to be Colin's golden opportunity; a fresh start where he could excel at sports without the stigma of being the 'hyper' kid. He told me he got teased about his clothes, that they weren't designer, but that's not what Colin wanted. And now he's been in a fight.

I thought he was on the right track. He gets up and is out the door every morning without a hassle. He does his homework. But his friends are at Capitol High, not at Sacred Heart. This can't be happening.

As I pull into the parking lot, the football game is in full swing. Students are cheering. The band is belting out Sacred

Heart's fight song. I see a knot of girls at a side entrance, and Anna Lucia is among them. She looks different from the last time I saw her. When she sees me, she runs toward the car. Her eyes are huge. She rubs her arms like she's warming herself, but it's not chilly.

"Coach took them inside."

"Anna, what happened?"

Her explanation is a jumble of words and sign language, but what I can make out is that Jake said nasty things about her. Colin completely lost it, rammed into Jake and pounded the daylights out of him. Apparently, Colin threw the first punch. Not good; the aggressor is always at fault, no matter how relentlessly Jake may have provoked him.

I tried to downplay Colin's impulsiveness and short attention span when he started at Sacred Heart, but it's no secret. It's in his record for anyone to see; anyone who took the time to learn about this fidgety new boy who doesn't quite fit in.

In the office, Colin and Jake glare at each other from opposite sides of the room. I see immediately that this was no minor schoolyard scuffle. Jake is holding an ice pack to the back of his head. His left eye is mottled and swollen. Colin stares at his hands, rocking slightly in the chair.

Before I have a chance to speak, an inner door opens and a wiry, bespectacled man calls us into his office. The school principal.

"Please sit, Mrs. McElroy, Colin," indicating the two chairs in front of his substantial mahogany desk. He looks over his readers at us, giving him an owlish appearance. He's not tall, but he stands ram-rod straight with an air of authority. He must be a voracious reader, for his office is lined with books from floor to ceiling.

"I'm Father Geary," he says, and I tell myself, *surely, this is a kindly man.*

"I'm Colin's mo...grandmother," I falter, realizing that I've had to be everything for him— mother, father, grandmother.

"Mrs. McElroy," he begins, hands folded neatly on the desk, "Sacred Heart operates under five core principles; Faith, Respect, Quality Education, Concern for the Poor and Social Justice. Colin and Jake's actions this afternoon clearly did not show respect. In cases like this our Discipline Committee will meet with all parties to determine the consequences for the students involved. You will be notified beforehand and both you and Colin are expected to attend along with Jake and his parents. Until the committee meets, both boys are suspended and cannot participate in any school-related activities. Do you have any questions?

Questions? I don't know what happened except what Anna has told me and I haven't had time to think about the consequences. Yes, I've got questions, but they won't be answered here, now. Best to stay calm and follow Father Geary's instructions. Depending on the way the hearing goes, Colin may need a lawyer. I've got to call Stuart as soon as we get home.

Stuart is reassuring. He says Colin doesn't need a lawyer.

"In a situation like this, Elaine, it's best to be open about Colin's past. His impulsivity is a big factor here. Mention that. If you run into a problem you can't handle, I'll come out there."

On the day of the hearing, I wish I had asked Stuart to come out and help. Colin and I are on our own.

The hearing takes place in an empty classroom. The desks are arranged in a circle. Father Geary's here. He's wearing a

Roman collar today. Jake's here too, of course, with his parents. The mother is a stunning blonde, the father one of those men who projects wealth and authority. Several adults, presumably on the Discipline Committee, and several students who witnessed the fight are here, too.

Father Geary clears his throat. He turns on a tape recorder and announces the purpose of the hearing. For the record, he lists the names of everyone in the room, including the Discipline Committee members and Colin's coach. My stomach clenches. Colin sits hunched, staring at the floor. Father explains that the committee members have had access to both boys' academic and discipline records and after today's hearing, they will make a recommendation. "However," he adds, looking first to Jake's parents and then to me, "the final decision rests with me."

He asks Jake to go first. The bruise around his left eye has fermented to a sickly purple. Jake stands confidently and begins reading from a prepared statement; his father nods in approval. It's not typical language for a high school freshman, with references to 'assault and battery' and 'bodily harm.'

Colin will not be reading from a prepared statement. I've tried to draw him out about what happened that day, but it's been a struggle. He is adamant that Jake started it by calling Anna a 'retard.' He says when Jake wouldn't stop bad-mouthing her, he lost control. Anna told me as much, back by the car, and added that Jake's comments were totally unprovoked.

"We weren't doing anything, honestly Mrs. McElroy, just standing around talking."

I believe her, of course. But will the committee? Colin is no more capable of making a convincing statement to this panel of adults than I am of pleading a case before the Supreme Court.

Jake finishes his statement and sits down. He smirks in our direction. Before Colin's turn, I ask Father Geary if I can say a few words. He nods.

I take a moment to collect my thoughts. Colin's story is in my heart. Putting everything that's happened to him so far into words seems impossible, but I've got to try. His future depends on it.

"I've raised Colin as a single parent since he was three years old," I say, hating the tremble in my voice. Am I defending him before a judge and jury? In a way, yes. This panel has the power to recommend expulsion, and Father Geary has the authority to carry it out. I clutch the turquoise and silver pendant hanging from my neck, a gift from Trish.

"He was orphaned, you see, after his parents were killed in a car crash in Ireland. His mother died instantly and his father lingered in a coma for months. When I brought him here to live with me, I decided to quit my nursing job at St. Vincent's Hospital to stay home and raise him. I'm fortunate to have a supportive family in Chicago and close friends here who are just like family to Colin and me."

Members of the committee start to fidget. Father Geary folds his arms across his chest, and they grow still.

"For most of my career, though, I was a school nurse in Chicago. That helped me recognize early on that Colin had issues that set him apart from other children. In day care he fought with the other children. He had trouble learning his numbers and letters. He needed more time to finish classroom work and homework, and more often than not the homework never made it back to the teacher. He's impulsive and high-energy and, well, it's been a challenge."

Poor Colin. He's sitting with his head down, clicking a ballpoint pen, his feet in constant motion under the desk. It feels like betrayal saying all this to strangers, right in front of him, but they need to know what led to the fight with Jake. What he did to Jake didn't happen in a vacuum. Things have been building up for a long time. Explaining the complicated puzzle that is Colin to Father Geary and the Committee is his best hope for fair treatment.

"When Colin was little, I took him to a pediatric psychiatrist. He told me how important consistency and routine would be to help him deal with his abandonment issues and attention problems. Colin has ADHD, attention deficit with hyperactivity. It's in his records from grade school. He took medication for a while, but when he worked for a landscaper this summer, it seemed he was getting better. Most nights he plopped on the sofa and watched television until it was time for bed. I'd read that as kids get older the symptoms sometimes go away. So I decided he could start school without medication and see what happened. Now, of course, I know that wasn't the best choice.

It turned out to be the worst idea, but unless you're a parent who's dealt with these issues day after day—year after year—you can't appreciate how improvement might be misinterpreted as a sign that a child has outgrown his symptoms. What Colin did to Jake was wrong, but Jake's comments were clearly meant to provoke him. Harassing Anna, Colin's girlfriend, who is hearing impaired, is more than harassment. It's against the law." Jake's father sits red-faced, blue veins visible on his temples. His lips are a tight cord. Mrs. Whitman stares straight ahead. Her perfect make-up can't disguise her ghostly pallor. "Anna is protected under the Americans with Disabilities Act. So is Colin."

Stuart said I shouldn't try to sound like a lawyer. Well, I've said what I have to say. The law speaks for itself.

The Committee members write furiously on their yellow pads. Father Geary frowns.

"Colin defended Anna, but in the wrong way. Unfortunately, with his inability to self-regulate, once the chain of events was set into motion there was no stopping it."

The room is silent. All eyes are on me. "I'm sorry for what happened." I look directly at Jake. He returns my gaze with contempt. I turn to Colin who looks up when he realizes I've stopped talking. "Colin?" I prompt him.

"I'm sorry," Colin mumbles.

I give him a look he knows too well.

"I'm sorry," he says, louder this time, looking at Jake who scowls back at him.

In the thick silence that follows, all eyes turn to Father Geary.

The rail-thin old priest steeples his fingers. "Well," he says with a sigh, "this sheds new light on the incident. But tell me, Colin, why didn't you stop? From what Coach and the others say, you just kept on even when Jake didn't defend himself."

Colin is at a loss. "I know I should have stopped, but I just couldn't."

Father Geary questions the students who were at the game. Each of them says that before Jake called Anna a 'retard' and 'a sweet piece of ass,' everything was fine. It was the name-calling that set off Colin, they agree. Next it's the coach's turn to give an account. He tells the committee he didn't see what led up to the fight, and he used the word 'rage' to describe Colin's attack.

As the room empties, Jake's parents snag Father Geary and chat like old friends. Colin and I feel like the outsiders that we are. On the way out, I try to get the attention of Jake's parents so that I can say again how sorry I am, but they finish with Father Geary and storm past us without so much as a nod.

My brain is on overdrive as Colin and I walk to the parking lot after the discipline hearing. What if he's expelled? After announcing his scholarship at his graduation party, I'll have to backtrack. *Bad news; it didn't work out, he got expelled.* I haven't told anyone, besides Chuck, about the fight, so it would be a double shock, out of the blue. I can just hear Denise; *We all thought he was doing so well. Have you told Mom yet?* This isn't about me, but it reflects badly on my parenting. I simply had *no idea* that Jake's bullying was so over the top. Colin never said anything and how was I supposed to find out? Interrogate him every night under a spotlight? Thoughts are racing through my head and I nearly walk head-on into Chuck who's standing next to my Toyota in the parking lot.

Seeing him, everything bubbles to the surface; fear, disappointment, frustration. I throw my arms around him and cry into his shirt for what seems like a long time. I want to stay here nestled in the warmth and strength of his arms. He strokes my hair and murmurs soothing words into my ear. Then he straightens up and looks at me with concern in his eyes. "Is it bad?" he asks. His compassion only makes me cry harder for a few moments until I'm able to pull it together. I'd told Chuck about the hearing and now he's here, offering his support. I could kiss him but for now I only want to shelter in his arms.

Colin's standing off to the side looking lost and uncomfortable. I throw him my keys, "Here, you can wait in the car." I tell him. Chuck offers me a bandana from his jeans pocket and I blow my nose and collect myself. "I'm not sure how bad it is. We won't know until the Discipline Committee reports back to Father Geary, the principal. He has the final say. He's a kind man, but I just don't know…" Tears well up again and

I tell Chuck between sobs how grateful I am that he came. "It means the world to me."

"Do you want to get coffee or a bite to eat?" he asks, holding my hands in his.

"Thanks, but I'm drained. I'm not good company right now."

"I hate to leave you like this." He says softly.

"I'll be okay. I need to clear my head, make a pot of coffee and put my feet up. This day has been brutal, defending Colin in front of strangers. I'll call you the minute I find out. I promise." I kiss him and rest my head on his chest for a few more seconds before turning to get into the car. "I'll call you." I say and close the door. Colin and I are silent on the way home. I'm not angry, just sad and disappointed. Colin stares out the window.

Despite all my worries, I feel safe and protected knowing Chuck has my back. That's huge, and worth more to me than anything—that I can depend on him. That's something I never had with my ex-husband. With Tom I never knew when, or if he would come home, especially when he got his paycheck. I'd wait up for him, or try to, call the local bars until the proprietors knew me by name, and generally make myself crazy. It was only after I joined Al-Anon, a support group for family and friends of alcoholics, that I learned I had to let it go. It was his problem, not mine. I didn't cause it and I couldn't control it. What a relief that was, living without feeling responsible for Tom's drinking.

I truly hope that Chuck and I make it as a couple. I'm grateful each time we're together, especially when I'm cuddling next to him after making love. I'll continue to live in the moment and try not to worry about the future, another twelve-step lesson I learned.

Colin and I don't have to wait long for the committee's decision. The following afternoon, the phone rings.

"Mrs. McElroy, its Father Geary." I hold my breath. If Colin is expelled, he'll have to transfer to Capitol in disgrace. "The Committee has made its recommendation and I am in agreement. Colin is suspended from school for two weeks."

I make the sign of the cross and mouth "Thank you."

"This was not a difficult decision. Two weeks suspension is the usual punishment for fighting on school grounds. However, I've added an additional requirement: Colin must see a counselor to help him deal with his anger issues. I have a list of referrals, if you wish. Also, I have to warn you that any more incidents and he will be cut from the team."

And he would lose his scholarship. End of story.

"Thank you, Father," I say, truly grateful. Then, because I need to know: "If you don't mind my asking, Father, what was Jake's punishment?"

"The same, two weeks suspension."

Two weeks at home with Colin. I'm incredibly relieved that his punishment wasn't worse, but our daily routine is out the window. Colin's playing a video game when I tell him.

"This is not a two-week vacation," I tell him. "Right now, there are some dead shrubs in the back yard I want you to dig up. And starting tomorrow I'll be stopping at school every day to get your work."

While Colin's outside I call Chuck to tell him the good news. He's probably at school so I leave a message. Then I begin calling the list of counselors Father Geary gave me. The earliest appointment I can get is Friday at five o'clock—and that's after telling the receptionist it's an emergency. I glance out the window. Colin is attacking the dead shrubbery with a shovel.

The following afternoon, Colin sits at the table long after the breakfast dishes are cleared and washed. From the kitchen, I watch him working out an algebra problem. He bites his lip, then stares into space, flips his pencil back and forth, and gets up for another glass of water. It's time to get him back on his meds. What was I thinking, letting him start school without them? I rest my hand firmly on his shoulder. This usually grounds him, at least temporarily. Math was never my strong suit. I think I'll phone Denise; she's the family math whiz.

"Col, there's a sandwich and some chips on the counter for your lunch. I'm off to the grocery store. Anything you want?"

"How about a driver's license and a red Corvette?"

"Very funny. Finish your homework so I can check it when I get back."

It's the typical mid-morning crowd at the store. Young mothers with babies and toddlers in tow, retired couples shopping together. Then there's me. I'll bet I'm the only grandmother with her adolescent grandson home on suspension. It could be worse. He hasn't broken any laws and he's not in trouble with the police. I'll have to redouble my efforts to get him through the next three and a half years. I can't afford to let my guard down for a moment, but with each passing year it gets harder and harder. Most people my age are planning for retirement and it dawns on me that next year I'll be eligible for Medicare!

"Anyone call?" I ask, schlepping two overstuffed grocery bags through the door.

"Yeah."

I start to put the groceries away. Maybe his counseling appointment's been rescheduled. Or maybe Christa called to fill me in on her latest adventure with Mercedes.

"Grandpa John called," Colin announces, "from Ireland!"

My heart stops. Out of the blue, a phone call from his other grandparents. After years of nothing but Christmas cards and birthday packages containing tins of biscuits, and heavy woolen sweaters that Colin never wears, John Casey calls.

"He wanted to talk to you. I told him you were at the store. Then he asked why I was at home in the middle of the day."

"What did you tell him?"

"I said it's a school holiday."

Good boy! Not that I condone lying, but this is a special case.

"Did he say why he called?"

My thoughts swirl. John's leaving the farm to Colin and wants him to come immediately? Maggie's finally died, after years of poor health? The farmhouse has burned to the ground and they have nowhere to go so they're coming here to live with their grandson!

"He said Grandma Maggie is sick and she wants to see me one last time. Grandpa left a number and wants you to call."

It takes a moment for all this to sink in. Meanwhile, Colin's shot up from the table and is jumping up and down with excitement. "Can I go? I'm already suspended so it won't matter."

"Hold on, Colin. It's not that easy."

I can't help thinking about the ugly confrontation with Maggie after Stephanie's death. Her idea of mothering Colin was that 'a wee sip' of whiskey would 'settle him' after the heartrending news. Imagine, giving whiskey to a *three-year-old* child! She backed down after I stood my ground, but she wasn't happy about it. When Maggie thought Christa and I were out of earshot, she complained bitterly to John that my Stephanie was a whore who threw herself at her son. I was livid. If it wasn't for Christa, the voice of reason, I'd have flattened Maggie on the spot. So I'm in no hurry to grant Maggie her final wish.

"It takes time to get a passport and book a flight," I tell Colin. "You'd only be there a few days before you'd have to turn around and come home."

Coming on the heels of his suspension, a trip overseas would seem too much like a reward. I don't want that, but I don't say "no" right off the bat. If I do, he'll only want it more.

"When? When can I go?" he shouts. Then, he adds, slyly: "I want to see Dora and Rosie and Marigold. Grandma Maggie, too."

So he wants to see the farm animals and, oh, his dying grandmother, too?

He was only three when he left Ireland and he's never been back. Still, for his first few weeks in America, he talked nonstop about the farm animals; there was Dora, a calf John Casey gave him, and Rosie and Marigold, Connemara ponies stabled at the farm, Nettie, the outdoor cat "who catches mice," and Russell, a big, barky dog that jumped all over me and Christa the instant we got out of the hired car. That was our official welcome to the Casey's dairy farm and it went downhill from there. We were nearly starving from our trans-Atlantic flight before Maggie served us tea and soda bread slathered in butter. Maybe she hoped we'd pass out from hunger and thirst. Well, that was over ten years ago. It's unlikely that the animals Colin remembers are still there. Things never live up to expectations, like going to your high school reunion and being disappointed by how small and lackluster everything seems.

Colin

Granma hasn't said "yes" but she hasn't said "no," either. Grandma Maggie and Grandpa John want me to come to Ireland and I want to go! No more shirts with collars, khaki pants, or homework assignments. I'll wear boots and old jeans and get covered with horse shit when I help Grandpa with the animals. Damn, I forgot to tell Granma something important: Grandpa John said he would pay for my ticket.

    She can't say no to that!

    That night, I'm in the kitchen when Granma calls the Caseys.

    "I'm sorry to hear Maggie's taken a turn, John, but a trip to Ireland is out of the question. Colin's nearing the end of his first semester in high school. I can't possibly put him on a plane now. He's on scholarship at a good school, a Catholic school. The principal is an Irish priest. Anyway, I don't want to do anything to jeopardize his education."

    Wait, she's not saying anything about the two-week suspension.

    "Maggie's a fighter with a will of iron. Tell her to hang on. The earliest Colin could come would be the end of the semester, around Christmas. It will give her something to look forward to."

    I'm going to Ireland over Christmas break. This is going to happen!

Elaine

Maggie Casey will probably outlive us all. Her "taking a turn" isn't reason enough to book a seat on the next flight. Besides, I can't reward Colin with an instant trip to Ireland after being suspended for beating a classmate to a pulp.

    Between now and the holidays, I let everyone know that Colin and I will be spending Christmas in Ireland. Sending him alone, with his poor judgment, is out of the question. More importantly, I have a sneaking suspicion the Caseys will to try to convince him to stay and help run the farm. They'll reel him in with promises that it will all be his after they're gone. What a legacy—a dilapidated farmhouse and all the work that goes into running a dairy farm. It's a grinding life. Letting the cows out to pasture, milking them twice a day, endless fence repairs, keeping the books, and who knows what else? Just look at what it's done to Maggie and John—they're worn out. They drink too much. Maggie lives on whisky, soda bread and strong tea with cream and sugar, which is the worst possible diet for a woman with diabetes. Colin can't possibly understand the commitment of running a farm. To him it's an adventure, a break from his everyday life.

After Colin's suspension is over, the remaining days of the semester go by in a flash. Our suitcases are sitting open on the living room floor. Stacks of clothes are piled on the sofa, waiting to be packed. My stuff takes up three times the space of Colin's, which consists of a single pair of jeans, a few T-shirts, and underwear. "Colin," I call through the closed door of his room, "what about socks? And your khakis and a good polo shirt for church. And a comb, a toothbrush, deodorant, and razors."

"Okay," he yells back, but I know it's up to me to finish the job.

At least Colin's been staying out of trouble. Once a week, I drive him to a session with Mr. Harris, a counselor who looks to be straight out of central casting. He strikes me as gentle-natured and scholarly, peering at the world through wire-rimmed glasses. Each time I walk Colin into his office, he bows to shake my hand, and no matter the weather, he is bundled in a cable-knit vest and tweedy jacket with leather patches at the elbow.

When I ask Colin what he talks about with Mr. Harris in his sessions, he answers vaguely, "Nothing, just stuff."

I persist. "What kind of stuff?"

Colin's sideways glance is code for, "Do you really think I'm going to tell you?"

If there's something I need to know, Mr. Harris will tell me. He's got to. After all, Colin's a minor and I'm his legal guardian.

In a few days we'll arrive at the Casey's farm. I try to tamp down the pain and grief that's resurfacing as our visit draws closer. They say time heals all wounds, but *they* don't know what it's like to return to the place where I lost my Stephanie.

Colin's attention issues are over the top. Last night during a phone call with Anna, he put her on speaker so he could play a video game. I would have hung up on him— she didn't. He's so revved up about the trip that he doesn't see it's really about endings; visiting the country where his parents died, and saying a final good-bye to his Irish grandmother. Well, who can blame Maggie? If the tables were turned, I'd want to see my only grandchild while I was still lucid. She's led a hard life and that accounts for her tough shell. I hope she'll offer Colin whatever tenderness she's got left.

Christa

When a co-worker tells me that she and her son, who's a bit younger than Deshy, will be building a birdhouse at the Home

Depot this Saturday, I get an idea. It's my week-end with Deshy so I call and reserve a spot, then I invite Mercedes to come along.

"...a birdhouse?" She seems confused. "I have a nail appointment on Saturday morning."

"You can get your nails done anytime. This is a chance for the three of us to do something together. C'mon, it'll be fun." I'm trying to sound more enthusiastic than I feel. What can happen? Plenty, but I sweep images of smashed fingers, spilled paint, and chipped nails out of my head. *I* know that Mercedes can be sweet and sensitive, and this is the perfect time for her to show that side to Deshy.

"Oh, alright." She sounds skeptical, but I love her for agreeing and give her a hug and kiss. "I can reschedule my manicure...I'll need it afterwards, for sure." She glances wistfully at her berry colored nails.

It's Saturday and when we arrive to pick up Deshy. He's dressed in jeans and an adorable fleece with reindeers on it, perfect against the early December chill. Trish looks past me toward Mercedes who's waiting in her red sports car. "Tell me there's a car seat for him." Trish demands, still staring intensely out the door.

"Don't worry; it's all taken care of." I say. *What does she think, that I'd let him ride in the car without one?*

Home Depot is humming with holiday shoppers buying Christmas decorations and that power saw that dads have been hinting they want. Mercedes gets second glances as we walk down the long aisle to the craft area. Her tunic top over leggings is perfect for a Saturday morning, but the knee-length calfskin boots with three inch heels attract attention, especially since everyone else is wearing faded jeans, sweatshirts and sneakers. Me, too. We find a spot at one of the tables set up for the project. The pudgy Home Depot guy with his uniform vest and name tag gives everyone a packet with all the materials needed for the birdhouse; pre-cut pieces of wood with a circular opening in the front section. The best thing is that there's no hammer or nails involved; it's a pre-fab birdhouse that snaps together! What a relief.

Deshy is sitting between Mercedes and me. He's shy around her and sidles up to me. It will take time for him to feel comfortable around her and more than that, to accept her as my new partner. Not that she'd ever take Trish's place in his heart. I hand her the packet to get started. She rips it open with her teeth and spreads the pieces and a sheet of visual instructions in front of Deshy. He catches on right away. That's my boy.

"This is the bottom," he says, holding up the largest square.

"Good job, Deshy," Mercedes says, and he smiles.

Next he begins snapping the walls together. He's the first one to finish at our table. The next step is decorating it. A separate table is set up with jars of paint; red, blue, green and yellow with a thick brush in each color. There are aprons, too, and Deshy's reaches to his feet. Mercedes and I each slip an apron over our head and roll up our sleeves. Mercedes in an apron and high leather boots is a sight to behold, tantalizingly provocative. She's the only woman I know who can pull it off—and look fabulous. Deshy takes each of us by the hand and leads us to the paint table.

"*I* want to paint it!" he cries, so we let him. The roof is red with smudges of other colors. The sides are blue and purple in spots where the red ran into the blue. It's a masterpiece. When he's done his hands, arms, hair and face are splotched with paint. He looks adorable so I snap a picture with my phone.

"My—our—little Picasso," I say, so proud of his handiwork.

Mercedes steps back as if appraising a priceless work of art. "It's the most beautiful birdhouse I've ever seen." She crouches to his level and kisses him on the cheek.

"It's for Mommy Trish," he says.

Mercedes stands and looks at me, her eyes wide and questioning, gauging my reaction.

"That's a wonderful idea," I say, not missing a beat. "It will be her Christmas present. And you made it yourself. She'll love it!" *I hope. But why wouldn't she? He made it with his own little hands.*

After a thorough scrubbing with soap and water and half a roll of paper towels, we've washed away most of the paint. It's time for lunch. I know Trish won't approve, but he begs for a McDonald's Happy Meal and I'm not about to say "no."

"McDonald's?" Mercedes says, screwing her beautiful face into a horrified grimace."Does it have to be McDonald's? How about Panera, at least there's nothing's fried there!"

"Sweetie, this is what parents do—make sacrifices for their kids." I say.

We're seated at a booth, Deshy and I are on one side and Mercedes is sipping coffee on the other. I reach across the table for her hand, and she squeezes mine in return, beaming. This day has gone far better than I had hoped. Deshy sees Mercedes and me holding hands, and he momentarily places his greasy fingers over ours, giggles, then resumes stuffing French fries into his mouth.

Perfection. I'm with the two people I love most in the world. It took a lot of pain and heartache to get to this place and I won't let anyone or anything take it away.

Trish

Christmas dinner at Elaine's has been a tradition for so long that memories of Mary Ellen and I volunteering at the homeless shelter, serving up slices of turkey with peas and mashed potatoes all covered in thick brown gravy seem like ancient history.

We worked the noon to three shift and when we were done, we each grabbed a plate of food and sat down with a homeless family from Mexico who were trying to get on their feet. We ate our fill and it felt gratifying that we had earned our dinner and helped out less fortunate people. Less fortunate, but not by much. On that particular Christmas, Mary Ellen and I felt like royalty, not wanting for anything. Sure, there were things we *needed*, like better paying jobs, a new coffee maker and nicer clothes than we'd buy at the thrift shop. But we were happy.

This year Elaine and Colin will be in Ireland, I haven't seen my family in years, and I don't know what Christa and Mercedes are planning. I'll be alone at Christmas and I'm partly to blame. After Christa and I got together, I didn't keep in touch with my old friends. Maybe they felt like I'd tossed them to the curb since I'd moved up in the world. That wasn't it, though. It's that my world was completely changed; moving into Christa's house and long hours spent planning Deshy's adoption. How short-sighted! I can't possibly go begging for a place at Mary Ellen or Rachel's table.

I've got to make the best of it, though, for Deshy, like keeping the holiday traditions that he'll remember; baking cookies on Christmas Eve, walking downtown to the Cathedral for midnight Mass, and waking up to presents under the tree. Even though I'm a "fallen away" Catholic, they don't ask for a membership card at the door and I'm not afraid of being turned away, even though Deshy and I might get sidelong glances. I'm not even sure I believe anymore, but the smell of incense, the sound of Christmas carols and the comforting familiarity of the Mass ritual feels like coming home. When I was a kid my entire family attended Midnight Mass and when we got home my sisters and I were each allowed to open one gift. That's when we were older and no one believed in Santa anymore.

Christmas morning dawns chilly and overcast. I light a fire in the kiva and make pancakes with a dusting of powdered sugar for Deshy, his favorite. I tell him it might snow later.

"Can we go sledding? Can we? I promise I'll wear a hat!" He says, delighted at the possibility of snow.

"That would be so much fun." I say, "If there's enough snow I'll take you, I promise."

It will probably be an inch at most, but I don't want to crush his hopes for a white Christmas complete with sledding.

After breakfast Deshy opens his gifts from Santa; a soccer ball, hand-held electronic game, and racing cars that run on a track. Without my job at Whole Foods I couldn't have afforded these extras, and I'm grateful that he's happy. Of course, there are no gifts under the tree for me and although I'm an adult and Deshy's mom, it still hurts, a hollow ache in my chest that I've been passed over by Santa and everyone else.

Before we brought Deshy home, Christa and I used to shop for our gifts together. One year we picked out exquisite stones for my jewelry craft; Sleeping Beauty turquoise, smoky topaz and black opals. I picked out a delicate gold ankle bracelet for Christa that she wore to work almost every day. *Deal with it, Trish,* I tell myself. *What's done is done. You're a big girl and you've gone through tough times before.*

The doorbell rings at exactly one o'clock. It's Christa to pick up Deshy. I feel myself falling apart, but vow to keep it together until he's out the door.

Christa is carrying a holiday gift bag that she pushes toward me when I motion her inside.

"Go ahead, open it," she says. "It's from Deshy."

Under white tissue paper is a little wooden birdhouse with a red roof and blue walls. "It's beautiful." I say, my chin quivering. My one gift, and it's from my son! I'm happy and sad, lonely and overcome with love at the same time.

"He made it all by himself," Christa says with pride, "a few weeks ago at Home Depot. I was keeping it for you."

It's difficult to find words. Christa was thinking of me, after all. I don't have a gift for her—unless I count not making a fuss about her and Mercedes spending the day with Deshy.

"Thank you," I say. Then I turn to Deshy. "Did you make this?" He nods and I give him a squeeze and a kiss. "I love it!"

"Well," Christa says, "we'd better go. I have a lot planned."

"Can Mommy Trish come, too?" Deshy asks, his eyes bright. No one speaks and I know it's up to me so smooth things over.

"You go with Christa," I say, giving him a final hug before he and Christa are out the door. "I have a lot planned, too. I'll tell you all about it tonight!"

My plan is to volunteer at the shelter, serving Christmas dinner to the homeless, addicts, and those down on their luck for reasons I may never know. When I was young my mother taught me that the best way to dig out of a funk was to help someone else, and that's what I intend to do.

The shelter smells of Pine Sol and years of cigarette smoke, even though smoking is no longer allowed. Residents and visitors sit at cafeteria style tables talking, playing bingo and waiting for the meal to be served. Someone says a prolonged grace extoling the virtue of charity, thankfulness for the food, and prayers to "A Higher Power" for peace on earth. Amen.

I don an apron, a hairnet, and a ladle to pour gravy over the turkey, mashed potatoes and green beans. Some things never change.

At six o'clock the shift is over. Some of the residents are assigned to clean-up and the volunteers are free to go. I head to the coat rack for my jacket and a woman with bushy red hair held in check by a blue bandana says to me, "A bunch of us are going to Denny's for some real food. Want to come along?"

"Sure," I say, and follow the crowd out the door. Besides Deshy's birdhouse, this is the best gift—not being alone on Christmas.

Elaine

Irish winters are wet and windy, especially along the western coast. Colin and I pause on the gravel drive, sweeping our gaze across the Casey farm, feeling the weight of a steel-gray sky and the slap of ocean gusts. Our driver deposits our luggage and roars off. I don't blame him. The place is desolate. The siding is dry and cracked; gutters dangle, shutters hang at odd angles. Lace curtains droop at the windows, dusty and yellowing. This house used to be Maggie's pride and joy. How sad.

From the barn, a barking dog announces our arrival. I climb a couple of steps and knock on the kitchen door while Colin bumps the suitcases up to the side porch. No one answers. A fierce wind whips around the house, cutting through our winter coats like they were made of tissue paper. We shiver and stamp our feet on the threshold. I knock again and push against the door. It opens. I stick my head in and call, "John, we're here. It's Colin and Elaine." Still no answer. I motion for Colin to follow me indoors. In the kitchen, we rub our hands together over the pot-belly stove that glows with welcome warmth. I'm relieved to see a teapot, mugs, and a thick slab of soda bread on the old wood table.

"John," I call again, this time louder. Maybe he's gone deaf, or he's out in the barn. Maggie's got to be here, though. Where else would she be? I take a look around.

The photo of Colin and his parents is still enshrined on the hall table alongside a vase of dusty silk flowers. I tip toe down the hallway, wincing at each creak and groan of the old floorboards, and peek into the bedroom. John is slumped in a chair, snoring noisily, having fallen asleep still in his overalls, thick sweater, and wool cap. The woman in the bed is hardly recognizable as Maggie. Her shrunken face is surrounded by a cap of white hair. In a restless sleep, she is clutching a down comforter to her chin. Arthritis has knobbed every joint of her fingers. Dear God, is this the woman who so intimidated Christa and me?

The room is stale and dusty, in need of a good scrubbing and airing. A faint medicinal odor hangs in the air. The old iron bed, a couple of unmatched dressers and the overstuffed chair where John is asleep are the only furniture. The faded floral wallpaper is peeling at the seams and the grimy windows could use a vinegar and water bath.

Colin's in the doorway, shifting his weight from side to side and digging his hands in his pockets. I take him by the arm and lead him into the room.

"Maggie," I whisper, bending low, "we're here."

She cracks open her milky eyes and stares into space, slowly awakening. "Jaysus, ye came."

Her voice is weak and hoarse. Even those few words leave her struggling for breath. She reaches for Colin with her claw-like fingers. He stands motionless, unsure of what to do. I take his hand and place it over hers.

"Thank the Lord you're here. I'm not long for this world, Liam," she gasps.

Good heavens, she thinks it's her deceased son.

Speechless, Colin quickly backs off and stumbles into his grandfather's chair. John wakes with a start.

"I must have dozed off. How long have ye been here? I wanted to greet ye proper like."

"It's all right, John," I tell him, taking care to keep my voice to a whisper. "We've only been here a few minutes. But Maggie—she thinks Colin is Liam and it startled him."

"Sure, she talks to Liam from time to time. I've heard her myself." He turns toward his wife of sixty years. "Doncha, girl? Talk to our Liam?"

"Yer an old fool, Johnnie, even when you were young. It's Himself I'm talking to, you eejit, it's me boy, Colin."

Maggie's feisty as ever.

John rubs the sleep from his eyes. Grasping the armrests for leverage, he hoists himself up and folds Colin into a manly embrace. "I'm glad ye made it," he says, tousling Colin's hair like he did when he was a toddler. "Yer almost as tall as me. Now when did all that happen?" John smiles broadly at the boy and Colin relaxes.

"How are you managing?" I ask. All I can think is that the man has aged twenty years in the last ten. Keeping a dairy farm going and tending to a chronically ill wife has taken its toll.

"Day by day," he sighs. "James is the only farmhand we've got left, thanks to Maggie who ran 'em all off."

When I was here ten years ago, I saw Maggie give James a good dressing down, probably not for the first time. I remember some cows strayed off the property when a fence blew down, and she blamed him, of course. Now he's the only one left to help out here. James must really need the work.

"Who takes care of Maggie?" I keep my voice low, wondering if she's able to leave the bed at all, even to use the bathroom down the hall. How much can one worn out man do?

"Sure, I've got some help. There's Brigid comes during the week, but on the weekends she helps out at her da's pub."

"Ah, that one," Maggie hisses. Apparently her hearing is still sharp.

"Keep a civil tongue, Maggie girl," he tells her. "Without Brigid you'd be lying in your own…"

"A barmaid in a public house, is what she is." Maggie slumps back onto her feather pillow, panting.

Really Maggie? You're in no position to quarrel about who wipes your arse.

"Colin and I will let you rest. We'll see you in a little while."

I wonder if Maggie is as close to death as John led me to believe. God forgive me, I don't trust her.

At the doorway, I stop to ask Maggie, "Would you like a cup of tea?"

"No. And close the door behind you."

Even on her sickbed, Maggie Casey doesn't have a kind word to say.

John shows Colin to the small bedroom across from the kitchen that he slept in as a toddler. I'm tempted to look in the dresser drawer to see if his crayons and coloring books are still there, for they've kept it exactly as it was. There's the narrow bed where he lay face-down years ago, a little boy mourning his dead mother. And the rocking chair where I held him and told him that his mother wasn't coming back. How he cried! My heart was ripped apart. I didn't think I could endure the pain.

I'm also assigned the same room as before; a chilly dormer upstairs. Remembering the damp chill, I packed a flannel night gown, thick robe, and fleecy slippers. I brought instant coffee, too, knowing full well that the beverages of choice here are strong tea and even stronger whiskey.

That night, sleep doesn't come easily. I'm not looking forward to spending Christmas here, in this drafty, sad farmhouse. I have to remind myself that I'm here so Colin can see his Irish grandparents before their time runs out. Tossing and turning in the creaky old bed, I stare up at paint chips peeling off the ceiling and contemplate the path Colin's life has taken. I've tried to raise him so that Stephanie would be proud. It's my unspoken promise to her. The terrible pain of losing her taught me two things:

Every day is a gift, and the future is not promised to anyone.

Colin

It's freezing! I burrow under the covers, but I still can't get warm. Besides, I smell bacon frying, and I'm starving so I pull on my jeans, a shirt, sweat shirt, and boots, and take a look in the kitchen.

"So you're here, then." A girl with laughter in her eyes looks up from the sizzling pan. Her skin is as white and smooth as the porcelain sink. Her hair is black and thick. It hangs in a braid down her back.

"Are you Brigid?" I thought she'd be older—wearing a white uniform.

"That I am." She turns to fill the dented tea kettle with tap water. "It's rashers and eggs for breakfast, then. You're hungry?" Her voice is like music.

Rashers? I have no idea what she's talking about, but whatever she's cooking smells delicious, and my stomach is growling.

"I'm starving." I don't want her to think I'm clueless—which I am.

"The tea will be ready shortly. There's cream on the table."

"I'm more of a milk guy," I say and she smiles.

"Here's the pitcher, help yourself."

The milk is rich and creamy, not like the kind Granma buys at home.

"I'm Colin," I say after gulping down a glassful.

"I know who you are," she says without looking up from the skillet. "I've been told not to interfere with their man from America."

What? Again, I'm clueless. "Their man from America?"

"Grandpa says you help take care of my Grandma Maggie."

"God knows I try," she sighs and shakes her head. "Some days she sends me packing, but Mister always begs me to come back, says he's got no one else and Jaysus, I can see why." She hands me a plate with rashers, fried eggs and potatoes. "I'm sorry, that was bold, yer bein' kin and all."

I dig into the food and pour myself another glass of milk. Granma comes downstairs shivering and pulling her robe tighter. She warms her hands over the pot-belly stove.

"Brrr…it's an icebox upstairs." She says then turns to Brigid. "Well, hello there. I'm Elaine McElroy, Colin's other grandmother."

"Brigid Ahern. Pleased to meet you, Ma'am. Breakfast, then, Mrs. McElroy?"

"Thanks, it smells wonderful. Has John eaten yet?"

"He eats after the chores are done."

Elaine

I've heard Irish breakfasts referred to as 'a heart attack on a plate,' but it's delicious and I can appreciate the amount of energy needed to run this farm. The tea, though, not so much. Too strong for my taste, even when laced with farm fresh cream. Colin brings his plate to the sink and thanks Brigid for breakfast. He's remembered his manners and I'm thankful.

"I'm gonna look around outside," he says. I can tell he's anxious to explore the place and check out the animals.

John didn't mention that Brigid is young and beautiful, but he wouldn't within earshot of Maggie. No sense risking a rant from her.

"Thank you for breakfast. I didn't realize you did the cooking, too." I sip my tea and pull the chair closer to the stove.

"Oh, yes, I care for the Missus and do what I can around the house." She sits down and pours herself a cup.

"That's a lot of responsibility at your age." I wonder, how old is she?

"Not at all. When I'm not working here I help at my Da's pub in town. It's called Ahern's."

I nod, listening for sounds from Maggie's room. Nothing. Maggie must be asleep. Otherwise she'd be barking orders like a field marshal.

"I noticed the bottles of pills on Maggie's bedside table."

"Oh yes, she gets her heart and blood pressure pills in the morning. I test her sugar three times a day and give her the insulin, too." She sits taller, seemingly proud that she's entrusted with Maggie's care.

I'm impressed. "Where did you learn to do all that?" I hope Maggie realizes how lucky she is to have Brigid. Otherwise they'd be paying for a housekeeper and a nurse.

"I was studying nursing at university when the money ran out and I was needed at home. That's when I learned that Mr. Casey was looking for someone to care for his wife." She's on her feet again, washing the mismatched plates and bowls, chipped at the edges, and setting them on the side of the sink to dry.

"Brigid! Brigid Ahern!"

It's Maggie. Brigid folds the tea towel and hurries to her charge.

I believe each of us is put on this earth for a reason. Maybe Brigid's calling is to serve others. I'd hate to see her sunny personality and determination eroded by Maggie's constant criticism, though. God bless the girl, it takes a certain person to minister to the likes of Maggie Casey. I couldn't do it, even with my nurse's training. Maggie is just too ornery.

I hear John clomp up the steps to the side porch. He pries off his mud-caked boots and sets them outside the door. When he comes in, his cheeks are scarlet. It must be the damp chill.

"Your breakfast is on the stove," I tell him. "I'll get it."

He devours the food and washes it down with two large mugs of tea laced with sugar and cream.

"So you've met Brigid, then?" he asks, wiping his mouth with the back of his large hand.

"She's a lovely girl. You're lucky; don't most of the young people leave for the city once they reach a certain age?"

"Sure they do. Just like our Liam did. Brigid wants to be a nurse, but her family's fallen on hard times. She's needed here, though, and needed at the pub, too, so she must stay."

"How old is she?"

"Surely, not more than twenty." He gives me a sly grin. "She's a looker. You thinkin' Colin might take a fancy to her?"

What?! Colin's fourteen, a freshman in high school.

Just then, Colin charges in the door, stomping and huffing from the cold. "Might take a fancy to who?" he says, warming his hands over the stove. "Is my calf Dora still here, Grandpa?"

And with that, I can tell his mind is whirling.

John patiently explains that farm animals serve a purpose; cats catch mice, dogs protect the herd, and the cows give milk and breed. Once cows outlive their usefulness, they're either sold or slaughtered.

"Dora went to slaughter about five years ago," John says.

Colin stares at the stove in silence. He has no frame of reference for animals that aren't cherished pets.

Brigid's standing in the hallway, her sleeves rolled up to her elbows, presumably after bathing Maggie. "Mr. Casey, I'll be needin' your help gettin' Missus up in the chair."

"I'll give her a hand, John. You sit for a while." I offer.

"Bless you, girl, I didn't have you comin' here to be nursin' my Maggie, but I surely do appreciate it."

"Mind her foot," Brigid instructs as she carefully lifts the blanket off Maggie's legs. Her left foot is sthickly bandaged with gauze and surgical tape. John didn't mention anything about this.

"What...?" But before I can continue, Maggie interrupts.

"What's happenin' is that they're hacking away at me piece by piece. Good thing ye got here when ye did—by the New Year there'll be nothin' left."

It's the end of the life she's known; a hard-working farmer's wife pulling her share of the never-ending chores. It's got to be difficult, depending on hired help for everything, even getting out of bed in the morning. It's not surprising, though. Maggie's been neglecting her diabetes for years.

"She didn't want me to say anything...didn't want you feelin' sorry for her." John says, standing in the doorway now. He lifts Maggie's frail frame onto the bedside chair. She's like a feather in his arms.

Maggie's amputated toes wouldn't be reason enough to lure Colin here, they decided, so John upped the ante saying that Maggie wasn't long for this world. Liars, both of them! What do I tell Colin? *Grandma Maggie's not really dying, although she's headed in that direction. She's had her toes amputated because she neglected to take better care of herself over the years. I tried to warn her about her bread and booze diet, but no way would she take my advice, or anyone else's.* Brigid tests Maggie's blood sugar with a prick on her finger and injects her with insulin. Add that to the list of things Maggie resents about her.

"I'll get your breakfast, Missus," Brigid says, leaving John and me alone with Maggie.

"Is this what ye came for, then, to gloat over me in my sorry state?" she says, her voice low and bitter.

I look toward John. We're both caught off guard. I wish Christa were here. She'd know how to shut this spiteful old woman up. But Christa's happily partnered with Mercedes now. They're enjoying their life together, and I wouldn't have it any other way.

"Enough, Maggie," John commands. "Elaine is our guest. We asked her to come."

"We asked *Colin* to come."

She is rotten from the inside out.

On the afternoon of Christmas Eve I put on every bit of warm clothing I packed and take a long hike around the farm, thinking about all the holiday traditions I'm missing. My favorite is walking to the Cathedral of St. Francis for Christmas Eve Mass. The Caseys, I've learned, celebrate Christmas Eve by driving to the local pub and knocking back glasses of Guinness with friends. But judging by John's somber mood, it's unlikely that there'll be much celebrating tonight. I offer to take Colin into town to buy a small tree and some decorations, but John dismisses this idea, so we settle ourselves at the table for a light supper of cold beef sandwiches. John reaches into a nearby cabinet and takes out a bottle and a single glass. I don't like the direction this is headed. What are we supposed to do, open presents while Maggie mopes in bed and John gets smashed in the kitchen?

John swallows a shot of whiskey. He's pouring a second when, behind him, like an apparition, Maggie stands upright with crutches.

"I'm ready, Johnnie," she says. "I'm ready to celebrate the birth of The Baby Jesus."

We gape at one another, stupefied. Maggie has miraculously risen from her sickbed, dressed herself, combed her hair, applied lipstick, and negotiated her way into the kitchen. Now that's a Christmas miracle!

John wheels around in his chair and grins ear-to-ear, for what he sees is a glimpse of Maggie before decades of hard work, hard drinking, ill health and the loss of her only child took its toll.

"I'm ready to go, Johnnie. Toes or no toes, I'll not lie in bed and miss out. We're going to the pub, like always, then to Mass at the church where we were married."

John is temporarily speechless, as are Colin and I. Maggie's transformation is as unexpected as a blizzard in July.

"Don't deny me this wee pleasure, Johnnie. It's all I've got left, me last holiday here on this earth." She turns to me and adds, "Sure, you're welcome to come along, and Colin, of course."

John's eyes moisten. He shakes his head with amazement and pride at his remarkable wife, his partner, friend and lover for God knows how many years.

"Give me a few minutes to change," I say. The only dress I packed is black, intending to wear it to a wake and funeral. I add a green scarf and gold pin. There, that's a little more festive. Good thing I made Colin pack his khakis.

Maggie remains in high spirits during the ride to Ahern's Pub. We're packed hip to hip in John's pick-up truck. The parking lot is jammed. The whole town, it seems, celebrates Christmas Eve at this place. Inside, a log fire crackles in the hearth. Colored lights loop overhead, tacked to dark wood beams. Welcoming cheers and shouts erupt as John carries Maggie across the threshold. Brigid greets us warmly and shows us to the last available table. Folks raise their glasses as we pass. Everyone seems to know about Colin, for one by one each man and woman raises a glass in a toast to "Your man from America." It's a close-knit Irish community and they're doing what the people of Ireland have done for centuries: gather at the pub to talk, eat, drink, and celebrate with family and friends.

Brigid brings frothy pints of Guinness for the adults and ginger ale for Colin, then moves to the next table where thirsty patrons are holding up their glasses for yet another round. Colin groans in disappointment; he wants his own pint.

"You can taste mine," I tell him.

"It's Christmas," John says. "Surely he's old enough."

When I stand firm, Maggie pushes her glass across the table to Colin, and fixes me with a challenging look. At the first sip of Guinness, he grimaces and hands it back.

"It's a taste you'll get used to," John laughs. "Come to love, even."

I know where this is going, and I move to cut it off right away. "He won't be here long enough to develop a taste, John."

"I'm just sayin' for the future, is all, and he's here now, isn't he?"

John stands, shouting over the noise. "Here now, a toast everybody, to my man from America, my grandson, Colin. *Slainte!* To your health!"

Awash in cheers, beaming with pride, John beckons for Colin to stand. For the Caseys, it's a priceless moment. And me? I'm wishing I was back in Santa Fe, preparing for a quiet dinner with my friends and family and a walk to church instead of knocking back toasts a world away.

Well-wishers flock to our table, tipping their caps, bestowing holiday greetings, and asking after Maggie's health. She sits up straight, clearly enjoying the attention. When word gets out that I'm originally from Chicago, people ask about their relatives in the States. Do I know Cousin Kevin who's a carpenter on the South Side or Uncle Patrick on the police force? They're disappointed when I explain that Chicago is a big city and I haven't lived there for years.

It's late, but the party's still in full swing. John sends drinks to his friends and Brigid brings rounds to our table from neighbors. Maggie is in a better mood than I've ever seen her. It's easy tonight to envision her as a young, fun-loving version of herself, out for a good time with her handsome husband.

It's all very festive, but I'm getting anxious about the drive back to the farm later. John has had too many drinks to count. Didn't I lose my daughter to a car crash on these very same country roads? It has to be John at the wheel, though. Neither Colin nor I know how to drive a stick shift, not to mention trying to drive on the wrong side of the road in the pitch dark.

"Brigid! Coffee!" I call out.

The party finally breaks up, just in time for midnight Mass. Thank God.

After the service Maggie announces, "We'll be stopping by me boy in the church yard. Colin should see where his da is buried and say a prayer."

Of course he should. We can all agree on that, at least.

At the cemetery, Maggie shuffles along the cobbled path on her crutches. John stays at her side, should she lose her balance. A vapor lamp clamped to an outer wall of the old church emits a weak yellow glow across the ancient cemetery. The ground under our feet is moist and fertile, but the only things growing are mossy headstones, worn by time and weather, bearing faint traces of the Celtic cross. Draughts of chilly night air settle over us like a pall. At Liam's grave, Colin and I kneel and make the sign of the cross. I say a prayer that Liam and Stephanie are reunited in the afterlife. Maggie hooks her arm around John's and they bow their heads, mourning their only child. The silence is oppressive, until finally Colin whispers, "What was my dad like?"

"Oh, he was a smart one, your da," Maggie says. "Always getting high marks in school, and got himself a scholarship to university, he did. Sure, we wanted him to stay on the farm, but we couldn't hold him back. Wouldn't be right in this day and age." She sighs. "Besides, there was no stoppin' 'im."

"Got himself a good job, too, right out of university, designing programs for computers with a big outfit in the city." John adds. "That's where he met your ma."

Maggie hiccups and sobs. John puts his arm around her middle and pulls her close. Tears well up in my eyes, not just for Liam, but for Colin's little family that was cut short. He's on one knee, his head bent. No one speaks for a while. The only sound is the buzzing of the vapor lamp. Finally, I can kneel no longer and I lean on Colin's shoulder to help myself up.

"I'm sorry for your loss," I whisper to the Caseys.

It's almost two in the morning by the time we get back to the farm, but John insists on showing Colin how to stoke the fire, and the boy manages to prod a few embers back to life.

I lay awake upstairs, shivering between icy sheets, thinking about how the Caseys revealed a softer side tonight, remembering their boy with pride. I hope visiting his father's grave will bring some closure for him, help him realize that Liam was a flesh and blood man who lived and died here in Ireland. Maybe now Colin will be more serious about moving forward with his life in Santa Fe. Wearing work clothes, tending farm animals, and getting dirty is new and seductive to him. He sees the drinking and camaraderie at the pub, but he hasn't experienced the day-to-day drudgery and loneliness of running a dairy farm. The Casey farm is nothing but a millstone that would keep him shackled here, but, of course, he doesn't see that.

On Christmas morning we all sit at the kitchen table, drinking tea and munching scones thick with fresh butter. Colin gives the Caseys our gifts to them; a flannel shirt and hooded sweatshirt for John, fleece-lined slippers and a robe for Maggie. They thank us again and again. They give me a lovely blue cardigan, which I plan to wear to the airport. Then they bring out Colin's Christmas gift, an authentic fisherman's sweater, knit from unbleached wool with a distinctive cable pattern. Maggie says that according to legend, each village has its own pattern, and that a drowned fisherman washed ashore can be identified by the pattern on his sweater.

Colin pulls the sweater over his head. My breath catches in my throat—he's so handsome, and he looks like a typical young Irishman. No doubt, that was the Casey's intention.

Two more days, and it's time to leave. The morning dawns like all the others, chilly and overcast. We don't indulge in long good-byes, for soon the driver is at the door. John wraps Colin in a bear-hug that seems to last forever. Colin bends to embrace Maggie, gently draping his arms around her slight frame. She whispers in his ear as she clutches his sleeve. He nods.

The plane pierces the blanket of clouds and levels off in dazzling sunlight. I relax, fully, for the first time since receiving John's call. Next to me, Colin is bobbing his head to the music in his earphones. I nudge his arm.

"What did Maggie say to you?"

I think I know, of course, but I need to hear it from him.

"The farm is gonna be mine. They want me to come back after I graduate and run it." With that, he smiles and puts his ear buds back in his ears.

That's no surprise. The Caseys and their damn farm have been lurking in the background of our lives for years, just waiting to lure Colin away from me. I've raised him, fed him, housed him, guided him through tough times at school, watched him excel at sports, taken him to doctors and counselors, and kept him safe every single day of his life. I swear, I couldn't love him any more if he was my own. I always thought, well, I always *hoped*, he'd be with me in Santa Fe. Or at least in America.

What are the Caseys offering? A bleak life as a farmer in rural Ireland. Is that his best hope for the future?

Whatever happens, whatever he decides, if and when he graduates from college, I'll be here for him, just as I was that day twelve years ago when I brought him home to Santa Fe.

Lulled by the drone of the plane's engines, I lean back and close my eyes. I try not to think about losing Colin to the Caseys, try to be happy that he's here with me now. I'll love him as long as I can, as long as I'm able, and as long as he'll let me.

May 2012

Elaine

I've stayed true to my promise of weekly Mass, as much as humanly possible given a bout of pneumonia last fall, followed by a mild case of shingles. And I have to believe as I sit here in the auditorium of Sacred Heart waiting for the band to play Pomp and Circumstance, that my efforts helped Colin along his journey. Sometimes, I'll admit, it felt like a death march, but I didn't give up on him—or myself, although the responsibility was a heavy weight on my shoulders. There were times when I lost sight of the fact that I could only do so much—Colin needed to do his part, too.

Chuck shows me the program with Colin's name among the list of graduates and as a member of the varsity soccer team, The Broncos, who won the state championship last year. Each graduate was allowed two tickets to the ceremony and Colin and I agreed that it would be Chuck and me. Denise, now retired, and Stuart are here in Santa Fe and have graciously offered to have the family celebration catered, an offer I gladly accepted.

I'm happy, but bone weary. I've kept my part of the bargain and at sixty-six I'm looking forward to a long rest. Chuck wants the two of us to rent a cabin in the wilderness and get away from it all for a while. I'm thinking along the lines of a week of pampering at luxury spa. Maybe we can do both.

Chuck has taken Colin under his wing, showing him the finer points of creating sculptures with Corten steel, his favorite medium. I've seen Colin don a protective helmet and under Chuck's guidance use an acetylene torch to weld massive beams together. Chuck's latest project is tentatively titled,

'Dessert Vista,' a grouping of abstract Saguaro cacti commissioned by a chain hotel slated to open outside Santa Fe. It's a feather in his creative cap that he hopes will result in rightfully earned recognition and further commissions.

I have to hand it to Colin—he's kept it together. He's been in a few minor brawls, all off campus. I probably would have never known if it weren't for a fat lip or black eye that he couldn't hide from me. He's not going to college, he's made that clear, and I accept his decision. He enjoys working with Chuck at his studio, a lot at an industrial park on the outskirts of town. Learning to weld and working with steel could be his ticket to a job in very high-paying trade. Let him figure that out for himself, though.

Helen, God love her, won't be here for the celebration. At 91 she's frail and her memory is failing. When the pot of oatmeal she left on the stove caught fire, it scared her—it scared all of us—and Denise and I agreed that we would try to keep her at home with a full-time care-giver for as long as possible. I have a new appreciation for my sister. She tackled the daunting job of interviewing and hiring a companion for Mom and checks in on them almost every day.

Roxy remains single and has relocated to the West coast for a better paying job. You'd think we'd see each other more often now that she's closer, but I can count on her for Christmas, at least. She's driving in for the graduation and says she has news. I can't help wondering what her 'news' might be, but she sounded positive.

The couple that I had the most doubts about, Christa and Mercedes, are still together and continually surprise me. Christa sold her home, Mercedes her condo, and together they purchased a luxury home in a gated community. After soul-searching and counseling, they decided to adopt a child. They will be joining the celebration later with their beautiful four year old daughter, Angelica.

After years of being estranged from her family, Trish learned from one of her sisters that her mother is dying from ovarian cancer. She and Deshy are on an extended visit to Michigan to reconnect with her family and help care for her mother. I cried when they left because I'll miss them and I believe that Trish, of all my friends, has suffered the most. She never fully recovered from her break-up with Christa. I watched her shrink back into herself, not trusting people, unwilling to risk another broken heart. I'll always be her friend, but she's pulled away from me, too. It makes me very sad.

Finally, Maggie passed away three years ago from a massive heart attack. She died peacefully at home. Ironically, despite my skepticism, Colin's visit really was her last good-bye. I'm thankful that he got to see her while she was still feisty and outspoken. John hired a full-time manager for the farm. It's too much for him, he says. Colin's planning to spend his summer in Ireland, helping out and learning about dairy farming. After that—who knows?

Father Geary steps up to the mic and announces, "Ladies and Gentleman, I proudly present to you the class of 2012!" The crowd cheers and applauds, and the band begins playing Pomp and Circumstance. Chuck squeezes my hand, and I lean into him as the graduates march down the aisle.

Photo by Tim Coughlin

About the Author

Kathleen McElligott was a nurse administrator, but admits that she couldn't wait to start her 'authentic life' after retirement. In 2015 she joined a group of intrepid women cyclists and journeyed by bicycle cross-country from San Diego, California to St. Augustine, Florida. It was a life confirming 58 day adventure that resulted in lasting friendships and a deeper understanding of our country's diversity.

Besides writing and cycling, she enjoys hiking Sedona's red rocks, kayaking, yoga, and spending time with her large family of four children and ten grandchildren. She lives in the Chicago area with her long-time partner, Ed.

Kathleen's work appears in numerous anthologies and websites. She has read her work at Printer's Row Lit fest and other Chicago venues.

1638 East Palace is the sequel to *Mommy Machine* (Heliotrope Press 2008), following the characters' life journeys as they seek fulfillment and love in their relationships. The final book in the trilogy will follow Colin into adulthood as he chooses between his inheritance in Ireland and his family in the States.

She would like to thank Whitney Scott for editing the final draft of *1638 East Palace,* Catherine Underhill

`Fitzpatrick for editing an early draft, and R.J. Nelson for reading the final draft.

For inquiries or comments, log onto her blog at kmcelligott.wordpress.com.